D1713521

The Ashburn Brothers Collection

MOUNTAIN MEN OF CARIBOU CREEK BOOKS 1-3

KALI HART

Cover Designed by Cormar Covers

Love on Tap

MOUNTAIN MEN OF CARIBOU CREEK
BOOK 1

"Grandma Hattie, I *know* you're not trying to climb those stairs." My grandma, the most stubborn woman in the entire state of Alaska, freezes. Her injured leg, still wrapped in an ankle boot, hovers above a narrow stair. One I clearly remember forbidding her to climb only yesterday. Just as I've reminded her every day for the past week. "Whatever you need, I can go upstairs and grab it for you."

"I want my quilting room," she huffs, lowering her booted foot to the floor. "Can you bring *that* to me?"

I close my eyes, focus on my breathing, and count to ten. I've dealt with my share of ornery patients, but she's really taking the cake. Why didn't I consider her capacity for spunky hostility when I agreed to oversee her in-home rehab? "We've discussed this. Those stairs are too narrow. You can't make it up there without tilting your ankle. You know. The one you fractured. Are you *trying* to make it worse?"

Her stern expression softens, as does her tone of voice. "I haven't been up there in *two* weeks, Riley."

"I can bring some of your quilting supplies downstairs," I offer.

"It's not the same." Grandma Hattie's nearing eighty-five, but until she slipped on some wet gravel while wrangling a fish at the creek, no one would've guessed it. My grandpa is the first to tell anyone that she's a self-sufficient woman who insists on doing everything herself.

Her stubborn pride is the same reason she refused to stay in Anchorage or Fairbanks for physical therapy.

She's reminded me at least a dozen times since I temporarily moved into the guest room that she's lived in this house for fifty-five years and has no plans on leaving. And because grandpa loves her so much, he's not the best candidate for overseeing her rehab. He'd let her get away with murder.

It's why I volunteered to come home after nearly a decade away.

Well, not the *only* reason.

I push away the worrisome thoughts. They'll

haunt me plenty enough later tonight when I'm lying in bed, staring at the ceiling. Right now, the most important item on my agenda is to figure out how to deter Grandma Hattie from her mischief without it requiring constant supervision. Or an ankle monitor.

"Is it the *room* you miss?" I ask, glancing up the staircase staged along the back wall of the living room. It leads to only one room, and that's Grandma Hattie's quilting room.

"I need the ambiance to finish the baby blanket for Huck and Penny."

At the mention of my brother's name, an idea pops into my head. "What if I switched my room with the quilting room? That way your room would be on the main floor."

Grandma Hattie's eyebrows draw in and her expression screws up, like I might've just suggested she paint the living room logs pink. She *hates* pink. The room at the top of the stairs has been her quilting room ever since I can remember. "What about the view? And the lighting? You can't bring those down here. I can manage these stairs—"

I bolt in front of her so quickly she doesn't have a chance to plant her good leg on the bottom stair. "Not a chance."

"You're lucky your grandpa's still at work—"

"Hattie, what're you up to now?" The sound of Grandpa Harold's voice is music to my ears. He looks tired from another day at the shop. He retired a decade ago, but he refuses to admit it. He likes tinkering with cars, ATVs, and machinery. The guys enjoy his company and appreciate his expertise. I imagine it brings him the same joy that quilting brings Grandma Hattie.

"I want to get up to my quilting room. I need to finish my grandbaby's blanket."

Grandpa drops a hand on her shoulder, then looks to me. My heart melts at the sheer love in his eyes. He'd do anything for Grandma Hattie, and probably has over the six decades they've been together. "Still too early for stairs?" he asks.

Huck and Penny just announced that they were expecting last week. I bite down on my bottom lip, trying to swallow my frustration before I speak, hoping my tone betrays none of it. I know he means well. "The stairs are too narrow. It's not safe right now. If they were wider—"

"I've climbed these same stairs for fifty-five years," Grandma Hattie snaps back, the exasperation in her tone hinting that she might be near throwing the white flag in this fight. For now. But one night of rest and she'll be back at it again. I have to get this handled tonight. It can't wait.

"I suggested we switch her quilting room and my room," I explain to Grandpa. "I was about to run down to the brewery to see if Huck can stop by after work. I'll need help to move the heavy furniture." If I thought a text would be enough to get my brother here, I'd try that. But he's stubborn and thickheaded. Not to mention totally in love. I'll have to do this in person so he understands the seriousness of the situation or he'll blow me off.

When thoughts of Zac Ashburn drift in uninvited, I try to push them out. But it's not so easy. He's Huck's boss. It'd be impossible to talk to my brother and not run in to his best friend. I made up my mind when I bought the plane ticket that I'd be avoiding Zac as much as possible during my stay. So far, I've been successful. The last time I saw him, I was fifteen and planted a wet one right on his lips. Spoiler alert: he didn't kiss me back. In fact, he looked downright mortified. His expression is forever burned in my brain.

"I can help you," Grandpa offers.

I wish I could take him up on his offer, but he's not quite fit as a fiddle anymore. And some of the furniture is crazy heavy. I don't need two grandparents down for the count. "I know you can, Grandpa. But someone needs to keep an eye on our wild child. She's out of control today. Maybe you could take her out for a drive or something?"

Grandma Hattie flutters her eyelashes at Grandpa, feigning innocence. I know he doesn't buy it, but he plants a kiss on her forehead anyway. Damn them and their cuteness. I'd kill to find someone to spend a lifetime with. Someone who'd look at me like I hung the moon in their sky, even when I'm a hundred. But when it comes to men, I have a knack at picking all the wrong ones.

"Hattie, you might like your quilts down here for a change. A different view could give you more...inspiration." Grandpa's always had a way with words. He can get through to Grandma Hattie like no one else can. He looks back to me. "Why don't you go see if you can grab Huck. I'll keep my sweetheart out of trouble. I'm craving a piece of Rose's blueberry pie."

I don't dare waste a second, even if the thought of seeing Zac Ashburn again after all these years makes me excited and nauseous at the same time. Of course, the nausea could be from something else entirely. *What a mess.* "I'll be right back. No funny business, Grandma Hattie."

"I assure you, the only funny business will be later, behind closed doors," Grandpa says, effectively moving my feet right out the door before he can say something that'll scar me for life.

If only Grandma Hattie's ornery behavior was my biggest problem, life might not be so bad. But the shitty reality is she's the least of them. I back the car out of the driveway, hoping Zac called in sick today. But I don't have that kind of luck.

CHAPTER 2

Zac

"One Caribou Creek Pale Ale and one Caribou Creek Pilsner," I say to the couple next in line at the bar, sliding two glasses to them. The brewery's been busier than usual for a Monday. I know it's good for business. A business I'm part owner of with my brothers. My livelihood depends on its continued success. But I'd be lying if I said I wasn't stealing glances at the clock, willing time to go by faster.

I let Decker, one of our part time bartenders, help the next person in line and return my attention back to the couple seated at the end of the bar.

I'm still shocked as hell that James Devano, playboy coast guard pilot and sworn lifelong bachelor, is here with a woman. He doesn't bring flings to town, or so he's told me. Maybe after all these years of resisting, a woman's finally got her hooks into him. From the interaction I've watched between them so far, I think she'll be good for him. She doesn't take any of his shit and isn't afraid to give it right back.

The ache I feel in my own chest is surprising. I push it away. I don't know that I have any business getting tangled up with a woman. Some days my head's a bigger mess than others. The flashbacks from Afghanistan plague me without warning for no fucking reason at all. Today has been one of those days. I yearn for the solitude of my cabin a couple miles from town. Out there, I can split wood until I chase them away.

"Don't rush me," the woman says playfully to James, bringing me back to the present.

Earlier, I set her up with a sample platter and took my time explaining the flavor pallet of each of the six brews we offer—Ben, my oldest brother who's in charge of sales and marketing, would have my head if I didn't. Sometimes he takes his job too seriously.

She's halfway through her samples before I realize I haven't offered James a drink. *Fuck, where* is *my head today?*

I turn to him. "Do you—"

"Is he here?" a woman demands, drawing my attention away from James and his date. I suck in a breath, prepared to lock my friendly smile into place so

I can politely put *her* in her place. We don't tolerate rudeness or assholes at our brewery. It's an automatic invitation out the door. But when I lift my gaze, I'm stunned into silence.

Dark auburn curls cascade over the front of her shoulders. My mouth suddenly dries. In her skinny jeans and muted green top, it's impossible not to notice and appreciate her curves. But it's those intense blue eyes that capture my attention and refuse to let it go. *Riley Kohl?* The last time I saw her, she was just a kid.

But there's nothing *kid* about her now.

Not even close.

She folds both arms over her chest, unwilling to offer me a smile. It's been well over a decade since I last saw my buddy's little sister. If it weren't for those eyes, I don't know that I would've recognized her. I'd heard she was in town. Nothing stays a secret in Caribou Creek. But I haven't run into her until now. And she does *not* look happy to see me. I can't figure out why that bothers me so much.

"Huck," she prompts snappishly, as if I'm not an old friend. "Is he here?"

"Your brother's cleaning out the fermentation tanks."

"How long will that take?"

I'm determined to rid her of that scowl. I can't

imagine why she's wearing it. She used to follow Huck and me around all the time when we were growing up. The three of us were thick as thieves. "Long enough for you to sit and have a drink."

"I'm in a hurry," she says, glancing around the brewery. I suspect the last time she saw the place, my grandparents were still running it. My brothers and I have made a lot of improvements since taking over. The rustic tin walls might be the only detail we didn't change.

"What are you drinking? We have six different—"

"I'm not." She moves to the edge of the counter and stretches up on tiptoe, as if that'll help her see over the saloon doors to the back. But they're too tall for her short frame. "Can you hurry him up or something? I have to get back before Grandma Hattie gets into more trouble."

"How is she?" I ask, recalling she fractured her ankle a couple of weeks ago.

"Stubborn as ever."

I can't seem to keep my gaze from raking over her curves. I haven't felt this drawn to a woman in ... ever. *Shit. Play it cool, Zac. Your head's a fucking mess. That's the only reason you're having these thoughts about Huck's little sister.* "You came back to help her out for a while?"

"I'm overseeing her at-home rehab, but I'm not

staying. I'm headed back to Orlando as soon as she doesn't need me anymore." She reaches into her purse and pulls out a ten-dollar bill. Slapping it on the counter, she says, "Give me an amber."

"Good choice," I say, refusing to take her money as I fill a glass and wonder what her life is like in Orlando. She always used to talk about leaving Caribou Creek and moving somewhere bigger. A city that never slept. But part of me thought she'd always end up back here. I thought all three of us would. "The amber's our most popular," I add, handing the glass to her instead of sliding it over. Which ends up being a big fucking mistake. A simple graze of our fingertips as we exchange the glass sends a jolt of electricity up my arm. *What the hell?*

Riley flinches. I give myself a whole second to consider that she felt it too. But she's looking at the glass of amber like it's poison and she doesn't know how it got there.

"Are you—"

"Um, I'll be right back." She sets the glass on the counter and hurries toward the restroom in the corner.

I force myself to shift my attention back to James, remembering he requested a to-go order to take back to North Haven. Luckily Decker has his wits about him and boxed it all up. "Sorry about that man," I say to James, setting the wooden crate filled with six packs

14

of the J-Squad's favorite brews. Though I try my damnedest to focus on my customers, I can't help but glance toward the restrooms, wondering if Riley's okay.

"Be careful with that one," James says, handing over his credit card.

So much for being discreet. "Don't I know it."

As James and his date leave, Riley reappears at the bar. I'm relieved she's not looking green, but still confused about her suddenly running off. But she doesn't waste any time explaining herself. "Is Huck done yet? I need his help moving furniture at—"

"Dude!" Huck bursts through the saloon doors, waving his phone. "She got it! Penny got the gig!"

It takes me a few seconds to remember what he's talking about, which is embarrassing considering he hasn't shut up about it all week. His wife, Penny, auditioned to open for a major concert in Anchorage. Though she doesn't sing professionally and doesn't want that lifestyle, her voice could win any music competition out there. "That's great, man! When is it?"

Huck looks up from his phone, a guilty expression spreading across his features. "This weekend. They want us in Anchorage tomorrow morning for press, rehearsals, and all that. I'll run it by Wes. Make sure I can take the time off —"

"No need." I'm not giving either one of my brothers the opportunity to turn down the last-minute request. Wes, the brew master, would probably approve even though he's shorthanded right now. But Ben will be a pain in the ass. Better for me to handle this now and deal with the repercussions later. "I'll talk to him."

"You can't leave yet," Riley says.

"Oh hey, sis. Didn't see you there." Huck's wearing his goofy, cupid-hit-me-in-the-ass grin that he's had on since he met Penny. I'm happy as hell for him, but I have to admit, I'm a little jealous. Huck didn't come home from Afghanistan with the same trauma I did. He had his whole heart to give. "Sorry, I have to go straight home. Penny needs help packing."

"I need help switching Grandma Hattie's quilting room with my room. She's been trying to sneak upstairs again. Do you want her to fall and break her other ankle? Or worse, her *neck*?" Riley folds both arms over her chest again, tapping her foot. When did she learn to put up such thick walls? Why did she? I feel something inside me bristle. *What asshole did this to her?*

"I can help," I hear myself offer before I've had a moment to think it through.

"You sure, man?" Huck asks.

"I'm free tonight. It's no problem at all." I meet

Riley's eyes for the first time since Huck erupted on the scene. I'm afraid my buddy'll catch me staring at his little sister like she's a dessert. A dessert I yearn to taste more by the minute. "That work for you?" I ask her, hoping like hell I sound calm and in control of my breathing. My pulse is another matter.

"How soon can you come over?"

"Give me an hour?"

"See, there you go," Huck says. "Problem solved."

"It'd go faster with all three of us," Riley adds, but it's no use. Huck's already turned his back and disappeared through the saloon doors. She stares at the swinging doors for several seconds before turning her baby blue gaze on me. "You might be in over your head. Grandma Hattie's out of control."

Riley adjusts her purse strap on her shoulder and about faces, abandoning her untouched beer. The sway of her hips as she marches toward the door causes my dick to twitch against my zipper. I discreetly stare at her amazing ass. My fingers itch with yearning to sink into her plump flesh. Yeah, I might be in more trouble than I realized.

"You good?" Zac calls from the middle of the staircase, sounding not nearly winded enough for all the trips we've been making between the two rooms. The mattress wobbles in my grasp, threatening to topple over the railing and into the living room. Though it wouldn't flatten my grandparents if it fell—Grandpa managed to convince Grandma Hattie to grab some pie from the local diner while we made the switch—it would definitely destroy a lamp or two.

"Remind me to get even with Huck when he gets back," I grumble, knowing my threat is empty. With how lost Huck seemed for the last few years, I'm happy he found a good woman. Penny's amazing. The only qualm I have about him leaving for Anchorage last minute is that the timing sucks.

"I would've rounded up more help, but we couldn't spare anyone else tonight."

Dammit, why does he have to be so endearing? I want to stay mad at Zac. Staying mad at him keeps my embarrassing teenage crush from resurfacing. I might not be the same awkward fifteen-year-old with braces anymore, but I'm not exactly a super model. I'm sure Zac gets hit on by every single female tourist who visits the CARIBOU CREEK BREWERY. For all I know, his bedroom is a revolving door.

"It's all good," I say, practically grunting the words. "We're almost finished. You'll be able to leave soon."

"I don't mind helping, Riley."

I ignore his words so I can't read into his tone and focus on maneuvering the pillowtop mattress into the oddly shaped room with random angled ceilings. We position it against the bedframe and let it fall.

Once it's in place, I drop on to the mattress and sigh. "Remind me to never buy a pillowtop mattress unless I'm paying someone else to lug it around. It's like sleeping on a cloud, but dammit this thing's heavy."

Zac rubs out a kink in his neck, but I pretend not to notice. The last thing I need to think about is those hands on my body. Or sex. Sex leads to bad decisions and just complicates everything in the end. No matter

19

what I find out when I'm finally brave enough to face things, I need to avoid sex for at least a year. Maybe longer.

"Never slept on a pillowtop before," Zac admits. "But after a year at a time on a cot, any mattress is better."

"You have to try it," I insist, patting a spot next to me before I think it through. Too late to revoke the invitation now without sounding like a jerk. Once upon a time, we were just innocent kids who wouldn't have thought twice about lying on the same bed. "Just lie down for a minute. I'm not going to bite." *Unless you want me to.*

Zac sits on the edge of the mattress, keeping a healthy distance from me, and slowly leans back. "Hey, this is pretty nice."

"Right?"

He props his hands behind his head and stares up at the ceiling. "I might have to get one of these."

For a moment, it feels just like old times. Before I developed my embarrassing crush on him, spending time with Zac was normal. It was always Huck, Zac, and me when we were younger. "Do you remember that time we thought we could catch the moose that was stealing raspberries out of Mrs. Johnson's garden?" I ask, wondering what else he remembers.

"You mean the time when Huck smashed half her

raspberries patch because the moose decided to chase *us* out of it?" Zac's chuckle is soft, little more than a puff of air. I feel my nipples harden, as if his breath is on them and not lost to the space above us.

"I'll never forget how *big* that thing was," I say, adding my laughter to his, remembering how fearless I used to be. It almost makes me sad now. With one bad decision after another, I have a hard time trusting myself these days. I live a very boring life outside of work. Any time I seem to stray from that safe, boring routine, I tend to find trouble.

"Huck's just lucky the damn thing didn't flatten him like a pancake. Your mom would've killed us if he got trampled." Zac turns his head, his brown eyes meeting mine. This close, I can see the familiar gold flecks in his irises. "How *is* your mom, anyway?"

"Remarried. Again." Mom moved to Arizona the minute I left for college. She'd moved to Caribou Creek when she married my dad, but he passed away when I was only nine. Didn't take long before Mom was itching to leave. She never really felt at home in Alaska. "Still in Arizona."

Zac shifts his body until he's lying on his side. He props his head in a hand. For some reason the way he's looking at me is making me feel more vulnerable than I already did. Which is the only reason my own gaze goes rouge, dropping to places it has no business dropping.

Wetness pools between my legs as I take in all the hard muscles suffocating beneath his tight t-shirt. I wonder what he's hiding in those jeans... "What about you, Riley?"

I clear my throat and pretend to fix my hair, certain I've been caught. "What about me?"

He pokes me near the shoulder hard enough to rock me, like he used to do when we were kids. Except the simple sensation of his touch has every nerve ending in my body on high alert. "Don't play dumb. You're better than that."

I'm not about to tell Zac Ashburn of all people that I might be pregnant. That the very sight of a glass of Caribou Creek Amber earlier freaked me out so much that I ran to the bathroom, afraid I might throw up—which I thankfully didn't. Or that I'm too chicken to pee on a stick and find out the truth. "I'm a physical therapist. In Orlando."

He rolls his eyes at me, and for some reason the carefree gesture makes my pulse double. So much for my teenage crush staying buried in the past where it belongs. It takes an embarrassing amount of restraint to keep my hands to myself. Damn the Army. It was obviously good to him and all those delicious muscles. "I already knew that."

"I live in an apartment with a lake view." I omit the detail about the cement factory on the opposite side of said lake, which is why rent is dirt cheap. "Thought about getting a cat."

Zac stares at me so intently it makes me feel naked. Uncomfortable. Afraid that if he keeps searching, he'll discover all my secrets. I didn't come home to fall for him all over again. Yet, in a matter of hours I'm already yearning to have him back in my life. I don't like this one bit.

"There's that look again," Zac says.

"What look?"

"The scowl you gave me earlier at the brewery. Did I do something to upset you?"

I'm not about to tell him that he's the reason I've avoided Caribou Creek for all these years. He's always been my kryptonite. If only I had a legitimate reason to be mad at him. But I'm only mad at myself. "Do you honestly not remember?"

"Remember what?"

Oh god. He's going to make me say it out loud. *Abort, Riley. Just abort.* "Never mind."

Zac scoots closer, making it impossible not to feel the warmth radiating from his body. The scent of his woodsy cologne rushes my senses. *That's new.* "Riley, what is it? You know you can tell me anything, right?" The familiar words from our childhood days create an ache in my heart. The tingling in my nipples is caused by something else entirely.

"You don't remember that I—"

"Riley? You home?" Grandma Hattie calls up the stairs, causing me to catapult off the bed as if she'd been standing in the doorway. Never mind that Zac and I weren't doing anything inappropriate. Or that we're both full-grown adults. "I brought you some pie."

"Coming." I don't wait for Zac to follow. I bolt down the stairs, convincing myself I need to keep Grandma Hattie from making another attempt to climb them. She *has* been extra spunky these past couple of days. That's totally the reason I'm in a hurry. It has nothing to do with getting space from Zac Ashburn.

"You still like apple, right?" Grandma Hattie asks, handing me a Styrofoam container.

"Still my favorite. Thank—"

"Zac, how lovely to see you," Grandma Hattie gushes, her attention one hundred percent shifting from me, her only granddaughter, to Zac. She always did like him the best out of the three of us. Probably because he's not blood related. "Riley, share your piece of pie with him."

"What?"

"I don't need any pie, ma'am." Zac saunters down the stairs, as if he has all the time in the world. As if we didn't almost share a moment up there. Not a trace of guilt etched on his perfectly chiseled face. "Thank you, though."

"Don't you *dare* call me ma'am," Grandma Hattie scolds playfully. "Ma'am will *always* be my mother, no matter how close to a hundred I get. It's Hattie."

"Yes ma'am—Hattie."

"Zac helped me move the furniture," I explain. "Huck's tied up."

"I heard!" Grandma Hattie's entire face lights up. "I hope they play that concert on the internet contraption. I'd love to hear her sing."

Zac and I share a quick amused glance that *should* be completely innocent. But the droves of butterflies erupting in my belly say otherwise. I'd swear there was a trace of heat in his dark eyes. Except it's more likely my overactive imagination is at work again. "I'll ask Huck if they're live streaming it," I say to Grandma Hattie.

But there's a dangerous twinkle in her eyes as they bounce between Zac and me. *Oh no. No, no. Down, Grandma Hattie!* "Zac, I can whip you up something to eat if you're hungry. Can't let all your help go unappreciated."

"I can't stay," Zac says, moving around me to get to Grandma Hattie. The brush of his shoulder against mine makes me a bit dizzy. Or maybe it's that delicious cologne. When I get back to Orlando, I'm buying a bottle and spraying it on my pillow. It'll be the closest thing I get to having a man in my bed for the foreseeable future.

Zac wraps Grandma Hattie in a hug. "You take it easy now," he says to her. "Don't give your granddaughter too much grief." He slips me a wink that causes those pesky butterflies in my belly to do loop-de-loops. "She's only looking out for you."

Shoving both hands in the back pockets of my jeans, I watch the first boy I ever had a crush on slip out the front door. Maybe in a different set of circumstances, this could be the start of something. But with the tangled mess my life has become, I can't entertain those thoughts.

No matter how badly I want to.

CHAPTER 4

Zac

I wake in a cold sweat, panting heavily and stomach in knots. The images from my nightmare flash faintly behind my eyelids. Memories from Afghanistan I'd rather forget. "Fuck," I mutter, angrily shoving the covers aside and hopping out of bed for the shower.

After the military, I did the responsible thing and sought help to deal with the plague of war. I thought I had a handle on it. For years, I've lived a mostly normal existence. But these past few months have dredged up some of my more traumatic memories, and I can't seem to put my finger on why.

I turn the water on and stand beneath the stream, willing my mind to wander *anywhere* else.

I'm not going to bite.

Though desperate to replace the warzone visions,

I'm shocked that Riley Kohl's voice pulls me out of my darkness. I blink for an extra-long moment, allowing her sweet image to replace the horrific ones. My heartrate instantly slows as a calm settles over me.

I try to reconcile the impossibility of it. Why *her*?

She's familiar. That's all. Her dark auburn hair in its long, lazy curls. The golden highlights framing her pretty face. Those startling blue eyes that have only gotten bluer with time. Her lips curl into a mischievous smile.

But the image doesn't stop there.

Oh no.

My wild imagination is clearly on a mission to distract me to the fullest.

I squeeze my eyes shut, resting my forehead against the tile wall as the hot water runs over my back. My steady heart rate begins to climb once again, but for an entirely different reason this time. I allow the forbidden fantasy to unfold. It's as if the camera lens that was focused solely on her face zooms out.

Riley stands before me in those skinny jeans and a sleeveless top that she begins to unbutton. Dear fucking god. I grip my cock—the fucker's already half hard—and begin to stroke it as my fantasy girl undoes another button. I'm teased by the hard nipples poking through the fabric. Another button undone reveals she's not wearing a bra. When did her tits get so *big*?

I stroke faster, shocked at how quickly my release finds me.

Hot ropes of cum shoot onto the tile wall before fantasy Riley works the last button of her top.

I'm panting heavily as my eyes pop back open, not sure what the fuck I should be feeling. I'm relieved that I was able to ward off the unwanted memories from my Army days. But to have them so easily wiped away with forbidden fantasies of my buddy's little sister isn't exactly great news.

I can't get involved with Riley.

I'm slipping on a t-shirt when I hear a knock on the front door. I live a couple of miles outside of town for a reason. To avoid people. It has to be one of my brothers. Probably Ben, who's pissed I let Huck take off without clearing it with him first. He makes the schedule, and not consulting him when there's changes really gets his boxers in a twist.

Pulling the door open, I launch right into my defense. "Ben, he didn't have time—"

"Not Ben."

I drop my gaze lower and find Riley Kohl standing on my doorstep, holding out a covered baking pan. My dick twitches in my pants, completely unaware that the shower was pure fantasy. Something that can never be realized in reality. "What's this?"

"Homemade caramel brownies. Grandma Hattie

insisted." She holds them out again. "Can I come in for a sec?"

"Uh, sure." I step back, allowing Riley inside. Because we're friends. It'd be rude not to invite a friend inside.

"Wow, this place is amazing." She tilts her head all the way up, admiring the vaulted log ceiling. "No way! You have a caribou antler chandelier. You always talked about having one when we were kids."

"You remembered." Finally, I free her of the brownies and carry them to the kitchen. She follows me, not shy about looking around.

"Of course I remember. The three of us used to sit on that old fishing dock, imagining what our lives would be like. What kind of houses we'd live in. What kind of cars we'd drive."

"Did you get your Mustang?"

"I did," she says, running her fingertips along my black quartz countertops. "But some jackass made a left turn on a red and t-boned me. Totaled it a week after I bought it." She lifts her baby blue gaze to me, and I nearly forget how to speak. I blame the unsolicited fantasy in the shower. One I'll have to take with me to the grave. "Do you *really* not remember what I did the day you and Huck left for basic training?"

This has to be why she's been mad at me since she saw me in the brewery last night. But for the life of me,

I haven't been able to figure out what I did all those years ago that's warranted her anger. "I'm sorry. I don't." I focus on the baking pan and help myself to a brownie. After my first bite, I realize I didn't offer one to Riley. But she turns it down.

"You don't remember me *kissing* you?"

I freeze at the words, instant panic flooding me. Did I do something that immature and stupid back then? "I kissed you?"

"No, *you* didn't." She covers her face with both hands and groans into them. "You know what, forget I said anything. I need to get going. If Grandma Hattie tried to get rid of me this morning, there's a reason. She's probably up to no good."

Riley's at the front door before I can register that she's trying to make an escape. I'm forced to run after her, catching the door with a firm hand before it closes. "Riley, wait."

She stops three feet from the front stoop, looking as mortified as I've ever seen her. "I really thought you remembered. I've just been wanting to apologize. Sorry I said anything. Just go back to forgetting—"

"If I ever get the chance to kiss you again, I promise I won't forget it. I doubt you will either." The bold words are out before I make the clear decision to speak them. I could blame my forbidden shower fantasy or a shitty night of sleep. But it's more than either of those things that's fueling the urgent need to bring a smile back to her perfect lips.

"You shouldn't say things you don't mean."

I'm prevented from a response because my oldest brother chooses *that* moment to tear into my driveway like he's being chased by a SWAT team. He's not, of course. He's too perfect to be in trouble with the law. He's probably just impatient and probably about to rip me a new asshole for giving Huck time off without consulting him.

"Riley—" But she's already in her grandpa's old beater truck, backing out of the driveway. Huck and I taught her how to drive in that truck. I stare after her. *Did she really kiss me and I don't remember?*

"I thought we had an agreement," Ben says, looking as pissed off as a taunted bull moose. "All time off goes through *me*."

"I'm sorry," I say, laying on the sarcasm thickly. I fold my arms over my chest and lean back against the door jamb. "I forgot Wes and I appointed you King of the Brewery at our last owner's meeting."

"Stop being a jackass." Ben looks over his shoulder. "What was Riley Kohl doing here?"

"Why do you care?"

"Fuck man. Do I have to remind you about *all* the rules?"

After the shitty night of sleep I had for the twentieth or thirtieth time in a row—I've lost count—I'm in no mood for Ben's shit today. "Did you really come here to lecture me about time off?" Though I wouldn't put it past him, I suspect he would've waited until I got to the brewery today to say something if there wasn't another reason he was here.

"You can't dip your pen in company ink, Zac."

I stare at him like he's grown two heads. "Riley doesn't work for us." Why that seems the more important detail to clear up and *not* that I didn't sleep with her, I don't know. Even if Riley were staying and Huck was cool with it, I'm too broken inside. Riley deserves better than the fractured pieces of me I could offer her.

"But her brother does. You think that through at all?"

My head is pounding, which isn't unusual after the nightmares. But it's getting much worse with Ben in my face. I haven't told either of my brothers that the PTSD is back. I don't need them monitoring me like I'm a bomb that could go off at any time. "Tell me why you're really here or I'm going back inside and locking the door."

"Because you don't answer your fucking phone," he grumbles. "Supply truck came a day early and kegs need to be cleaned. Since you sent Huck to Anchorage without telling anyone, you get to pick up the slack. Get your ass down to the brewery an hour ago."

"Let me grab my keys. I'm right behind you." I slam the door closed before he can get another jerkish jab in. It's pointless to remind Ben that he's not the boss. The three of us make decisions together and have equal sway in our family-owned company. I also don't need any more lecturing about Riley Kohl. Should I have made that comment about kissing her? Probably not. But would I take it back given the chance? No way in hell.

Riley

"What do you mean I can't stay here?" I watch Grandma Hattie pull down wine glasses from the cupboard near the sink, ready to pounce if she drops something. Maybe I've been hovering too much for the past couple of days. But it gives me an excuse to stay in. To avoid Zac Ashburn and his dangerously tempting words. "It's just a bridge game."

Grandpa Harold lets out a good laugh as he enters the kitchen. "Just a bridge game," he mumbles, shaking his head. He sets a hand on Grandma Hattie's shoulder and kisses her forehead. "You've been gone too many years, pumpkin," he says to me. He redirects his attention to his wife. "Need anything before I head to poker night?"

"Yes." Grandma Hattie points a glare at me. "Get

rid of my parole officer. What will the ladies think if she's hovering around me all night, watching my every move? It'll throw me off my game. I can't let them smell weakness."

I hide a laugh behind my hand, realizing I'm going to miss Grandma Hattie's spunkiness once I return to Orlando. I make a mental note to get over my damn self, and my pitiful crush, so I can visit once in a while. While I still can. *If they don't disown me first.*

I *should* head to the grocery store or gas station and get a pregnancy test. Rip the band-aid off. But in a town as small as Caribou Creek, there's no way I can make such a purchase without a rumor spreading like wildfire. "Since you won't invite me to play cards, just where am I supposed to go?"

Before Grandma Hattie can list off some suggestions, a knock at the kitchen door turns all our heads. Her bridge ladies aren't supposed to show up for at least an hour. Huck and Penny are out of town—

"Zac, come on in!" Grandma Hattie wraps her arms around his waist, unashamedly resting her head against the middle of his torso since she's not tall enough to reach his hard chest. Completely unaware that my pulse has tripled in a single breath. I had hoped the space would help me get my head on straight when it comes to Zac Ashburn. But clearly, it's had the opposite effect. My damn nipples are pebbled in seconds, reminding me of the promise that left his lips. One about a kiss neither of us would forget.

"I brought back your brownie pan," he says, lifting it as evidence.

"You're just in time."

"Oh no," I chime in before this gets any crazier. "Grandma Hattie, don't you *dare*." I should've seen it the other night when that dangerous twinkle was dancing in her eyes. She saw *something* when she looked between Zac and me. The sly devil is trying to play matchmaker.

"Are you busy tonight, Zac?" she asks.

Grandpa Harold plants another kiss on her temple, throws me a wink, and slips out the door. Leaving me to fight my own battle. *Gee thanks.*

"Got the evening free, actually. Did you need me to help move more furniture?"

"Not tonight. The ladies are coming over for bridge." She loops an arm through his and subtly guides him in my direction. "Which is why I need Riley to leave. All her fussing is sweet, but it'll ruin my concentration. I'm on a winning streak."

"Are you sure this is a *bridge* game?" I ask, highly suspicious that these old ladies are gathering to gamble. Maybe that's why Grandma Hattie wants me gone. She doesn't want me to find the poker chips or black jack table. "Never mind. I don't want to know," I add, holding up my hands. "Grandma Hattie, can I really trust you not to overdo it? Your ankle—"

"Rose'll keep me out of trouble. She was a nurse before she bought the diner, you know." Somehow, she's finagled herself and Zac to within arm's reach of me. She pats my arm fondly. "We all have former lives, you know. She's on her way over right now."

"Sounds like your grandma has everything handled," Zac says, wearing a half smile that threatens to undo me. I haven't been able to stop thinking about what he said when I left his place yesterday. It's not enough that my traitorous body can't keep itself under control at the sight of him. But I've been fantasizing about that kiss. One that wouldn't leave me embarrassed and hiding until he left town.

"You're going to entertain me?" I challenge.

"I think that's a grand idea!" Grandma Hattie's eyes are twinkling again.

"I have an idea," Zac says, holding out his hand for mine. "Do you trust me?"

I stare at his hand for several long beats before flicking my gaze up to his. "The last time you asked me that, I ended up covered in mud from head to toe."

"But you had fun, right?"

The memory of me holding onto him tight as he four-wheeled it through the bumpiest, muddiest trails in history still warms me from the inside out. It was the day I realized I had a crush on him. I could've been covered in moose crap and still been stupidly happy. "I don't want to get dirty tonight," I say, pointing a stern finger at him.

Zac grabs my hand, causing tingles to skitter up my arm. "No promises."

"Zac!"

A knock at the door announces the arrival of Rose Clayton, owner of THE CARIBOU CREEK DINER. "Out you go!" Grandma Hattie ushers us both toward the door. "Don't come back until the stars come out."

I'm two steps out the back door before it dawns on me. "The stars don't come out this time of year—"

Zac drapes an arm over my shoulders, guiding me away from the house. Something he's done hundreds of times in our youth. But this is the first time electricity zings up and down my body like a damn lightning storm is happening inside of me. I steal a quick glance at his lips, wondering if I'll get that second chance to try them out tonight. Wondering if a kiss, now that we're older, will lead to more.

"Where are we going?" I ask as he holds the passenger door of his truck open.

He winks at me, causing those pesky stomach butterflies to throw a dance party. "Now what fun would it be if I spoiled the surprise?"

CHAPTER 6

Zac

Though I told myself I only stopped by Hattie's to drop off the brownie pan, I knew it was a lie. I haven't seen Riley since yesterday morning, when she practically ran away at the mention of a kiss I still don't remember. Her absence since has left me feeling restless and antsy, and I don't like it one bit. The need to see her was too overwhelming to ignore.

"The old boat dock is still here?" she asks, her eyes lighting up when I pull up to the edge of a graveled area. A spot where the three of us used to drop our bikes. We used to come out here all the time when we were kids. We'd fish, not that we caught anything, and waste an entire day eating junk food we snuck out of their mom's pantry. My favorite part was always the daydreaming. Our plans. Our big what ifs.

"It is."

"Is it safe?"

"Yes." I cut the ignition and push open my door. "You coming?"

"If I fall through a rotted board and get wet—"

"Though I wouldn't mind seeing you soaked from head from toe, the boards are new. I fixed it up a couple summers ago." I close the door and head toward the dock, leaving her to catch up. Putting me far enough in front of her so I can't see her expression. I'm left to wonder if she caught what I was really saying.

"Why would you do that?" she asks, stopping at the point where the grass meets the wooden planks. "*How* did you do it and not get shot? Wait, is Old Man Jenkins...*dead*?" She gasps, her wide eyes and panicked expression so damn cute. It makes me yearn for things I've convinced myself I don't deserve.

"He retired. Moved to Charleston."

"Who owns it now?"

At the dock, I turn and look back at Riley. She hesitates at the edge, as if she can't quite trust she won't end up in the water if she dares to join me. It gives me an extra moment to discreetly rake my gaze up and down her curvy body. Damn, she's filled out in all the right ways. What I wouldn't give to watch her unbutton that top and reveal her bountiful tits for my viewing pleasure. The part of me that knows I shouldn't be thinking these things about Huck's little sister has apparently checked out tonight. "I do."

"*You* own it?"

"Old Man Jenkins sold it to me when he left town."

She takes a couple cautious steps forward, picking up her pace when she accepts it's safe. "How could you afford it?"

Old Man Jenkins got dozens of solid offers over the years, but he wasn't as interested in money as he was in selling it to someone who appreciated the land. On each deployment, I tucked away as much money as I could. "There's a lot you don't know about me, Riley Kohl. That happens when you disappear for fourteen years."

"You weren't in Caribou Creek the whole time," she says, narrowing her eyes at me.

I kick off my shoes and sit on the edge of the dock. I pat the space beside me, but Riley doesn't sit. "I don't bite," I say, repeating her words from the other night. "Unless you want me to."

She rolls her eyes at me before quickly turning away. But she's not fast enough to hide the redness creeping up her neck at my words. The one thing that's been undeniable since we laid eyes on each other in the brewery Monday night is the chemistry that's crackling between us. A pull so strong that physical distance will no longer be enough to keep us apart. I know she feels it too. It's the heat dancing in her eyes. We'll crave each other no matter how many miles or obstacles separate us.

Finally, Riley kicks off her sandals and joins me, dangling her toes in the water. I feel her tension as if it were my own. Something is troubling her. It'll trouble me too unless I can help her. But Riley Kohl is as stubborn as they come, second only to her grandma. "Did you accomplish any of those dreams you dreamed up out here? Besides the Mustang."

"I don't have the million-dollar mansion overlooking the ocean," she admits, offering a weak smile to the creek. "I didn't marry Justin Bieber and have his babies. Thirty was my cut-off. Considering that's only a few months away, it's probably too late to accomplish that dream. Unless I'm unknowingly carrying his triplets—"

She stops abruptly and clears her throat. Trouble flickers in her eyes. Never in my life have I wanted to bring someone peace as much as I want that for Riley. I'd endure a thousand years of war nightmares if only she could smile without reservation. Whatever is eating at her, it's more than some kiss I don't remember. It's much more. "Riley—"

"What about you? You obviously took over the

family brewery with your brothers. You always talked about doing that."

I lean back on my hands, daring to slide one closer to her. Not touching, but close enough that I can feel the heat of her dancing against my thumb. It takes every ounce of restraint I have not to run my hand up her arm. What I wouldn't give to caress every inch of her naked body and commit the feeling to memory. "We took over ownership from my grandparents three and a half years ago when they decided to retire and move south. They live in a bungalow on a white sandy beach, just like Grandma always wanted. And Grandpa gets to fish all day, every day."

I dare to graze my thumb against hers, caressing with a feather's gentleness. She stares down at my hand but doesn't pull hers away. "Sounds like it all worked out, then."

"Yeah, I guess it did."

"Is it hard? Not having them in Caribou Creek?" She lifts her gaze to mine and dammit if my pulse doesn't double on the spot. Those baby blues, filled with compassion, reach inside me to depths I never thought a person could penetrate.

"I still have my brothers." I slide my hand atop hers. She turns her hand, offering me her palm as our fingers thread together. My dick twitches against my zipper, reminding me of the many forbidden fantasies starring Riley Kohl and very little clothing. Fantasies that have been on repeat since the morning I stroked myself in the shower to her image. "You're still going back to Orlando?"

"My whole life is there."

I scoot closer to her, resting our joined hands on her thigh. "Your job. Your apartment. Your theoretical cat."

"His name is Mr. Whiskers."

"How original." My gaze drops to her soft lips, wondering why the hell I can't remember her kissing me all those years ago. Not that it could've led anywhere. I was eighteen, leaving for basic training. She was fifteen and my buddy's little sister. But now that we're older, the three-year age gap means nothing. Everything about this moment feels...natural. As if we've been here a thousand times before. As if we'll be here a thousand more.

"It's *my* theoretical cat. I can name him whatever I want."

I dare to lean closer, reaching for a stray lock of hair the breeze is set on teasing. I tuck it behind her ear. I should pull my hand away. But I've already come too far to turn back now. I know there'll be some complications with Huck, but we'll work them out when he gets back. I have to have Riley Kohl for my own. I need her as badly as I need oxygen. I know I'm a broken man, but maybe what I need to heal is sitting beside me, parting her lips in anticipation.

"Ready for that kiss you'll never forget?" I ask in a heated whisper, tucking my fingers beneath her jaw and tugging her closer. I don't give her a chance to answer the question before I brush my lips against hers. I pause, giving her a moment to pull away. But she doesn't. She reaches for my cheek, tugging me closer.

The kiss deepens as our lips press harder together. I thread my fingers into her hair, certain she'll give me shit later for messing up her ponytail. I run my tongue between her lips, begging for entry she willingly grants.

She softly moans into my mouth as our tongues do a dance.

Before Riley Kohl showed back up in Caribou Creek, I never would've guessed she was The One. But suddenly it makes sense why it never worked out with anyone else. I can blame my war trauma all I want, but deep down I knew something was missing with the women I dated. *She* was missing.

With one kiss, I know my fate with Riley is sealed. There'll never be another for me. The sudden realization should scare me more than any IED ever did, but instead it has the opposite effect. It brings me peace.

I drop a hand to her neck, relishing in the softness of her skin.

"Stop!" Riley pulls back so suddenly she nearly topples into the water. I catch her by the waist to keep her from tumbling in. "I'm sorry. I can't—" She looks me square in the eyes, that familiar tension returning. My stomach twists in knots at what she might confess. "I might be pregnant."

CHAPTER 7

Riley

My heart stops beating for an alarming number of seconds as Zac stares at me in disbelief. It's unsettling for many reasons. But the biggest is that I'm afraid I've ruined any chance of whatever was happening between us from going further. Going anywhere. *Way to ruin the moment, genius.*

"Pregnant?" he repeats, the word hardly a whisper as it escapes his lips. Lips that felt so damn good moving against mine only moments ago.

"It's a pathetic story," I say, pulling my hand away from his warm cheek. As badly as I want to kiss him again and pretend like I never blurted this embarrassing confession, he deserves to know what a mess my life is right now. "Boy meets girl. Boy pursues girl. Girl is fooled by his charms and gives in. Girl ends up the butt of a terrible joke."

"You don't know for sure?" he asks.

I let out a sigh, staring off across the creek. Hoping that some caribou might creep closer to the water and divert this mortifying conversation. "I'm too chicken to find out. I'm not exactly in the best location to buy a pregnancy test without half the town starting a rumor. I'd never forgive myself if Grandma Hattie had a heart attack on my account." The orthopedic surgeon I let charm his way into my pants is very married despite his claims of a divorce being nearly finalized. Apparently, the divorce was complete fiction. A fact I learned the hard way when I caught him banging his actual wife in an exam room.

"What will you do if you are?"

"Good question."

"You're still going back to Orlando?"

I can't imagine anyone being thrilled to find out I'm carrying a married man's child. *If* I'm pregnant. Considering I missed my last period completely and I've been nauseous off and on, I don't consider my odds of *not* being pregnant too great. Grandma Hattie is a wonderful, loving woman. But I don't know how she's going to feel about this. I doubt she'll continue to offer me a bed if she finds out the details. I won't be welcome here. "I think I have to."

All I want to do is rest my head on his shoulder and drink in his warmth. Wrap his comfort around me like a blanket. Zac feels like the safety and reassurance I crave but definitely don't deserve. But I can't let him get tangled up in all this. It's too much to ask of anyone. "This is my mess. I have to deal with it, and I will."

"You don't have to face all this alone, Riley."

Damn the man for being so sweet and sexy all in the same heart-stopping glance. I pull my toes out of the water and hop to my feet. I can't stay here any longer. If I do, I might crawl into his lap and slide my hands under that too-tight t-shirt so I can feel those muscles ripple against my fingers. Even if Grandma Hattie locks me out of the house until her bridge night is over. "I'm a big girl. I've got this." *I totally don't got this*.

"Riley—"

"And no one knows about this, okay? Not Grandma Hattie. Definitely not Huck."

"I won't say a word."

"Thank you." There's something happening between us that goes beyond physical attraction. And make no mistake. There's *plenty* of physical attraction sizzling in the air between us. I'd give nearly anything to go back to his place and get naked with Zac Ashburn. To feel his hands roam all over my body. To

LOVE ON TAP

taste every inch of his warm, hard skin with the tip of my tongue. To feel him inside me, taking me to places I've never been. That earthshattering kiss is going to rev up the intensity of my naughty dreams tonight and probably many nights to come.

But until I know what my fate is, I can't drag him into my tangled web. He deserves better than to be caught up in my mess of a life.

"Is there anywhere to get ice cream this late at night?" I ask, certain there's not since Rose is at Grandma Hattie's.

Zac hops to his feet and grabs his shoes. "The gas station has a pretty surprising selection of Ben & Jerry's."

I'm so relieved for the normalcy that remains between us. Zac could be completely freaked out right now or ready to run a hundred miles in the opposite direction. Instead, that familiar bond of friendship reassures me he's not going anywhere. "What are we waiting for? Lead the way."

51

Zac

"You sure you don't mind?" I ask my buddy Decker as we pull into Hattie's driveway unannounced. I don't have any idea how this'll go down. Riley might feel like I'm pushing her and hate me for it. But I can't stand back and do nothing. I need her to know that I'm here for her. That she can remove that tough-girl armor and allow me to lessen some of her burden. "Hattie Kohl can be a handful."

Decker smirks. "I'm sure I've dealt with worse."

We walk up to the door, but before I can knock, it flies open. "Zac, what are you doing here?" Riley glances at Decker. "And you brought...*company?*"

Grandma Hattie peeks over her shoulder, the same mischievous twinkle in her eyes that she's been wearing since I helped Riley move the furniture. When I'm her age, I hope I enjoy life half as much as she does. "It's very thoughtful of you Zac, but you know I'm a happily married woman. Going on fifty-six years."

"Grandma Hattie!" Riley scolds.

Riley's shocked expression does things to me. Just the memory of her kiss awakens a part of me that I thought was permanently dormant. I wonder if she thought about me last night as much I thought about her. If she touched herself while thinking about me like I did while I was thinking about her. Did she imagine my hands on her body? My lips exploring every inch of her? "I *did* bring Decker by for you, Hattie, but it's not a date. I don't want to get on Harold's bad side."

"Smart man."

"I need to borrow Riley for a while."

"We haven't gotten through all her morning exercises," Riley says immediately.

"That's why I brought Decker," I explain.

Her arms are across her chest again. I can't help but drop my gaze to the perfect tits she keeps trying to hide. "No offense, Decker, but I don't see how bartending qualifies you to oversee physical therapy."

"Before I started working at the brewery, I was a medic in the Army for ten years." The mention of the military makes me stiffen with unease. Vague images are all it takes to unsteady me these days, but

I take a deep breath and shift my focus to the present. "Some physical therapy exercises are a piece of cake compared to what I'm used to," Decker adds. I notice he has Hattie grinning from ear to ear. But whether it's his charm or her approval of me stealing away Riley for the morning, I'm not sure.

"See," I say to Riley. "He can help Hattie run through her exercises *and* keep her out of trouble. Right, Hattie?"

"Of course, he can." Hattie agrees so readily I can't help but hope she's on my side. That she sees the spark between Riley and me and is trying to help fan the flames into something that will make Riley stay. "He's lucky I'm a married woman or that *trouble* part might be a stretch."

"Grandma Hattie!" Riley gasps again.

Hattie winks at me, reassuring me that, yes, she's on my team. Before Riley came back to Caribou Creek, Hattie wasn't shy about her opinions. She told me more than once that I needed to find a good woman and settle down. Even if Huck blows a gasket, at least Hattie approves.

"I only have the morning," I say to Riley, hoping that'll coax her from the house. "Have to be at the brewery after lunch."

"Don't just stand around everybody," Hattie

exclaims. "Riley, go get your purse. Decker's got things covered, right soldier?"

"Yes ma'am."

Hattie narrows her eyes at him. "We'll have to straighten a few things out. But I think we'll manage just fine. See you later, Riley. I promise not to run up the stairs while you're gone." She crosses her finger over her heart. "Scouts honor and all that."

Riley is practically shoved out the door a moment later. Finally, the two of us are alone. I yearn to pull her into my arms and revisit that smoldering kiss from last night. But outside the possibility of a very nosy audience, I can sense her hesitation and hold back. "I'm sorry to ambush you," I say.

"Are you though?" It's the playful graze of her fingertips against my bicep that eases away the tension. The hints of flashbacks have subsided completely, allowing me to breathe easier. Or maybe it's just that Riley is standing so close that the morning breeze can hardly wedge its way between us.

"C'mon," I urge before I give in to the temptation and pull her against me, kissing her like there's no tomorrow. Before things get physical again, there's something she needs to decide on first. "I've got some fresh coffee in the truck."

"I could kiss you." She blurts the words before she seems to realize their impact.

"Again?" I tease.

"Zac—"

"I know. I know. That's why I'm here."

Once we're both in the truck, she looks at me. "I don't understand."

"Do you trust me?" I ask, reaching for her hand and squeezing.

"I've always trusted you." Her worried expression softens, that familiar twinkle reappearing in those baby blues. "That was usually my downfall, you know. If I didn't end up covered in mud or soaking wet from falling in the creek, I was stranded in a tree with an irritated moose on the prowl or—"

"I lured that moose away, in case you forgot." I wait for her easy smile before I broach the more serious topic. "I'm not going to push you. But I also know one of the reasons you haven't found out if you've got a bun in the oven is because you can't buy a pregnancy test without the entire town knowing by noon."

A mile from town, I slow for the turn onto the private dirt road.

"We're going to your place?" she asks as I follow the half-mile drive to my cabin.

"I didn't think you'd want to pee on a stick at Hattie's." My attempt to tease falls flat as her expression goes blank. "Look, you don't have to do anything you don't want to. You don't have to share the news with anyone—including me. I just wanted—"

"Did you buy it in town?"

I relax, understanding her reservation now. "Of course not." Unable to sleep, I got on the road at four a.m. and headed south to the nearest gas station large enough to carry such a thing. I'll probably pay for that early morning four-hour round trip midway through my shift at the brewery, but I couldn't sit still. I had to do *something* to help.

Riley reaches for my hand, her blue eyes shiny with gratitude. "Thank you."

I try to pretend that her touch doesn't ignite every nerve ending in my body. I've always considered myself a patient man. But with Riley Kohl, I feel time ticking away all too quickly. If I want to convince her to stay in Caribou Creek, I can't drag my feet about it.

I park my truck in front of the cabin, glancing her way before I open the door. Even with the reassurance that no one in town knows, I can tell she's nervous as hell. My hand cups her jaw before I think it through, my thumb caressing her silky soft cheek. "What you do is up to you, sweetheart. There's no pressure, okay?"

"Okay."

I stare at the three different boxes displayed on Zac's kitchen island.

No pressure.

Right.

My palms are sweaty, my pulse erratic, and those butterflies in my stomach are drunk. Not silly drunk. No, they're about-to-throw-up drunk. Nausea assaults me, forcing me to grip the counter.

"Hey," Zac says, resting a reassuring hand on my shoulder. "If you're not ready, that's okay too."

I allow my eyes to fall closed and focus on the sensation of his touch. I breathe in his woodsy cologne, inviting the distraction it provides. If it's the only thing I accomplish before I leave Caribou Creek, I'm going to find the bottle responsible for making Zac smell so damn good. Maybe steal a t-shirt doused in the intoxicating aroma.

"I'm not ready," I finally say, my words quiet and wobbly.

I'm not ready to face reality. I'm not ready to find out if I'm carrying a married man's child. Not ready for everyone I care about to turn away from me. I never should've believed him when he told me his divorce was almost finalized. I should have been more diligent in finding the answers for myself before I succumbed to his charms.

"You want pancakes?"

I feel the tension in my shoulders ease as Zac slides his hand away. "Pancakes?"

"Pancakes make everything better, right?"

His effortlessly sexy smile erodes the rest of my dread. I stare at his mouth, remembering how perfect it felt against my own. But the untouched tests remind me I should keep my hands to myself until I'm brave enough to face reality. "Not hungry," I admit. Well, *not for pancakes*.

I move from the island, eager to put some distance between those tests and me. Though the only direction I yearn to go is right into Zac's arms, I force myself to travel in the opposite direction. I stop at a side table against the far living room wall. It's covered in framed photographs of men in Army uniforms.

I reach for one and study the picture that includes Zac, my brother, and a couple other GIs. "Wow, you *really* fill out a uniform."

"That was in another life." He takes the framed picture from me and sets it back down. The graze of his fingers scrambles my brain. He's standing close enough to blanket me in his heat. I shouldn't lean into it, but it's too late. My back is pressed against his chest, my neck tilted in offering, and my hand reaching for his cheek before I even realize what's happened.

Zac nuzzles my neck, his beard tickling my sensitive flesh.

I sink into him further, forgetting by the second why I'm supposed to resist him.

His warm hand slides down my arm and settles on my stomach, holding me in a way that feels possessive. The wetness pooling between my legs outs me. I like it. I like it *way* too much. A soft moan escapes my parted lips, begging him to kiss me again.

"I'm sorry if I pushed you," he says in a low, heated whisper against my ear.

"You didn't." I comb my fingers through his beard, willing his lips to find mine. "I appreciate what you're trying to do."

"I want you to know something, Riley."

"Yeah?"

"No matter what you find out, I'm not going to

leave you high and dry." He doesn't give me a chance to respond because his lips are on mine. Moving in that seductive way that makes it impossible to think straight. I snake my hand around his neck as my bones turns squishy and hold on as our tongues swirl together.

"Sweetheart?"

A thrill shoots through me at the tender nickname. "Yes?"

He moves his hand to my hip and digs his fingers in. "If I move too fast, you just have to tell me."

In this heated moment, I can't imagine anything being too fast. I'm soaked between the legs, desperate to feel his hands on every inch of my body. There's a faint whisper in the back of my mind, reminding me that I'm supposed to stay celibate, but I drown it out with a moan. How long have I waited for exactly this moment? Fifteen-year-old me never dreamed up more than a sultry kiss. But in the years I stayed away from Caribou Creek, I never completely put Zac Ashburn out of my mind. "Zac?"

"Yes, sweetheart?"

"You have more than a cot in your bedroom, right?"

His low, deep chuckle has those drunken butter-flies in my stomach all aflutter as they bump giddily into one another. "Why don't you come see for yourself?" He slips his hand in mine and guides me down the hall.

He allows me into the bedroom first. But I only have time to register its massive size and the too-small bed before he steps up behind me and wraps his body around mine. "Better than a cot, right?"

At this point, the floor would do.

I spin in his arms, draping my arms around his neck and inviting his lips back to mine. In the passionate frenzy, I end up against the door with half my clothes missing. Zac's shirt is gone, allowing me the pleasure to run my hands up and down his chest. Every inch of him is deliciously hard.

He leads me to the bed, tugging off my jeans before we fall onto the mattress. I'm left in nothing but my bra and panties, feeling suddenly shy around the first boy—now *all* man—I ever crushed on. He's hard, cut muscle. I'm soft, generous curves.

"Don't do that, sweetheart," he says, hovering his glorious body above mine.

"What?"

"Second guess your beauty. You're better than that." He fuses his mouth to mine as his hand slides between my legs. Stroking wet silk with just the right amount of pressure to drive me wild. I rock my hips against his touch. I love the way his simple words instantly renew the confidence I lost a few months ago.

Zac kisses a trail from my lips to my belly as he tugs away my panties. I gasp as I realize what's about to happen.

"I need to taste you, Riley," he says in a near growl.

I've never had a man go down on me, though I've fantasized about it a lot. To have Zac Ashburn be the first turns me on in ways I never thought possible. I spread my legs wider for him in offering.

"Good girl." He rewards me with a drag of his tongue through my folds. I let out a long, drawn-out moan as I sink completely against the bed. Becoming one with the mattress and pillow beneath my head as his mouth performs some kind of magic spell against my pussy. He licks, suckles, and gently nibbles my clit. His tongue carves its way through every fold, tasting every bit of me.

When his tongues plunges into my channel, I buck my hips against his face. Fuck, that's...amazing. His deep laughter vibrates against me, intensifying every sensation. How the hell have I gone my whole life without experiencing this? My eyes fall closed as I rock in rhythm to his mouth.

Zac scoops his hands beneath my ass, fusing his mouth against my pussy so tightly I'm sure he's cut off his oxygen supply. It doesn't stop me from fisting my hand in his hair and pressing him harder against me. He laughs again.

"Oh my god, you're trying to kill me with that rumbling laugh of yours," I mock complain.

"There are worse ways to go." Those are the last words he speaks before he intensifies *everything*. The pleasure happening between my legs is dizzying. My toes and fingertips start to tingle as I reach that magnificent edge of the cliff. As I soar over the edge, crying out his name, I'm certain I've never experienced anything quite like this.

It's like flying.

I never want to come down.

I secure the front door lock of the brewery and cut the power to the neon *open* sign. Fridays are typically one of our busiest days of the week, but this one was insane. Dozens of tourists exploring Denali National Park took a bus to Caribou Creek and spent the day in town. Many of them hung out at the brewery from the moment we opened until last call.

"What a day, huh?" Wes calls out to me as I head back to the counter and wipe it down.

"Went by fast." I leave out the fact that I feel completely depleted for fear my mild complaining will summon Ben from his cave. He's been tasking me with extra shit to make up for Huck being out of town. And I've been doing his bidding just to keep Huck from getting the brunt of Ben's wrath when he gets back. Doesn't mean I'm not still irritated that I missed hanging out with Riley last night because Ben decided we needed to clean the fermentation tanks. *Again.*

Riley invited me over to watch the live-stream concert tonight with her and her grandparents. But with how fucking tired I am, I'll probably be passed out before Penny finishes her first song. Time is going by too damn fast. How long before Hattie doesn't need in-home rehab? How quickly will Riley get on a plane and head back to Orlando?

Unless I can convince her to stay here.

"I'm checking out a house on Fifth Street," Wes says, pulling out his phone and quickly typing out a text. "Interested in tagging along?"

"Not tonight. Got things to do. And I'm wiped."

"Wiped, huh?" Wes lifts an eyebrow in suspicion. "You're falling for her, aren't you?"

Leave it to my middle brother to see right through me without any effort. He's too perceptive for his own good. Sometimes it's downright eerie. But I'd happily deal with Wes over Ben. "Don't you have enough rental properties?"

"Only three," he says, studying me too closely for me to believe he's going to drop the whole thing with Riley. "I like even numbers."

"So do I," Ben announces, appearing at the end of the bar to count the drawer. "Preferably ones in the green."

For once, I'm happy to see my grumpy brother. He's just the distraction I need for Wes to zip it. The last thing I want is for rumors to spread around town about Riley and me. Especially with Huck still in Anchorage. He'll be back Sunday, and I still haven't figured out what to say to him about his little sister. I haven't come up with anything that guarantees he won't give me a black eye. But it doesn't stop a grin from forming at the memory of licking her sweet pussy. The taste of her still lingers faintly on my tongue.

"We're always in the green," Wes points out.

"We haven't been in the red," I add.

"We've been close enough." Ben doesn't offer a hint of a smile. I'm convinced if he tried, outside of the schmoozing his job requires, his face might crack and shatter.

I can't remember the last time the three of us hung out and just enjoyed an evening together. Ever since we signed the paperwork to take over the brewery from our grandparents, Ben seems to have lost all his joy. It makes me question if we made the right decision.

Or if he just needs to get laid.

"You want to come with me to see a new rental?" Wes asks him.

"Can't."

"Won't," Wes corrects him. "You mean *won't*."

"I need to run numbers."

"I already did," Josie Bennington, our administrative assistant, appears at the end of the bar. She's slipping on a hoodie with our logo. Ben pretends not to notice, but I catch him stealing a side glance as she wriggles into her oversized sweatshirt. Though he'd never admit it, he's crazy about her. But he'd also die before he bent his own rule about dating employees.

"You did?"

"I emailed you the report," she adds, offering him a soft smile he pretends to ignore. Wes and I have a bet on how long it'll take those two to give in. Wes thinks it'll happen before the summer's over. Convinced Ben moves slower than a snail wading through molasses, I bet two years. "Did you need me to do anything else before I leave?"

Wes and I share a knowing look, neither of us missing the hopefulness in her tone.

"No." Ben pretends to focus on the register. "You can head out."

Her smile falls, but she gives a nod. "See you all Monday."

Wes waits until Josie has slipped out the front door and I've relocked it before he drills into Ben. "Dude, what is your problem?"

"No problem." Ben pulls the drawer out of the register and sets it on the counter to start counting.

"Don't waste your breath," I say to Wes. "He won't listen."

"You should fucking talk," Ben snaps at me. "I thought I told you to stay away from Riley Kohl."

I bristle at his commanding tone. Sometimes Ben can be a real dick. My fists ball at my sides, ready to defend Riley's honor. Ready to tell my oldest brother to fucking butt out. "When you stop lying to yourself about Josie, *then* you can talk like you fucking know something." I don't wait for him to bark back at me. I don't give him the pleasure as I grab my keys and head out, leaving half the bar counter for him to clean.

It's not as if I don't know this whole situation with Riley is fragile. There are so many road blocks in the way of a happy future together. But unlike my brother, I'm not afraid to face them head on.

I'm falling for Riley Kohl.

For the first time in weeks, I wasn't stirred awake last night from nightmares. No, just the raging hard on she gave me in my dreams. I'm falling for her, whether I like it or not. Whether anyone else likes it or not. The way she kissed me back yesterday tells me I'm not alone in this. The only thing that matters is how am I going to convince her to stay in Caribou Creek? Because I *have* to. I can no longer imagine a life that doesn't include her in it.

My body hums as I park in front of Zac's cabin. Last night, he fell asleep on the couch with his arm draped over my shoulders as we watched the live-streamed concert with my grandparents. Never in my life would I have thought such a simple thing could feel so...special. Or that I would crave so many more of those simple things.

I yearned to go home with him.

But I settled for walking him to his truck and stealing some very handsy kisses in the shadows before he promised to text me after he got home safe. All night long, I felt his hands on my body and remembered the talented stroke of his tongue through my folds. The way his beard felt brushing against the insides of my thighs. Needless to say, I'm about to spontaneously combust.

I should be alarmed at how easily I'm falling into this fantasy life, knowing that soon I'll have to return to Orlando. As much as I want to stay in Caribou Creek, things aren't so simple. Even if Huck doesn't freak out about Zac and me, I don't know what I would do for work. It's highly doubtful the clinic could support a full time PT. And then there's one important matter that still needs addressing...

It's why I've decided that tonight, I need answers.

I'm going to stop being a chicken and pee on all three of those sticks just to be sure, one way or another. I still haven't had my period, going on six weeks now. But the lack of morning sickness gives me a small bubble of hope. I'll love all my babies no matter what. I just don't want to be tied to Chip if I can help it.

I nervously knock on the door, uncertain if I'm feeling jittery because of the pregnancy thing or because I'm dying to climb Zac Ashburn like a tree. Grandma Hattie sent me on my way with a bottle of wine and a promise that I wouldn't drive home drunk. I think it's her secret blessing to get myself a fix of the hunky military veteran.

When there's no answer, I twist the knob and call out for Zac.

I hear the faint sound of running water, and step inside. It takes concentrated restraint not to shed all my clothes and join him in the shower. *Focus, Riley.*

I set the bottle of wine on the counter and pick up one of the pregnancy test boxes. If two pink lines show up, will Zac really stay true to his word? Though I'm incredibly touched by his offer, it's not fair of me to extend that burden to anyone else.

At the sound of footsteps, my nervous fingers drop the box. Zac waltzes into the kitchen, drying his hair with a towel that obstructs his vision but leaves every other delicious inch of him on full display. I try to be respectful, but my traitorous she-wolf eyes drop right to his most impressive part. *Is that thing legal?* He's half hard, which leaves my imagination to wonder two naughty things; one, what was he thinking about that aroused him, and two, how much bigger does it get? *Is it hot in here? It's hot in here. I should crack a window.*

"Riley, hey."

"Oh, hey." The words come out as a squeak as I busy myself with the kitchen window latch.

"It doesn't open."

"Oh."

"I need to fix that." I catch him wrapping the towel around his waist out of my peripherals but still wait a few extra seconds before I turn around. My cheeks are no doubt a deeper red than his kitchen towels.

"Grandma Hattie sent wine," I say, thrusting the bottle forward in an effort to draw his attention away from my sudden awkwardness. But it doesn't stop me from wanting to lick those stray water droplets from his skin. "Said it's not responsible to drive home drunk."

Heat flares in Zac's eyes as a devilish smile curls his oh-so-kissable lips. Lips that know their way around my body. I'm so focused on them that I don't realize he moves around the island until he's standing in front of me. "Probably better spend the night here then. Just to be safe."

"Probably."

"Riley, you keep looking at me like that, we won't get to the movie."

I reach a hand to his side, digging my fingers into his warm skin. The simple gesture pulls us closer and raises my internal temperature a thousand degrees. All I can think about is molding my body with his. "What movie?"

He combs a hand into my hair, tilting my face up. "You're cute when you're flustered."

"I'm not flustered."

"Your denial's cute too." He doesn't give me a chance to retort because his lips are on mine. Fire ignites inside my body, roaring to life and awakening every nerve ending in one quick swoosh. I grip his hips

KALI HART

with both hands, meaning only to pull him closer. Except, the towel falls away. As does any chance of Zac hiding his eagerness or my ability not to stare at his now fully hard cock.

"Oops," I say, feeling my cheeks flush. I bend to grab the towel and crash my face right into his length. I freeze, feeling foolish and turned on all at once. My forehead rests against his swollen head. I could stick out my tongue and tickle the base with the tip. I already can't think straight with Zac this close to me. But with his giant cock unleashed, I've turned pure hussy.

"Riley," he growls.

I reach for the towel, but don't grasp it before my tongue darts out and licks his shaft. A fierce tingling between my legs begs me to it again, so I wrap my hand around his base and explore him with up and down strokes of my tongue. "This is fun," I say, my words spoken against his cock. With the groan he makes, I can only assume the vibration of my voice is doing to him what he did to me yesterday each time he laughed with his mouth fused to my pussy.

I drop to my knees as Zac wraps my loose hair around his hand, pulling it out of the way. I'm so fucking turned on by the way he grips my hair, as if he's going to control the situation. *Good luck, buddy.* I take his swollen head into my mouth and suck him like

74

a lollipop. "Mmm," I moan purposefully to increase the sensation.

"Fuck, Riley. You're going to make me come."

"In my mouth?" I flutter my eyelashes at him, enjoying control I've never had when it comes to Zac Ashburn. My inner she-wolf has roared to life, and I'm loving it.

"Is that what you want, sweetheart?"

"Yes." I tease his head with the tip of my tongue before I suck him into my mouth again, taking in more of him this time. His guttural groan makes me so damn wet I can hardly stand it. As I pull my mouth away, I twist his shaft with my hand. With one quick breath, I take him into my mouth again. Trying to swallow him as much as I can. But dammit, he's so *big*.

I use both hands to help pleasure his entire length as I suck his cock like it's my life's mission. Surprised that for the first time in my life, I'm not only enjoying this, but turned on by it. Who knew giving a blow job could be so much fun?

"Babe, I'm going to—*come*!"

Hot ropes of cum fill the back of my throat, and I swallow every last drop.

When I stand, I find Zac leaning against the island and panting heavily. I have to admit, I was hoping to get laid tonight. But I don't regret a thing. For the first time, I feel like I've fully embraced my sexual side.

What else could I explore with Zac if only I found a way to stay in Caribou Creek?

"That was fun," I say, playfully biting my bottom lip.

"Fun?" he pant-laughs. "It was fucking amazing."

"I'm a little sad I wore you out, but—"

"Wore me out?" Zac's eyes darken instantly. He tugs me against him by my belt loop and cups my cheek possessively. "Sweetheart, I'm *far* from worn out when it comes to you."

CHAPTER 12

Zac

"I—I should take one of those," Riley says, nodding toward the pregnancy test boxes on the counter, despite her roaming hands promising the only thing she wants to do right now is go to the bedroom. "Don't you want to know first?"

"Sweetheart, I already told you. I don't care what you find out. I'm not going anywhere."

"But—"

I silence her with a kiss as I slide a hand inside her shirt to get it off. I undo her bra and let it fall to the kitchen floor. I tug her against me, loving how fucking good it feels with her tits pressed against my bare chest. "If you don't want to do this Riley, tell me and we'll stop."

Her eyes widen in surprise. "I don't want to stop."

A devilish chuckle escapes my lips. "Good to

know. Because I have some plans for you tonight, and none of them involve sleeping." I unzip her jeans and dive a hand inside, loving how the damp silk feels against my fingers. Remembering how she tasted as she came on my face. My dick roars back to life, ready for more.

When I lead Riley to the bedroom, she's not wearing any clothes.

We collapse on the bed, and I crawl up her body like a hungry animal. I gently press my hips into hers, resting my hardening cock against her belly. She combs her hands through my hair as I prop myself up on my elbows. I lower my mouth to a nipple and take my time giving it all the attention it deserves. Fuck, I could spend hours—days even—just exploring her curvaceous body.

Riley reaches between us, wrapping her silky fingers around my cock. There's nothing fucking better than the feel of her hand holding my dick. I groan against her nipple, sucking in a breath to keep myself under control.

"There's a condom in my nightstand drawer," I say to Riley. "Can you grab it?"

There's a flicker of disappointment in her eyes I don't quite understand, but she reaches for the foil packet before I can figure out what's wrong. "Want me to put it on?" she asks, biting her lower lip.

"Go ahead, sweetheart." What I really want is to plunge my cock inside her without a rubber. But I won't risk knocking her up and adding another complication to her life. Not until we know what those tests in the kitchen have to say. Of course, the second we know I'm fucking her with nothing in between us. I'm claiming what's mine. But I have to admit, there's something erotic about watching her roll the rubber onto my cock.

I sit back on my heels and tug her hips toward me, spreading her legs for my viewing pleasure. "What a pretty pussy." I yearn to drag my tongue through her folds, if only to taste her again. But I want to watch her as I bring her to her climax. I slide a finger through her folds, pressing against her clit. "So fucking *wet*."

"That's your fault, by the way. I've been this way for *days!*" She moans the last word, her voice jumping an octave as I hook a finger into her channel and search for the spot that I know will drive her wild. Her high-pitched whimpers tell me I've found it.

I plunge in a second finger, using my other hand to give some much-needed attention to her swollen button. Every movement is slow but deliberate. I don't want to rush anything with Riley Kohl. I wish I had a lifetime to learn every little thing that turns her on and brings her pleasure, but I know it's not guaranteed.

"Oh my *god!*" she practically sings, rocking her

hips faster to urge me to pick up the pace. "I—I—I'm going to—"

"Let go, sweetheart. I promise to keep you safe."

She surrenders to my promise, exploding seconds later. Her body shudders hard against my hands as she comes. She cries out my name loud enough to scare off the wildlife. I don't let go until she stops jerking.

I give her a few seconds to catch her breath, but no more. I pull her hips closer to mine and line my cock up at her entrance. She bites down on her bottom lip as her expression lights up. "Finally," she says as I push my swollen head into her slit.

"Fuck," I groan. "You're so fucking *tight*." I shackle her hips to control the motion, filling her inch by inch. I pull out slowly between each plunge, but it's torture when all I want to do is fuck her senseless. She must read the agony in my expression.

"I'm spending the night, you know," she says, running her fingertips over my hand. It's all the permission I need to stop holding back. I bend forward, lining up our bodies, and thrust in and out of my sweetheart like it's the most important mission of my life. She holds on tight, letting out a chorus of sexy noises as I pummel her pussy over and over. The bed frame creaks and all the blankets fall to the floor. But I don't dare slow down.

She comes the moment my dick starts to pulse.

The sensation of her pussy convulsing around me is all it takes for me to lose control. I thrust one final time, holding myself as deep inside her as I can go and release my seed. The only thing that would make this moment more perfect is if the condom wasn't between us. The need to claim Riley for my own is overwhelming. I won't be sated until I can come in this tight pussy and stake my claim.

I wake naked and wrapped in Zac's arms. There is literally nothing better than this feeling. Well, except the feeling of him inside me. I thought his cock might split me in two, but instead, it took me to one pleasureful euphoria after another. Heights that I never knew existed. Over and over. It's a wonder my legs aren't completely numb.

It's a bigger wonder that wetness drips down the inside of my thighs as the feel of his hard cock presses against my back.

I'm sore in the best way.

I should be exhausted.

But instead, I'm insatiable.

I lift my thigh up and over his leg, pulling his cock between my legs from behind. I spread my folds and press him against my pussy, rocking my hips in just the right motion to drive me crazy.

"Mmm." His warm hand slides down my shoulder and wedges beneath my arm until he has a handful of boob. He reaches around me to grab the other. As I use his cock as my personal toy, Zac kneads my boobs with his rough, calloused hands. "You're so fucking *wet*."

"*Still* your fault." I take my time stroking my pussy against his cock. Pushing his fat head against my clit and wiggling it around. I've never done this before. Never felt brave enough with anyone. But Zac has broken through all my walls. He's not only okay with me being *me*, he's turned on by it.

"That's it, sweetheart. Come on my dick. I'm going to come with you."

I rock my hips harder, using my palm to press him firmly against me. We gyrate together as he continues to tease my boobs and nuzzle my neck. The sensation of his beard against my skin reminds me how it felt between my thighs. That quick image is all it takes for me to lose it. I cry out his name as my hips jerk violently against him. Seconds later, he comes in my hand.

When we've both caught our breath, he nibbles my earlobe. "Soon sweetheart, I'm coming in that pussy of yours without anything between us." His heated promise causes shivers on anticipation.

I'm on the pill. All I need to know is whether or not I'm pregnant.

Familiar dread fills me.

What if I am?

It's one thing for Zac to say he'll stick by me. Quite another to follow through.

"I'm going to start a pot of coffee." He kisses my forehead. "Want me to bring you a cup?"

I *should* get up and get this whole peeing on a stick thing over with. But the temptation to steal a few more minutes in his bed, memorizing his scent, wins. "That would be great."

He turns my face with a single finger, drawing me in for a kiss that nearly makes me forget my name. I lost count of how many times I came last night. How many times we went at it. The night was a long, continuously erotic fantasy. "I'll be back."

He pushes off the bed and struts to the door buck naked.

Even his ass is perfect.

Of course it is.

I pull the covers over me and inhale deeply. If it's the last thing I do, I'm finding out what the name of his cologne is. A yawn escapes, coaxing me to stay in bed. Well, maybe I'll search his bathroom after a quick nap.

I give in to the urge to sleep, hoping Grandma Hattie's staying out of trouble. Grandpa Harold promised he'd look after her this morning since the shop is closed on Sundays. They're no doubt at the early church service. The thought makes me smile. I want what they have. Over fifty years together and still going strong.

Can Zac and I really have that?

It's the sound of my brother's voice that disrupts my otherwise perfect morning. "Did you get my sister *pregnant*?"

CHAPTER 14

Zac

"It's not what you think, Huck." His instant anger is understandable considering three pregnancy test boxes sit unopened on my kitchen island. That Riley's clothes are all over the floor doesn't help my case any.

"You fucking knocked her up?" Huck looks mad enough to punch a wall. Or my jaw. One swing and I'll no doubt lose a couple of teeth. If I'd known he was going to get back from Anchorage this early, I would've made sure Riley was gone. This isn't how I wanted him to find out. I wanted to talk to him, man to man. To let him know my true intentions with his sister.

"Huck," Penny warns, getting through to him like no one else can when he's upset. It's the same way Riley keeps me grounded.

Huck turns to his wife. "Do you have another explanation?"

Riley appears in the kitchen wearing nothing more than one of my t-shirts. It comes down to her knees. If this moment wasn't so fucking tense, I'd tell her she looks damn cute in it. But that comment would definitely earn me a black eye.

"He didn't get me pregnant you idiot," Riley says, marching toward the coffee pot and pouring herself a cup.

"Huck, do the math," Penny adds. "Riley hasn't been in town that long."

Riley sucks in a deep breath that lifts her shoulders. I resist the urge to draw her into my arms, hoping not to poke the angry bear named Huck. Worse than him finding out we've been sleeping together is that the pregnancy tests are out in the open. The one secret she trusted me to keep is exposed thanks to me.

"Do you want to explain this?" Huck asks Riley, sounding more like an angry, protective father than a compassionate, caring brother.

"Huck, calm down," I plead.

He glares at me hard enough to shut me up. It's a look that promises he'll deal with me later. My heart thunders in my ears at the heavy tension in the room. Flashes from Afghanistan try their damnedest to get in my head. It takes every ounce of fight to keep myself grounded in the present.

"Are you okay?" Riley asks me in a whisper.

I give a terse nod, laying my palm flat against the counter. I focus on the cool granite against my skin. *I'm at home. In Caribou Creek. In my house. In my kitchen.* I allow the hard surface in my kitchen to center me. To reassure me I'm not in a warzone anymore. I need to stay present to defend the woman I love.

"Riley?" Huck asks, his tone growing more impatient by the moment.

Riley touches her soft hand to my bicep for several seconds before she passes by me and all my senses distill into one. Her warmth. Her touch. Her smell. Like my whole damn world has been washed clean after a spring rain.

It's *her*, I realize. She's the reason I haven't been having nightmares. I figured out they started up again after Decker got to town. We served a tour in Afghanistan together, and it was brutal. Seeing him after all these years has unexpectedly triggered some bad memories. He and I went through a lot of bad shit together.

But it's Riley who's kept me grounded.

"I don't know if I'm pregnant," Riley explains to Huck and Penny. "I've been too afraid to find out.

And before you start lecturing me or shooting questions at me like a firing squad, let me at least get dressed." She gathers her clothes from the floor and disappears into the bathroom.

"You knew?" Huck practically growls at me.

"She only told me a couple of days ago. I was trying to help."

"By *sleeping* with her?"

"I care about her." I love her, but I'm not about to let Huck be the first person to hear those words. "I'm not just fooling around. I want to build something real with her."

"She doesn't live here, in case you forgot," Huck fires back. "And I doubt you're moving to Florida."

"Would you two stop fighting?" Riley snaps, her tone exasperated. The lack of sleep shows at the corners of her tired eyes. I want to tell everyone to fuck off and take Riley back to bed. Cradle her in my arms and let her get some solid sleep before she faces the shit-show she doesn't deserve. But Huck won't let this rest until the truth is out.

"Riley, why didn't you tell me?" Huck asks, his tone gentler.

"Tell you that I might be knocked up by a married man? Yeah, I'm sure *that* would've gone over real well."

Her words hit me like a sharp slap to the face. A *married* man? There has to be a mistake. Riley

wouldn't...would she? The room feels like it's spinning. The faint echoes of another time and place grow
louder in my ears. I try my damnedest to ignore them
because I need her to clear this up. *Not the fucking
time, PTSD. You asshole.* "You didn't tell me that part,"
I say, my words hardly above a whisper.

"Fuck, Riley. You were screwing a married guy?"
Huck runs a hand through his hair, messing it up.

"An orthopedic surgeon I worked with, if you
must know. One who isn't the best at keeping his pants
above his ankles." She turns to face me, her eyes shiny
with tears. "He lied to me. Not that it really matters,
does it?" Her eyes fall to the tests on the island counter.
"I might be carrying his child. I told you; you don't
want any part of this. I should've pushed you away."

I feel myself unraveling from the inside out. The
stress of the situation has triggered my PTSD more
than I realized. I feel the familiar symptoms from years
ago creeping back in. In minutes, I might put everyone
in harm's way and have no control over it. I need to get
help. Again. But first, I need to make sure everyone is
safe. "Get out," I shout. "Everyone. Out!"

"Zac—"

"*Go*, Riley."

"It's not what you think," she says, her words
fragile.

It makes me feel like a complete asshole to turn her

away, but I'll never forgive myself if I do something to harm anyone in this room. I need everyone gone so I can calm the fuck down. The fucked-up circus happening in my kitchen is overwhelming my senses. I need solitude to get myself under control. "Everyone get the fuck out now!" I yell the words to get the point across, and finally, they go.

CHAPTER 15

Riley

"Whatever's wrong, it's nothing that a slice of blueberry pie won't fix," Grandma Hattie says, carrying a plate to the kitchen table and setting it in front of me. The twinkle that's pretty much resided in her eyes since the night Zac came over to help move her quilting room downstairs has faded, along with my hopes of a future with him.

"Thanks, Grandma Hattie."

I pick up the fork and prepare to eat my feelings. *Zero regrets.* At least about the pie.

I should've been honest with Zac from the first. If only I'd confessed the whole truth after that toe-curling kiss, I might've saved myself from completely falling in love. From conjuring crazy secret schemes that involved moving to Caribou Creek and poten-

92

tially finding a new career. From getting my hopes up that Zac and I had a real future together.

Grandma Hattie takes a seat next to me and covers my free hand with hers. "You wanna talk about it?"

"Not really." I let out a heavy sigh. "But you deserve better than confusing silence."

"Oh good. You came to that conclusion on your own. I thought I was going to have to attempt the stairs to get you to spill the beans."

I laugh for the first time in hours. I've missed Grandma Hattie so much. Though I talk to her on the phone at least once a week, it's not the same as spending time with her in person. In a couple of weeks, she won't need me anymore. The thought saddens me. These are moments I'll never get back. "I may have made some less than ideal choices back in Orlando," I admit, hoping my confession doesn't give my sweet, albeit mischievous, grandma a heart attack. I shovel in a hefty forkful of pie and take my time chewing and swallowing before I add, "I let an orthopedic surgeon seduce me. A *married* one."

"Oh dear."

"In my defense, I believed the jackass when he lied and told me his divorce was almost finalized. But that doesn't excuse my behavior. I should've known better. I should've seen through him."

"Bet he was quite the charmer," Grandma Hattie muses.

"He's better at that than being a doctor," I mutter.

Grandma Hattie chuckles, and I find myself relaxing. I thought I'd scandalize her. Well, I still might when I finish this confession.

"I haven't had my...cycle—"

"Period. You can say the word, dear. I may be old, but I'm not a total prude. If I told you what your grandpa and I were up to last night—"

I hold up a hand, effectively silencing here. "TMI, Grandma Hattie."

"You're pregnant?" she guesses.

"I don't know. I've been too chicken to find out. I'm a couple weeks late." She squeezes my hand tight, offering comfort I don't deserve. "It could be stress," I say. "Or—" I look down at my belly, "—a baby."

"Does Doctor Man Whore know?"

I nearly spit out my bite of blueberry pie. I should know better than to eat in Grandma Hattie's presence. "No. Contrary to what he told me, he's *very* married. I don't want to complicate things. His wife is a little scary."

"Well, if she murders him in his sleep, that's not *your* fault. He's the one who couldn't keep his man snake in his pants." Another bite gets stuck in my throat. Grandma Hattie pushes up from her chair to fetch me a glass of water on account of my repeated choking.

I set down my fork, giving up on the eating until I have some alone time. "Man snake, Grandma Hattie?"

That familiar twinkle reappears in her eyes. "I won't tell you what else I call it."

"Thank for you that," I mumble under my breath.

"No matter what you find out, you know you have a home here, right?"

"Really?"

She drops both hands on my shoulders and squeezes, resting her head atop mine. "Of course, Riley. We'd never kick you out. That punishment is too easy. It's much more fun making you deal with me when I'm cranky." She plants a kiss on my head and moves around the table to the sink. "I was talking to Mary Lou yesterday. Sounds like they might be looking for a part time physical therapist at the clinic."

"Really?" Part time won't pay the bills, but it *is* something.

"You want to tell me what happened with Zac? Obviously, you didn't get drunk last night."

"Not on wine." My smile quickly fades when the memory of him shouting fills my head. I'd never seen him like that. So stressed and on the verge of losing control. How could I have known one detail would upset him so much and make him take back his promise? We haven't seen each other in fourteen years. Maybe the boy I once knew has completely changed into a stranger.

"Oh, sweetie. He'll come around."

"Doubtful."

"He loves you."

"How do you know that?" I feign nonchalance, but my pulse races with undeserved hope that Grandma Hattie knows something I don't.

Before she can answer, there's a knock on the kitchen door. But Grandma Hattie isn't out of her seat before a bunch of people burst inside. Huck, Penny, and Zac file inside. I take a quick scan of the boys, surprised neither one is sporting a shiner. In fact, they seem to be...getting along?

I stare at the pie, certain I'm hallucinating. *What is in this?*

"I'm sorry I overreacted," Huck says, dropping his hand on my shoulder and squeezing. "You didn't deserve that."

"I did."

Huck steals my fork, so I offer up my half-eaten pie. As delicious as it is, it's proven to be a choking hazard this afternoon. I pretend to focus on the plate's blue flower border, but it's no use. Zac catches my glance more than once. He shouldn't even be here. He should be at the brewery working.

"I'm sorry for how I acted this morning," he says, nudging Huck out of the way to stand closer to me. He slides into the chair opposite me and turns it to face me. Our knees brush as he reaches for my hand. I don't realize I'm shaking until he caresses my hand with his thumb. "I have secrets of my own. I didn't come back from Afghanistan unscathed. I had a pretty severe case of PTSD. I got help for it. I thought I was through the worst of it and knew how to handle the rest. But this morning..." He squeezes my hand. "I made an appointment to address my recent issues."

I'm stunned to silence.

This whole time, I thought he was pissed at *me*. Replaying the events of this morning, remembering how out of it he seemed in moments, it all locks into place. The chaotic situation overwhelmed him. "You sent us away to protect us?"

"It was a precaution. If anything had happened to you—"

"But it didn't."

"Huck, Penny," Grandma Hattie says with a wave. "I want to give you something. And these two clearly need a minute."

We wait until the kitchen is clear. "Can I come with you?" I ask. "To your appointment? I want to know how to help."

"You already help more than you know." He cups

my cheek and I melt into his touch. This is a hand I know would never touch me in harm. I know it in the depths of my soul. We belong together. I think we were always meant to find our way back to each other. To build on the foundation of childhood friendship with love. "Since I kissed you, I haven't had the nightmares. You bring me peace."

"Except earlier," I mutter.

"Well, that had some extenuating circumstances. But that's why I made the appointment. If you want to come with me, you're more than welcome." He pulls me closer still. "I want a future with you, Riley. No matter what the stick says. You're it for me." He sets a shopping bag on the table. "If you're ready, I'd really like to know the answer."

"That eager, huh?"

He leans closer, until our cheeks touch. His lips tickle my ear as he whispers, "As soon as you know the answer, I plan to take you home and fuck you with nothing between us. I'm claiming you for my own, Riley Kohl. No matter what you find out. You're mine." He kisses a trail to my lips, leaving me dizzy and breathless when he's finished.

It's time.

CHAPTER 16

Zac

It takes all my restraint, and several deep breaths, to stay seated on the couch with everyone else. Penny and Hattie gush over a baby blanket while Huck and Harold talk about some old car they want to fix up together. But my mind is racing too much to be a part of any conversation.

I'll take care of Riley no matter what.

If she's carrying a child, I'll help her raise him or her as if they were my own. I meant what I said. I'm in this for the long haul. But it doesn't ease the nervous tension not to know. Once we know, we can make plans for our future. I can help Riley figure out how to build a life here in Caribou Creek that makes her feel happy and fulfilled.

Finally, after what feels like hours but has probably been roughly ten minutes, the bathroom door bursts open. "*Not* pregnant!" Riley announces, holding up all three tests. Her smile is filled with relief. A collective sigh fills the room. Grandma Hattie clutches her chest. There's a twinkle in Riley's eyes that's reserved for me.

I give the women a few moments to gab before I gently take Riley's hand into mine own. One simple glance causes heat to darken her eyes. She squeezes my hand in confirmation. It's time to make this future official. "Grandma Hattie, we'll be back later, okay?"

"You just found out she's *not* pregnant," Huck says, feigning disbelief. "Don't be trying to knock up my sister already, man." The room erupts in laughter as Riley and I head to the door.

Huck and I had a long talk after I chased everyone away this morning. As soon as he dropped Penny off at home, he came back to check on me. He was there when I was going through the worst of my PTSD years ago and knew how to help.

I told him how I felt about Riley. That I planned to marry her.

He admitted he wanted to slug me, but that was before Penny talked some sense into him. He left me with a threat to feed my body to the bears should I ever hurt Riley, which only seemed fair.

"I'm so relieved," Riley says as I speed through town.

"Do you *want* kids?"

"Of course I do." She reaches for my hand as I turn onto my private dirt road. Soon to be *our* private dirt road. "But when I'm ready. When *we're* ready."

We hardly make it inside the door before I have her pushed up against it. The urgency between us is intense. Our lips blaze hot trails as I strip away her jeans and panties. She tugs on my zipper, pushing my jeans and boxers to the floor. She fists my cock, causing me to groan.

"Nothing between us this time?" she asks, biting down on that bottom lip of hers in a way that drives me wild.

I scoop my hands beneath her ass and lift her up against the wall. She wraps her legs around my waist, guiding me to her entrance. "Never again, sweetheart. I'm coming in your pussy and claiming you for my own. I won't share you. *Ever.*"

She wraps her arms around my neck, holding on as she arches her hips against me to push me inside. "Good. You're the only one I want, Zac. I love you."

"I love you more."

"Not possible."

I flash her a wicked smirk before I pummel into her pussy in one powerful thrust. "I'm about to prove to you just how possible it is. Better hold on."

Epilogue

ZAC

About nine months later...

"Are you happy with *six* rental properties?" I ask Wes as I twist in the last lightbulb over the kitchen sink. His new tenant will be arriving any minute, which was a couple of days earlier than he expected. It's the only reason I agreed to dip out of the brewery early and help him to finish up a few things before she gets here. Well, that and Ben is being a total pain in the ass these days.

"Six is an even number," he says, as if that's an answer.

"It's a lot to keep up with. You're not going to hire anyone to help?"

He shrugs and squeezes out a sponge in the sink. "I like staying busy. And it's investing in my future."

"There are other ways to spend your time," I say, half ribbing, half serious. Wes hasn't dated anyone since he moved back to Caribou Creek a couple years ahead of Ben and me. He hasn't talked much about the woman who stomped on his heart, but it's obvious that it changed him.

"I'm working on a new brew," he says, as if that's what I meant. "But don't tell Benny-Poo. I don't want him to get his panties in a twist. You know how he is about change." Wes gathers the last of the cleaning supplies and drops them in a bag. "Thanks for your help, man. I'm sure your *wife* is eager for you to get home."

At the mention of Riley, a cheeky grin spreads across my lips of its own accord. "I have to pick her up from the clinic on my way home."

"You guys decide on a name for the baby yet?"

Once Riley officially moved back to Caribou Creek, we didn't waste much time. We were married within a month and pregnant two months after that. With my PTSD back under control and no longer wreaking havoc on my life, we decided enough time had been wasted during the fourteen years we spent apart. "Not yet."

"Liar."

"If I told you, Riley would kill me."

"Fair enough." Wes heads to the door. "I'm happy

for you, man. Truly. Excited to meet my nephew, *Wesley*."

"Nice try."

"Hey, just remember, I'm the brother you like."

Before I have a chance to say something back, a rickety car pulls into the driveway. One I'm shocked made the drive to Caribou Creek. "Where did you say your new tenant was coming from?"

"Fairbanks."

"Good thing it's still summer."

A woman a couple years younger than Riley steps out of the car, shouldering a duffle bag. I'm about to tell Wes I'll see him later when I notice he's frozen in place and staring. Uh oh. "You know it's a bad idea, right?"

"Says the brother who was sleeping with his buddy's little sister and then *married* her."

I pat him hard on the shoulder, my way of wishing him luck before I head to my truck and leave the two of them alone. I recognize that stupid, goofy look on his face. I've worn it myself. He might not cave right away, but sooner or later he'll be in some serious trouble.

I head to the clinic, forgetting all about my brother the moment I see Riley step outside. With her six-month baby bump and radiant glow, she's never looked sexier. Some days I still can't believe I was lucky enough to snag her. Lucky enough to call her mine for the rest of my life.

"Hey, sweetheart," I say, greeting her with a kiss at the passenger side. She snakes a hand around my neck and yanks me down hard before I can get her door open. God, I love this woman so much.

"I'm crazy horny," she admits after she breaks apart the kiss.

"Good to know."

"Zac?"

"Yeah?" I open the passenger door and help her inside.

"I'm not kidding. I'm going to maul you the second we get home. So...drive fast?"

I don't even try to hide my wicked smile. "Anything you want, babe."

Bonus Epilogue

ZAC

Bonus Epilogue: about five years later...

"How long do I have to wear this blindfold?" Riley pats the silk sleeping mask covering her eyes as I pull out of the gas station. I've filled up the truck, bought enough road snacks to appease our entire family—though we left the kids at home with my grandparents—and insisted she pack an overnight bag suitable for any occasion. All to throw her off the trail of my real plans.

"Until we're out of town, and you can't figure out which direction I went."

"The highway only goes two ways—north and south."

"Pretty confident, aren't we?"

One corner of her mouth lifts. "I've had my coffee."

Life has been blissfully chaotic these past few years. We've had three amazing kids, Riley's been working full time at the clinic because Caribou Creek has proved it needs a physical therapist who's readily available, and business at the brewery is doing better than ever. So well that Ben no longer scowls over the numbers.

But in recent months, Riley and I haven't made a lot of time for just the two of us. I've been eager to get my wife all to myself. To remind her that she's still the center of my universe and deserves to be pampered.

Which is why when my grandparents told me they were coming to Caribou Creek to visit all their grandchildren, I convinced my brothers and a couple buddies to help me finish my surprise project ahead of schedule. Riley has no idea what I've been up to, and I can't wait to see the look on her face when she realizes I built a cozy getaway cabin near our special dock.

"Do I get any hints?" she asks as I turn on to the private dirt road.

"What fun would that be?" I tease.

"If I end up covered in mud—"

"No mud," I promise. "But I'm not guaranteeing you won't get wet. Very, *very* wet."

I roll the truck to a stop in the gravel area near the dock, pointing the truck toward the cabin. When I shift into park, Riley voices her immediate confusion. "Why are we stopping? We've only been on the road like ten minutes. I mean, I'm all for a pit stop if you want to get frisky, but someone from town might see us."

I take Riley's hand and squeeze it. "There will be plenty of time for *frisky* in the next twenty-four hours. Make no mistake about that." I lean over the center console, cup her cheek, and press my lips to hers. Savoring the taste of her. Taking my time as our tongues do a slow dance together.

When I break the kiss apart, I gently pull off her blindfold.

"What are you—" She gasps, bringing both hands to cover her mouth as she stares straight ahead.

"I have a surprise for you, in case that wasn't obvious."

"We're—this is—it's a cabin."

"It's *our* cabin."

Her excited eyes are shiny with unshed tears. For years, we talked about building a cabin along the water. One that our little family could escape to on the weekends, or even just for a night around a campfire. A cabin she and I could spend some alone time in together without one of the kids screaming that another one hit him or stole his toy.

"Do you want to see it?"

"Of course I do!" She's out of the truck so fast I can hardly keep up. Halfway to the front door, she spins in a full circle, taking in the wooded surroundings, the creek our town is named for, and the dock where we spent so much time daydreaming.

"Even got the wooden rocking chairs you wanted," I say, nodding toward the covered front porch. It points west, her favorite direction, and I can already picture us savoring a thousand sunsets on it.

"It's perfect, Zac!"

I unlock the front door and allow her to go inside first. I try to rein in my own impatience as I give her a tour of the two-bedroom cabin meant to accommodate our family whenever the mood strikes. But when we make it to the master suite, the urgency between us crackles in the air. It's been a long time since we've been alone together outside of lunch breaks and naptimes.

"This is a *nice* bed," she says approvingly, slipping her arms around me in the doorway.

"It's a pillow top."

Her laughter is infectious. It warms me from the inside out. "It's like sleeping on a cloud," she says.

I comb the hair back from her cheek, tracing her jaw with my fingertips. "Wanna try it out?"

"You know I do."

She moves toward the bed, but I hold her back. She looks at me as if to say *what now?* "I heard it's better if you're naked." I tug her into my embrace, holding her tight against me as I crush my lips to hers. Her fingers comb through my hair as she moans into my mouth. My hands drop to her ass, squeezing her cheeks. Grinding her against me.

"You going to get me naked or what?" she asks between kisses, her eyes hooded.

I run my hands up her back, slipping beneath her shirt. It falls to the floor seconds later, followed by her bra. Though I'm eager to get to the bed and inside my wife, I can't resist suckling a tit. Not wanting the other to feel left out, I give it equal attention. All the while, my wife is stripping me from the waist down.

When her hand circles my cock, I make quick work of getting both of us the rest of the way naked.

We're a tangle of arms, lips, and all our favorite body parts as we collapse onto the bed. We roll as one, our hands and mouths roaming, tasting, and savoring. There's nothing better than the way Riley feels against me, skin to skin.

"You like the bed?" she asks, hands framing my face.

I roll her onto her back and nudge her knees apart, lowering my throbbing cock to her entrance. "We haven't really broken it in yet." I push into her channel, filling her slowly and completely. Sliding home until our bodies meet and my balls graze her sensitive flesh. "Listen," I whisper to Riley.

"To what?"

"Silence."

"You're right!" She wraps her legs around my lower back, locking her body to mine with her ankles. Spreading her thighs wider and allowing me in just a little deeper. Fuck me, this is paradise. "No one's screaming or crying or tattling. Nothing's breaking. I could get used to this," she admits with a devious smile, running those soft fingers along the back of my neck and into my hair as I set a leisurely pace. I plan to take my time enjoying my wife every minute we're here.

"Sweetheart?"

"Hmm?"

"For the record, you don't have to be silent. Not even a little bit."

I drop my lips to hers as I pick up the pace just enough to make her whimper. Each thrust is deliberate. She rocks her clit against me every time our bodies join.

"Fuck, you feel so good," I groan.

She digs her nails into my neck, kissing me harder. Inviting my tongue in for playtime. Distracting me so effectively that I don't realize she's rolled us until she sits back. Hands pressed against my chest, tits dangling temptingly, and that wicked smile promising she's up to no good.

She leans forward only enough for me to take her tits in both hands. I knead and massage them as she sets a steady rhythm riding my cock. Each time she sinks down on me, she rubs her button against me.

How the hell did I get so lucky?

"I want you to come on my cock, sweetheart." I pinch her nipples at the same time, sparking her into action. She fills herself with me fully then starts to grind hard against me. Up and down. Up and down. It's the hottest fucking thing. "That's it, Riley. Make yourself come on my dick."

She comes apart seconds later, her pussy convulsing around my length as she lets out a series of moans that no doubt scares off the wildlife for miles. It's been so long since we've just been able to let go and not worry about waking babies.

When she starts to catch her breath, I roll her onto her back again. She wraps herself around me like a pretzel and I thrust hard and fast, headed for my own release. I slam into her again and again, feeling myself nearing the edge.

"Come in my pussy!" she cries out.

Her dirty words cause my dick to pulse. I pummel into her channel once, twice, three times and still inside her. Shooting hot ropes of cum into her depths. Claiming my woman for what must be the millionth time since the first. Knowing there will be a million more ahead of us.

"I love you," she says, cupping my cheeks with both hands. "Thank you for doing all this."

"I'd do anything for you," I say to her, dropping a kiss to her forehead. "You know that, right?"

"Yeah, I do."

"I love you, Riley. Now and always."

I pull out and drop down on the bed beside her, still trying to catch my breath.

"You know something?" she asks.

"What's that?"

"The bed didn't creak. This thing is solid."

"Cedar frame. Pillow top mattress. I went for the best, sweetheart."

She draws me in for a tender kiss, but when she goes to pull back, I tug her right back to my lips. Crazy how a single kiss can recharge me in an instant.

"You know what?"

"What, sweetheart?"

"I bet you twenty bucks we can get this bed to

creak before we leave." The mischievous twinkle in her eyes promises she's already up for round two.

"Twenty bucks, huh? You know this thing is crazy solid."

"Maybe," she says with a shrug, reaching between my legs and wrapping her hand around my cock. "But it'll be fun trying either way."

I have a hard time arguing with that. "You're on."

THE END

Love Drunk

MOUNTAIN MEN OF CARIBOU CREEK
BOOK 2

CHAPTER 1

Avery

"You're my favoritest teacher ever, Ms. Nichols." Little Tyler Parsons launches himself at me, wrapping his tiny arms around my legs with such force I nearly topple backward. He's had a rough day involving a, thankfully, failed attempt to eat blue paint. It ended up down his shirt instead, which is why I'm expecting a phone call from his mom later when Tyler forgets to give her the note I put in his backpack explaining what happened. She won't be happy to discover that he looks like a Smurf at bath time.

It's been a long day. But compared to what my life looked like a few months ago, these are the problems I welcome.

"Don't forget to give your mom that note," I call to him after he bolts to join his older brother who's already half a block away. The sun has warmed away the cool, crisp air from earlier this morning. But with the leaves rapidly changing color, it won't be long before the snow comes.

Secretly, I'm thrilled for winter and the promise that it'll be harder to travel through the mountains. *Harder to find me.*

"That your paint eater?" Trinity Stark asks, joining me on the sidewalk outside the lone school building in Caribou Creek that houses K through twelve. She teaches high school English, but our overlapping lunch break helped spark the first true friendship I've found since moving here.

"That's the one."

"I don't know how you do it." Trinity stares after the last of the kids. "I'd be exhausted if I had to wrangle kindergarteners all day."

"I'd lose my mind if I had to deal with high schoolers and all that attitude."

"Hey, there's a kick boxing class tonight. Want to come with me?" The hopefulness in Trinity's eyes nearly makes me cave. It's the same look she's given me the last three times she's asked. But my determination to avoid the instructor, who also happens to be my incredibly hot landlord, makes it easy to turn the offer down.

"Not tonight."

"You painting your bathroom ceiling again?" Trinity teases, though I don't miss the edge of suspicion in her voice. She's both curious and concerned. It's sweet of her to look out for me, but I'm trying really hard to find my independence. Getting close to someone and sharing the details of my nightmarish past isn't high on my list. If I take her up on her equally repeated offers of kickboxing or happy hour at the CARIBOU CREEK BREWERY, I know I'll divulge too much.

After a toxic relationship gone *way* wrong, I promised myself I wouldn't rely on anyone ever again. Realizing I might've been a little dramatic on that declaration, I revised it to a more realistic year. Just one year to prove to myself that I can survive without leaning on anyone else.

Though a kick boxing class is hardly a threat to my plan, Wes Ashburn definitely is. Because my resolve also includes a non-negotiable no-dating policy.

Not that Wes has asked me out.

But the way he looks at me whenever we run into each other makes me feel like he wants to. Makes me feel like I'd like it if he did. That I'd find it difficult to tell him no. Avoiding him is much easier. Even if it means staying away from the brewery he owns with his brothers or skipping out on kick boxing classes I really want to try.

"I'm really tired. It's been a long day with the blue paint catastrophe and all."

"All the more reason to come. I promise you'll feel so much better after you kick around a bag for an hour."

"Maybe next time."

"Okay, I'll stop pushing." Trinity offers me a kind smile that suggests she truly wants to be my friend and isn't intimidated by all my kicking and screaming about it. She doesn't even seem to be keeping track of how many times I've blown her off. "But one of these days, I'll convince you to come."

In my classroom, I take my time gathering my things and cleaning up. I wait until I see Trinity's car drive away and hear only the squeak of the janitor's cart down the hall before I sneak out. I don't want to admit my car wouldn't start this morning and I have to walk home. I need to get a new battery, but I also need to make my rent payment this week. It's not one of those have my cake and eat it too kind of weeks.

With fall in the air and the sun warming my face, I don't mind the walk. The fresh air helps ease my worries away.

Caribou Creek is packed with small-town charm and friendly people. Though I'll never stop locking my door at night or looking over my shoulder at every little sound, I do breathe easier here. I don't know how long the peace will last. Eventually, Lucas will find me. It's inevitable. The only way I might've prevented that was to move to the lower forty-eight. But I wasn't going to let him chase me out of Alaska. I love it here too much.

"Ms. Nichols, how lovely to see you," Hattie Kohl greets as I hold the door to the grocery store open for her. Her grandmotherly smile is warm enough to thaw even the coldest hearts. "I hear great things about our new kindergarten teacher. The kids sure do love you."

"Thank you, Mrs. Kohl. That's very kind of you to say." The compliment makes my heart swell. All I've ever wanted is to find a place that accepted me as one of their own. I thought I had that in Fairbanks, but it was mostly an illusion I created to keep myself sane when the reality was really sideways. "Making something good for dinner tonight?"

"Chicken pot pie. Buttering Harold up before I tell him we've added an extra bridge night to the calendar this month."

If I wasn't only twenty-five or allergic to socialization, I might ask to join them. I've heard whispers that their bridge nights are really a cover for something more scandalous. It's anyone's guess who isn't in their immediate circle. I think they're playing black jack, but I've even heard rumors about strip poker. "That sounds wonderful. Have a good evening."

Hattie sets her hand on my shoulder, and looks me

in the eye, as if she wants to make sure I hear what she's about to say. "You're home here, Ms. Nichols. It's okay to believe it." With those words of wisdom, she strolls to her car.

Home.

I *want* to believe it.

But it's going to take some time for me to unpack that duffle bag beside my bed.

I gather a few ingredients to fulfill my spaghetti craving and continue on my way. I don't mean to pass by the fitness studio, but it cuts two blocks off my walk. My feet are starting to ache from having been on them all day.

Or maybe what I really want is a glimpse of Wes Ashburn.

I see him through the glass front. Hands behind his back as he walks back and forth watching his students kick and punch padded cylinders. In his tight black t-shirt and gym shorts, all of his hard muscles are on display. I've longed to comb my fingers through his dark beard more than once. Especially in my dreams where I can't seem to get myself under control.

I don't realize I'm staring until his gaze locks with mine. A smile slowly spreads across his perfect lips and he nods. My pulse doubles at the attention I shouldn't want. At the thrill I shouldn't feel. At the way my nipples pebble, the damn things pointing in his direction because they're aching for his touch.

I send him back a pitifully quick wave before I hurry down the sidewalk and turn the corner. Running away like the chicken I am.

If only I didn't have such a fucked up past I needed to recover from, maybe I could entertain a crush on the sinfully hot brew master. But I can't afford the distraction, no matter how badly I may want to climb Wes like a tree.

CHAPTER 2

Wes

"You get all that residual grain cleaned out of the top of the tank?" I ask our new hire, Tanner. It's only his third day working at the brewery, so I'm cutting him a little slack with remembering everything. But I'm not going to let him get out of the work that needs to be done. He's a smart kid. Well, *kid* to me because he turned twenty-one a week before starting. Twelve years younger than me makes him a kid.

"Oh, right."

"Make sure you get it all. Liam's coming to pick it up for his livestock tonight."

"Cows in the mountains," Zac says with a head-shake as he strolls inside the brew house. "Do you really think his herd's going to make the winter?"

Cows aren't unheard of in Alaska, but they're rare.

"It gets colder in Fairbanks. They manage." I glance at Tanner, just to let him know I'm watching. "But they're hungry," I say to the kid.

"Got plenty of grain for them," he answers with a thumbs up.

I look back at my youngest brother. "It slow in the taproom or you just trying to sneak out early again?" Zac is the first of us Ashburn brothers to become a father. He's still not back to working full time hours—much to our oldest brother's disdain—but my nephew is only two and half months old. Something Ben can't quite grasp with his too-logical, unemotional brain.

"Need to head out early, but don't tell The Grinch." It's no secret that Ben is a growly pain the ass. He only knows how to smile when he's interacting with clients and vendors. Not even his hoity-toity city girlfriend seems to make that permanently etched frown go away. But I know exactly why that is. Hell, Zac and I both do. But Benny Poo, as I call him because I love how pissed off he looks when I do, won't do shit about the real problem. So, he remains permanently grumpy.

"You do know you're one third owner, right?" I remind Zac. "That means one third in charge."

"Who's in charge?" Ben appears like a bad cold—undetected and unwanted until it's too late to do anything about it.

Tanner looks like he's about to answer the question, but I catch him with a stern look. He might mean well, or maybe he's trying to be funny, but the kid doesn't need to be on Ben's shit list his first week. It's a hard list to get off of.

"Grandma June sent me a text," Zac says, wisely shifting the conversation to a topic Ben can't resist. Despite his brooding nature, he *does* love Grandma June. "She and Grandpa just landed in Anchorage. They're picking up a rental car and heading to town tonight." Zac folds his arms over his chest and looks to Ben. "Which is why I need to head home. I need to help Riley get their room set up. She didn't get any sleep last night."

As expected, Ben's hardened expression doesn't change.

"Give it up," I say to Zac. "There's block of glacial ice where his heart should be."

"Knock it off," Ben growls, not entertained at all by our ribbing. Which, because we're brothers, only makes us want to up our game.

"They could stay with you," I say to Ben, "But Grandma June and Kat would probably pluck each other's eyes out within a day." Zac and I have a bet going about how Grandma June's going to feel about Ben's girlfriend. And how long it takes her to call bullshit on the whole relationship. Grandma June is not known for biting her tongue when she has an opinion. I only hope I have the popcorn ready when the fun begins.

"Got someone to cover?" Ben asks Zac, ignoring me entirely.

"Decker's covering the front."

After the few seconds it seems to take him to process, Ben nods. Never mind that the decision is not his. We're equal owners. We can come and go as we please. Even without us hovering, there are more than enough employees to cover. But that doesn't mean I'm about to announce to Ben how often I slip out for an hour here or there to make quick repairs on rentals I own.

"Kat coming to town soon?" Zac asks Ben. "Grandma June will want to know for family dinner."

My stomach rumbles at the mere thought of her cooking. I have many talents, but cooking isn't one of them. I can't remember the last time I had a good, home cooked meal I didn't have to buy. "Is she taking requests?"

"*Katherine's* coming in the morning." Ben's scowl only deepens because he's asked us not to call her Kat more than a hundred times since the sham relationship began. One I'm certain is a whole lot more about business than anything else. A five-year-old could guess that there's no love between them. Or even affection.

Before I can get in a jab about it, my phone vibrates. I pull it from my pocket and damn near drop it when I see Avery Nichol's name on the screen. She's the most low-maintenance tenant I have. I never hear from her aside from monthly rent payments. Though a part of me wishes that was different. *Very* different.

Avery: My kitchen sink's leaking. Can you come take a look?

I know how complicated things could get if I got involved with one of my tenants, but Avery's done something to me I can't begin to explain. Since the first day I met her months ago, she's managed to worm her way into my thoughts, my fantasies, and my dreams. My pulse triples every time I run into her in town. It damn near went berserk last night when she walked by the fitness studio and waved.

Wes: Be there in 5

I leave my brothers arguing and instruct Tanner to clean out the tank once he has all the grain out. Promising I'll be back in an hour to inspect his work, I feel Ben's scowl burn into the back of my head as I leave. But I don't bother looking back. Avery could've requested I come change a burnt-out lightbulb and I would've left with the same urgency.

I try to tell myself it's curiosity. She's so closed off from everyone. Surely, if I was able to peel back the layers, I'd lose interest. Right?

I haven't dated anyone since I moved back to Caribou Creek a few years ago, and for good reason. The last thing I should be entertaining is getting involved with a woman I hardly know. A woman who's clearly keeping secrets.

So why does she seem to consume my every waking thought?

CHAPTER 3

Avery

My sweatshirt is soaked completely through. As is the upper half of my jeans and most of my hair. I'm damn near in tears, but only because I finally admitted defeat with the stupid pipe under the kitchen sink. What started out as a simple drip has turned into a complete catastrophe.

I had no choice.

I had to text my landlord.

Wes shows up so quickly I don't even have time to change. Which is just as well, because I'm *not* trying to look my best for him. If I look like hot mess—well a wet one anyway—maybe he won't look at me with that hint of desire and longing. A look that's plagued my dream for weeks now.

"You okay?" he asks the instant I open the door and he spots me.

It takes incredible restraint not to look him up and down. To pretend that the sight of him in that tight t-shirt and low-slung jeans isn't doing funny things to my insides. All the Ashburn brothers are attractive, but Wes is definitely the hottest of the trio.

"Believe it or not, the pipe under the kitchen sink is in worse shape." I step back, allowing him inside. I clutch the door with both hands, realizing he's the first person I've allowed past the front stoop since he handed me the keys. Or maybe it's because Wes is invading my personal space, which in some of my dirtiest fantasies starring the brew master, is exactly what I crave most.

"Mind if I take a look?"

"Go for it." I did manage to mop up the river of water making an escape, but I've left a trail of every towel I own in its place. "I shut the water off," I tell him, hoping he won't think I'm completely clueless. I learned how to do a lot of things on my own. Having only one parent who was more interested in her revolving door of boyfriends than anything else left me to fend for myself a lot. But even my go-to YouTube channels couldn't help me out of the mess I created today.

"Smart girl," he says, flashing me an approving

KALI HART

smile that makes me weak in the knees. Hotness this lethal isn't fair.

To my amazement, Wes doesn't flinch or fall over from shock when he sees the kitchen. He simply turns to me, offering a reassuring smile. "I've got this. Why don't you get changed? You have to be freezing."

I don't need to look down to know my damn nipples are hardened into peaks and reaching toward Wes. Despite the embarrassment that sends me scurrying to my bedroom to change, a wicked thought still wriggles in as I change. I bet Wes' mouth would warm my nipples right up.

Calm down, Avery. You just want what you can't have.

I use a t-shirt to dry myself off since every towel I own is currently on the kitchen floor mopping up water. In my ensuite bathroom, I catch the first glimpse of myself in the mirror since water exploded from the kitchen pipe and nearly scream. Makeup runs down my cheeks in streaks. My smeared eyeshadow makes me look like something out of the eighties.

Washing away the clown disaster on my face, I resist the urge to reapply my makeup. Reminding myself that the objective is *not* to draw Wes's attention.

"You need some new coupling nuts. I didn't realize yours were rusted through," he says from beneath my sink when I step into the kitchen. His shirt rides up his

132

stomach, revealing those very defined abs. Making my mouth water and my naughty imagination hum to life. "I'll see if Mike has some at the hardware store."

"So, I can't use my sink?"

"I'm working on a temporary fix." Wes pokes his head out from beneath the sink and locks his gaze with mine. "And I mean *temporary*. I need to come back Monday and fix this or it'll be a lot worse."

I slip into a chair at my tiny kitchen table and pretend I'm not freaking out inside. I don't let people in my space. Not anymore. Not until I know I can trust them, and trust is in very short supply. Especially when it comes to trusting myself.

Yet, the one man I trust myself around the least needs to come back. Go figure. "Can't we grab that hardware tonight?"

"Mike's closed up for the weekend," Wes says, his hips shimmying with whatever he's doing beneath the sink.

"Oh."

"Hey," Wes says, again lifting his head from under the sink until our eyes meet. "I'm not *that* terrible to be around. Unless you ask my oldest brother. Then you might get conflicting information." He returns his attention to the piping, leaving me more curious than ever about him. I've heard a few things, of course. Impossible to be in a small town and *not* hear about everyone in some capacity. But there's a lot of gaps I've been filling in with only my imagination.

"Where did you learn to fix plumbing?" I ask, afraid that if I can't keep the conversation going my overactive imagination just might get me in to trouble.

"When I lived in Portland. I was there for school, to learn the science behind brewing. But in between that and my drill weekends, I worked a lot of odd jobs. One of those was a summer helping a guy flip houses. He taught me a lot." Wes slides out from under the sink, his t-shirt soaked. The light fabric sticks to his skin. But instead of him looking like a hosed-down cat, he looks like a fucking firefighter calendar model.

"Is there anything you *don't* know how to do?" My pathetic attempt at flirting doesn't completely backfire, but my words come out high-pitched and squeaky.

At least Wes has the decency to pretend not to notice. "Cook."

"Cook?"

"I can't cook to save my life."

"You can brew beer, but you can't cook?"

"Correct." He wipes his hands against his jeans. "Remember what I said. You can use your sink if it's for something quick, but don't use it more than you have to. I need to come back tomorrow and fix it or you might flood the place."

"Oh. Okay." Hard to argue with that since I don't

have renter's insurance or the money to pay for a catastrophe of that size.

"Now, what's up with your car?"

My pulse doubles at his unexpected question. One that makes me feel as though my privacy were invaded. Or maybe it's just my pride that's being taken down a notch because he noticed I've been walking. "I never said anything about my car."

"You didn't have to."

Nervously, I twist the bracelet on my wrist. I bought it the day I graduated college with my teaching certificate. Something to celebrate all that I'd overcome. "It's just a dead battery. I'm getting it fixed."

"I can take a look." He steps closer to the kitchen table, making me feel tiny with his broad shoulders and tall frame. I should feel cornered, like trapped prey. But the only thing I feel is the tingling between my legs. "Maybe you just need a jump."

I instantly conjure an image of me jumping Wes, except in that fantasy scenario, we're missing all our clothes. I gulp a swallow and try to look anywhere other than those gentle yet intense eyes. They make me feel entirely too vulnerable. "I don't want to bother you."

"It's no bother," he says. "Might save you a few bucks."

The sooner I get Wes on his way, the sooner I can

let out the breath I've been holding all this time. I know it's the worst idea to crush on my landlord, even if he's hotter than sin. But it'd be a whole lot easier to convince myself of that truth if the man were gone. If only my bank account didn't beg otherwise. "Keys are on the counter."

CHAPTER 4

Wes

I can't count the number of things wrong under the hood of Avery's car. It's a miracle it survived this long. I remember the day she first pulled into the driveway behind the wheel. Avery had driven from Fairbanks, and I was shocked she'd been able to make the trip without breaking down.

"So, about that jump?" Avery asks, appearing at the side of the car. The glow of sunlight illuminates her already gorgeous figure. I'm momentarily speechless at the sight of her. Her dark hair is twisted at the back of her head, but a couple of tendrils have escaped and are kissing her soft cheeks. What I wouldn't give to pull the rest of it loose and let her hair fall over her shoulders. "Wes?"

My hand slips and my knuckle scrapes against a

nut. *Fuck*. I wince, but keep myself from muttering aloud.

"You okay?"

"Mind getting me a shop rag out of my truck? There's an open bag on the passenger seat."

I'd be lying if I tried to pretend I wasn't watching her ass shake as she hurries to my truck. It's a nice, plump ass I'd love to get both my hands under. I'm so entranced that she nearly catches me staring.

"You want me to get out the jumper cables?" she asks, handing me a clean shop towel. "I'm not completely useless—"

"Avery," I say gently, ducking out from under the hood to face her. Looking her in the eyes before I deliver the bad news. "A jump isn't going to do anything, I'm afraid. Your car has some...issues."

She presses her lips together, as if that single act is holding her together. Keeping her eyes from becoming any shinier with tears than they already are. I can tell she doesn't want to cry in front of me. Though Avery Nichols has been one of the most elusive people in Caribou Creek, I've still watched her from a distance. She doesn't like to accept help or display signs of weakness. She has something to prove, and I suspect she wears a thick coat of armor because of it.

"Half the spark plugs are bad."

"Maybe they just need a time out. That works for

most of my kindergartens. Unless they're named Timmy. Then they're a lost cause." I can't help but laugh at her rambling attempt at humor, if only to help ease the tension I sense she's feeling.

"Timmy Carlson?" It's not hard to guess that one. I've seen the kid throw some epic tantrums in the grocery store and behind the stands at the local ballpark when his brother's playing baseball.

"How'd you know?" The shininess softens in her eyes, intrigue sharpening her gaze.

"Everybody knows everybody in Caribou Creek." I dare to peer into those emerald eyes. They're the deepest shade of green I've ever seen. They're mesmerizing and dangerous. They wield the power to bring me to my knees. Those eyes alone are the reason I should run in the opposite direction. Yet, my strongest impulse, however irrational, is to surrender to them. To surrender to Avery. "Anyway, some of these spark plugs are exactly like Timmy. Time out's not going to work, I'm afraid."

"What else is wrong with it?" Avery asks in a tone that implies she wants the band-aid ripped right off.

"You're out of oil."

"Okay. Add more oil. That doesn't sound so bad."

"You've been out of oil for a while. It's done some damage."

She covers her face with both hands for several

beats and finally lets out a heavy, groaning breath. "Let me guess? Timmy level damage?"

"Imagine if someone gave Timmy a Red Bull and a bucket of ice cream—"

The pitiful laugh that escapes her lips is filled with despair that twists my heart. I hardly know Avery Nichols, but I've been drawn to her since the first moment I laid eyes on her. It's a pull I can't explain. Unlike anything I've ever experienced, even with a woman I once thought I wanted to marry. It's a pull that demands I do everything in my power to help her. "Hey, I have two trucks. Why don't you borrow one until you get things sorted out with your car?"

"I can't do that."

"Sure you can."

She crosses her arms over her chest, unintentionally drawing my eyes to her bountiful breasts. Even beneath her sweatshirt, it's impossible to notice the massive tits she's hiding beneath it. What I wouldn't give to take them in my hands and squeeze... It takes my best effort to look away before she catches me staring.

"Why would you do that?" Avery asks.

"Because I don't need two trucks right now."

"I don't mind walking."

"You might next week. There's half a foot of snow in the forecast." Sensing she's going to fight me on this,

I change tactics to give her time to adjust to accepting my offer. "Let me clean up what I can under the hood. There's a couple minor things I can do to save you some money when you do get your car to the shop."

"I've already taken up enough of your time, Wes."

Something jolts inside me at hearing my name leave her lips. Like a shock to the system, but one I like. Way too much. "It'll be quick. I'll be out of your hair before you know it."

"Fine. But at least let me get you something to drink. I don't have any beer. You have anything against lemonade?"

"Not at all."

I dive back under the hood, searching for anything I can do to help save her a few bucks later.

Avery hurries inside and shuts the door so quickly it slams. The woman intrigues me. I'm good at reading people, but she's proven to be a greater challenge than anyone I've met before. Though I might be able to pick up on small cues, the deeper stuff is out of my grasp. The desire to know everything about her is growing stronger with each minute I stay.

I hear tires crunch against gravel. An engine roars then dies.

I hardly have time to pull myself out from beneath the hood of her car before I see Avery on the front step. Holding a glass of lemonade and standing stark still.

Fear flashes in her emerald eyes, quickly replaced by anger.

A car door slams, drawing my attention to the unsolicited visitor.

"Lucas, what the *hell* are you doing here?"

"You thought I wouldn't find you. You were wrong." A tall, lanky man who's in desperate need of a shave marches forward. The whiff of alcohol is strong as he unknowingly passes by me. "Now stop playing—"

I don't think. I spring into action. "Babe, you got my drink?" I step forward, posing as a barricade to Avery. "Can I *help* you?" I ask this Lucas, unable to keep my fists from balling at my sides. If he so much as lays a finger on her, I'm prepared to put my hand-to-hand combat training into action.

"Who the fuck are you?" Lucas spits at me, taking another step forward.

I move, standing in front of Avery. "I'm her boyfriend."

"C'mon," Lucas says, rolling his eyes so hard it seems to throw him off balance. He stumbles but catches his step. "You ain't with *her*. Look at her. She's—"

I'm in his face in half a second, daring him, with one hard look, to finish that sentence. I wouldn't stand for this behavior from anyone, no matter who they were disrespecting. But that he's targeting Avery makes me see red. "You need to leave."

Lucas shoves me by the shoulder, but his pitiful attempt doesn't move my firmly rooted footing an inch. The surprise in his eyes would be humorous if I didn't want to murder the guy. I return the favor, shoving him in the same place. Only Lucas stumbles back several steps and damn near falls on his ass.

Avery comes up behind me, clutching the back of my arm like a lifeline.

"Leave," I say again. "If you don't want me to call the cops, you'll get your ass out of town."

Lucas stumbles to his car, practically ripping the door open. "This ain't over, Avery. You know it ain't. We're meant to be together. Forever. You told me that." He cranks the ignition and slams on the gas, nearly taking out a mailbox across the street before he speeds off.

I turn to Avery and pull her shaking body into my arms. She clings to me in a rare moment of vulnerability. Her brave front is hiding more than I suspected. I comb a hand over the back of her head, tucking her protectively against me. "You okay, sweetheart?" I ask in a gentle whisper.

"I'm..." She takes a deep inhale and lets it out slowly, wriggling free from my embrace. It pains me to let her go, but I don't want to spook her. She's obviously been through a lot with this asshole. "I'll be okay."

I pull out my phone and shoot a text to my buddy Garrett, letting the police chief know there's a drunk driver in his town. "I want you to pack a bag."

"Why?"

"Because it's not safe for you to stay here tonight." If Garrett doesn't catch Lucas, the asshole just might find a way to stick around. I'd never forgive myself if he showed up in the middle of the night and hurt Avery. "You're staying at my place until we know he's actually gone."

"Your place?" Her widened eyes are cute as hell, but this isn't the time for smiling. I need Avery to know I'm serious.

"I have an empty guest room." Though I'd like nothing more than to have Avery nestled in my arms as we slept, and nestled in other places as our bodies tangled between the sheets, I'd never put that kind of pressure on her. "I want to keep you safe, Avery. Nothing more."

I watch the fight dancing in her eyes, but it only takes a few moments for her to relent. To realize that she could be in real danger here all alone. "Okay."

CHAPTER 5
Avery

Sleep is impossible.

The encounter with my ex is unsettling enough. I'm afraid to think about what might've happened if Wes hadn't been there. The street was deserted. I have no idea where my entire neighborhood was, but I don't know that a scream for help would've been heard in time. I left Lucas the night he punched a hole in the wall an inch from my head. Though he never hit me during the two years we were together, I knew it was coming if I stayed.

But it's not that alone that has me awake.

It's Wes Ashburn.

Knowing he's sleeping just down the hall from me is almost more than I can take. I've been fighting my attraction to him since the day he handed me the keys to my rental. After the way he stood up for me and came instantly to my rescue without missing a beat by pretending to be my boyfriend, I'm finding it a lot harder to fight these unwanted feelings.

Especially after the way he cradled me in his arms and held me tight.

Never in my life has a man's embrace felt so safe and reassuring—or any embrace, for that matter.

Nor has it turned me on quite so much.

I crawl onto the couch and toss a throw blanket over my lap. Wes lives a couple miles from town in a cabin on at least four or five acres. The windows in this room, which stretch all the way to the vaulted ceiling, offer a breathtaking view. Mountains peek behind a heavily wooded area and there's a hint of a creek in the distance. *This* is the type of place I always dreamed of living someday.

"Meow!"

I startle at the unexpected sound, but quickly relax. A tabby cat the size of a small mountain lion pounces onto the couch and struts across the cushions to me. "So you're the elusive Mr. Sprinkles, huh?" Wes mentioned a cat when we first arrived. One named by a girl in last year's kindergarten class. But until now, I hadn't met him.

The tabby crawls into my lap, pressing the back of

his head and neck into my hand. His purring is louder than my clunker car's engine. Well, when it's actually running. Mr. Sprinkles kneads his front paws into my leg and finally settles.

"He likes you." Wes's voice causes me to start, but I refrain from whipping my head around. There's no telling what the man sleeps in. What if he's in a pair of boxers and nothing else? I need a minute to prepare myself. Just in case.

"He's a good kitty, aren't you?"

Mr. Sprinkles purrs louder.

"Couldn't sleep?" Wes guesses.

There's no point in lying to the man who seems to read me better than anyone else. "Not really."

"I have a cure for that."

My breathing is suddenly heavier, imagining all the ways Wes could lull me back to sleep. One delicious orgasm at a time. I dare to look over my shoulder, almost disappointed to see him standing behind the couch in a t-shirt and shorts. Not that I'd actually entertain the idea of having sex with my landlord. No matter how mind-blowingly hot it might be. "What's that?"

"Banana pancakes."

"It's after midnight."

"That's the best time for 'em."

"I thought you couldn't cook," I rebuttal.

"I can't." He flashes me that warm, mischievous smile that has heat shooting to all the naughtiest places inside me. "That's why you need to help me."

I hug Mr. Sprinkles before dislodging him from my lap, which earns me a disgruntled moan. "I'll cuddle you later," I promise, winning him right back over by running a hand down the length of his spine.

When I meet Wes in a kitchen straight out of one of the Alaskan dream home magazines, I can't help but laugh. "You can't cook, but you have a kitchen that'd make most people drool with jealousy." I shake my head as I take the variety of ingredients he hands me one by one as he pulls them from their homes. "I'm a little surprised that you didn't work for a chef during your jack-of-all-trade years."

"I did, actually."

I start to measure out pancake mix. "You're lying."

"I only lasted three days before he fired me. I guess after starting two kitchen fires, he was over it."

"You're making that up."

Wes turns to me wearing a goofy grin that both puts me at ease and makes me yearn to comb my fingers through his beard. Cooking together, in such close proximity, is a terrible idea this late at night. We're both sleep-deprived. My shield against this insane attraction is weakened. Yet, there's nowhere else I'd rather be.

"In my defense, the fires were small."

I whisk together the batter as Wes peels and slices bananas. He tells me a story about his restaurant days as he works, his voice relaxing me in ways I can't even fathom. It's amazing how easy we settle into each other. How effortlessly we work together. I try to ignore the heat radiating from his delicious body, but it's hotter than the burner on the stove. One accidental brush turns into two, then three. I lose count.

When Wes starts to put away the ingredients, I feel the absence of that heat in a big way. In a way that promises I'm going to be in trouble if I don't tread carefully. But when he comes up behind me and peers over my shoulder into the frying pan, I forget all about playing it safe. I start to fall back against his chest. My eyes fall shut as I tilt my neck to the side. His breath tickles my sensitive skin. Slowly, I begin to turn my face. Hoping for a kiss I shouldn't want.

My lips part.

I feel his beard graze the side of my cheek.

"Avery," he says in that deep, sexy voice.

"Mmm?" I melt a little more into him, relishing in the feel of his hard chest pressed against my back.

"Avery, the pancakes. They're burning."

"Shit!" My eyes pop open and I spring into action,

flipping the small pancakes over. The bottoms are burned black. "Oh no," I groan.

"It's okay. I'll eat them."

"I'm sorry."

"Avery, it's okay." He drops a hand to my shoulder, those warm fingers caressing my neck. Making me forget all about destroying our midnight meal. "They'll taste great, you'll see."

It's only when he moves away and starts to gather plates and silverware that I realize how peaceful I feel around him. If I'd burned pancakes with Lucas, he'd remind me for weeks afterward. He was notorious, not only for pointing out my screw-ups, but also for making me relive them. "I can make you new ones," I say to Wes in one last attempt to right this situation. More than being afraid of backlash later, I don't want *this* to be his first impression of my cooking. "We have more batter."

Wes grabs one of the pancakes from the plate and takes a big bite out of it, locking his gaze with mine as he chews. Not once does his face screw up. In fact, he looks like he's enjoying his burned bite. "These are great. Really, you should try one."

This moment alone isn't enough to make me want to say screw this year of being single. But all the moments combined with this one are certainly testing my resolve. Wes has been nothing but wonderful since he saved me from Lucas and brought me to his place. He's made sure I've wanted for nothing, including enough blankets to ward off the coldest winter nights. He also turned up the thermostat after he caught me shivering, which I suspect he rarely does.

Now the incredibly sexy man is eating my burnt pancakes like they're some rare delicacy.

My heart is officially melting.

Mr. Sprinkles weaves his soft body through my ankles, letting out a loud *meow!*

"Here's the real test," Wes say, breaking off a piece of pancake. "If Mr. Sprinkles turns his nose up at your cooking, well, there's nothing I can do."

"Hey!" I playfully protest.

Mr. Sprinkles quickly chews his bite, undeterred, just like Wes, that it's burned.

"I didn't know cats ate pancakes." I run my fingers along his spine once more. When I stand, Wes is closer than I remember him being. If I simply reached out my hand, I could run my fingers along his hard chest. The temptation is overwhelming.

"Mr. Sprinkles is...special." Wes carries our plates to the island, breaking the spell. At least for now. I force myself to catch my breath while he's several feet away. I need to focus.

I only ended things with Lucas a few months ago, but it was something I should've done a long time before I did. I was too afraid. I need to make sure I can stand on my own two feet before I entertain the thought of falling for someone else.

I can't fall for Wes Ashburn, no matter how badly I want to.

CHAPTER 6

Wes

I've hardly taken a sip of coffee when I hear pounding at the door. I bristle at the very real possibility that Ben's at my door, demanding I come into the brewery on my day off to make up for leaving early yesterday. I was supposed to go back and check on Tanner, but I had to do it with a phone call. My brother is no doubt irked over it.

But there was no way in hell I was leaving Avery alone.

I still haven't gotten confirmation from Garrett that he's been run out of town.

When the doorbell starts going off like a sugar-sated kid is ringing it, I set down my mug and march to the door.

"Wesley!" Grandma June gives me no warning before she tackles me in a bear hug. She squeezes me so tight it's a wonder I can breathe. "Oh, it's so good to see you! It's been two years, you know. *Two* years." She finally lets me come up for air, but doesn't give me a chance to speak before she continues. "How've you been? How do you like being brew master? I heard you're buying up rental properties left and right. Oh, I brought cinnamon rolls." She reaches for a saran-wrapped pan she set on a deck chair. "Let me come inside. See what you've done with the place."

"Do you want some coffee, Grandma June?"

"Do you have my favorite creamer?"

"Caramel?"

Grandma June's entire face lights up. "You remember."

"Of course I do. I'm not your favorite grandson for no reason," I tease.

But the expected response doesn't come, because Grandma June is frozen in place. Staring down the hall.

Avery stands at the opposite end, looking like a deer in headlights.

"Grandma June, this is—"

"Wesley, you didn't tell me you had a girlfriend!" If I thought Grandma June was excited about coffee, it's nothing compared to her delight at this supposed discovery. I send an apologetic expression to Avery over the top of Grandma June's head, but it's not enough to keep her from rushing back into her room and hiding.

"Uh, Grandma June, why don't you fix yourself a cup of coffee while I check on Avery."

"Avery!" Grandma June coos. "What a lovely name."

I set caramel creamer near the coffee pot and hand her a mug. "I'll be right back."

I hurry down the hall and knock gently on Avery's door. As I wait, I can feel Grandma June sneaking a peek down the hall. I flash her a smile and mutter against the door, "Avery, I'm coming in." I don't have a choice but to open the door, though I do keep my eyes shut out of respect.

"Why are your eyes closed?" Avery asks, her tone a mixture of panicked and comedic.

I close the door behind me before our conversation carries down the hall. Grandma June might be a few years shy of eighty, but her hearing is scarily sharp. "Can I open them?"

"Yes."

Avery stands a couple feet in front of me, wearing the same sweatshirt and pajama shorts she wore last night. Shorts that showcased her legs and made it so damn hard to keep my hands to myself. "What's going on?" she hisses, pulling me back to the present dilemma.

"My grandparents are in town. Grandma June surprised me with cinnamon rolls." I rub my hand along the back of my neck. "Um, she wants to meet you."

"What?" Avery shakes her head adamantly. "No. No way."

"Look, it'll be easier if you just go along with this."

Avery lets out a laugh that says it all—I've got to be fucking crazy. But she doesn't know Grandma June. She doesn't realize what we're up against. Last night, the only thought I had was keeping Avery safe. I forgot my grandparents were coming to town. Or that Grandma June would probably show up with some goodies the first chance she got. "Look, I'm grateful for last night, but *this*—"

"These cinnamon rolls are best enjoyed while they're fresh," Grandma June calls, her sing-songy voice growing closer. "You two can canoodle once I leave. Come on out here so I can meet the woman who's finally stolen my dear grandson's heart!"

I clasp my hands together, knowing I look clichéd and ridiculous but I don't care. "Please?"

Avery doesn't get a chance to answer before the door flies open. I hop back to avoid being hit with it, colliding into the curvy beauty who's making it hard to think straight. I drape an arm over her shoulders, tugging her close.

Surprisingly, she doesn't squirm.

"Grandma June, this is Avery Nichols. She's the new kindergarten teacher."

"Oh!" Grandma June invites herself right into the room and makes a beeline for Avery. She wraps her in a warm hug, stealing her right out of my grip and probably suffocating her. "I've heard so many wonderful things about you, dear!"

"You have?" The words come out strangled.

"Grandma June, she needs to breathe."

"Sorry, dear. I'm a hugger. I also don't do anything half-assed. Ask any of my grandsons."

"She's right," I admit, tugging Avery back to my side. Hoping she won't hate me for what this ordeal is going to mean. There's no getting out of this now that Grandma June has put it in her mind that I've found a woman after all this time alone. But maybe this'll work in both our favors. Grandma June can leave Alaska believing I'm in a happy, committed relationship and she doesn't have to worry about me. Avery will be surrounded by family during the day and down the hall at night. In other words, completely safe. "Those cinnamon rolls are torturing me all the way back here."

"I'll get out the plates. Now Avery, you *must* tell me all about you!"

Grandma June rushes ahead of us, a ball of energy if ever there was one. Old age hasn't slowed her down at all. Avery turns a slightly frustrated, but mostly scared, look to me. "It'll be okay," I whisper against her ear. "Trust me."

"Trust you." Avery repeats the words, as if she's trying them on for size.

Before I can tell her why, Grandma June calls to us. "Hurry up you two love birds. I have to get back to Zac's before your grandpa realizes I gave away all the leftover cinnamon rolls to you and Ben."

"How is Benny Poo this morning?" I ask, hoping to divert the conversation away from Avery. Hoping that it'll put her at ease if Grandma June isn't prying into her life, no matter how well she means.

"He looked tired," Grandma June says honestly.

"That's because he works all the time."

"Even when his girlfriend's in town?" Grandma June shakes her head. "Something's not right there."

It takes a lot of restraint to bite my tongue, but this isn't the time to air out Ben's dirty laundry. Grandma June will figure out the problem with one visit to the brewery. All she'll have to do is see Ben and his administrative assistant Josie in the same room, and she'll know what the rest of us do. "We don't know Kat all that well," I admit.

"I invited Katherine to dinner." Grandma June slides two plates across the island, both barely containing heaping cinnamon rolls. Her pinched lips morph into an instant smile when she looks up at Avery. "Oh, Avery. You must come too!"

"To what?" Avery asks as she pulls apart a piece of cinnamon roll, the warm icing spilling across her thumb. What I wouldn't give to suck the sweet frosting from it. To run my tongue along—

"Why, family dinner tonight of course!"

"What? I couldn't possibly—"

I drape an arm around Avery's shoulders, hoping to soothe her. "What Avery's trying to say, Grandma June, is that this is pretty new between us. I haven't even told my brothers yet. I don't want to ruin what's blossoming here by subjecting Avery to their scrutiny."

"Nonsense!" Grandma June persists. "Avery, he's just trying to scare you. Please say you'll come. I'm only in town for a few days." Grandma June pulls out the big guns and reaches across the island for Avery's hand that isn't covered in icing. She squeezes it until Avery looks her in the eyes. "I've waited so long to see dear Wesley find someone who makes him happy. He deserves someone truly special after what he went through with—"

"Grandma June, your coffee's getting cold," I interrupt, not wanting my past dredged up. Grandma June knows more than anyone about my life imploding in Portland, but that doesn't mean I want to relive any of it. And definitely not in front of Avery.

"Oh, you're right it is. But you know, I better be running along before your grandpa pitches a fit about the cinnamon rolls disappearing." She shoulders her purse and hurries to the front door. "Dinner's at five-thirty. Don't be late!"

"This is a bad idea," I mutter as Wes pulls his truck into a spot outside a cabin similar to his own. It's tucked away in the woods, but higher up in the mountains than Wes' home. Three trucks are parked side-by-side, and the realization of what we're about to do makes my heart race with panic.

"Hey," Wes says, reaching for my hand. The simple touch makes it possible to breathe again. Which is a completely separate problem I'm not willing to face right now. "This is for your benefit too. If Lucas is still hanging around, which I highly suspect he is, you're not safe at your house. But it *is* a small town. People will talk. So why not let them think we're dating? In a couple weeks, we can stage a mutual, boring breakup. Once I know you're safe."

"You make it sound so simple."

"Because it *is* simple." He strokes the back of my hand with his thumb. Completely unaware how turned on I am by the simple gesture. Tingles skitter up my arm and spread all throughout my body. "I'm not trying to take advantage of this situation, Avery. I promise that. I'd never do anything you don't want me to." He lifts one corner of his mouth in a playful smile. "Besides, Mr. Sprinkles would probably shit on my pillow if I did anything to upset his new best friend. He's loyal like that."

"You sure you're not using me for my cooking?" I tease.

"I can't answer that." His devilish smirk does funny things to my belly. "Now c'mon. We sit out here much longer, they're going to thinking we're *canoodling*."

I laugh, and wow does it feel good. Though I'm a little on edge about attending this intimate family dinner and being found out as an imposter, I haven't felt this at ease in a long time. It's Wes. His presence calms me. Makes me feel safe.

"Grandma June is a phenomenal cook," Wes says as he takes my hand on the covered front porch. "I promise the food will make up for everything else."

I don't have a chance to ask for clarification before the front door flies open. Grandma June pounces, wrapping both Wes and me in a hug. "You made it. I'm so glad! Come. Come inside. We're just about to eat." She shackles her hand around my wrist and tugs me forward. Wes threads his fingers through my other hand. A promise he won't abandon me.

I shouldn't trust any of this.

When I let my guard down, bad things happen.

But the instant chatter of conversation and echo of laughter warms my soul. How many nights did I lie awake as a kid, staring up at my ceiling, praying that I could wake up the next day to a normal family? One where my mom actually cared that I was there and took an interest in me. Cooked me breakfast. Gave me hugs. Invited my grandparents over for Sunday dinners.

"You okay?" Wes whispers against my ear, pulling me from my past.

"Yeah."

"Sit down at the table, everyone," Grandma June announces.

I recognize Wes' brothers, Zac and Ben. Though I avoid the brewery because I don't want to run into Wes, I've seen them around town. Riley, Zac's wife as well. She offers me a warm smile from across the table.

"Ms. Nichols, right?"

"Avery."

"Avery, it's nice to meet you. We didn't know Wes was dating anyone."

"I don't tell you lot everything," Wes teases. His arm goes around my shoulders, offering that protective comfort I'm getting too accustomed to. It goes against my determination to figure things out for myself. But it feels too good to deny. Especially since we're both supposed to be playing a part.

"You're the new kindergarten teacher, right?" Zac asks.

"Yes."

"A darn good one from what I hear," Grandma June offers.

"You're one of Wes' tenants, right?" Ben asks, his lips a hard line. His tone is unsettling, warning me that Wes and I are under scrutiny. When he warned me about his oldest brother, I thought he was kidding. Now I believe him.

"Yes, I am."

"You think this is wise?" Ben continues, and I'm not sure which of us he's scolding.

"Ben, knock it off," Wes warns, his fingers digging into my opposite shoulder and tugging me closer to him. I lean into him, unsure if we're playing a part right now or not. But it feels too nice and allows me the excuse to catch a deeper whiff of his enticing aftershave.

"Where's Kat?" Grandma June asks as she sets a covered casserole dish on the table.

"*Katherine*," Ben corrects.

Grandma June just stares at him.

"She's taking a phone call. She won't be long."

"Go *get* her. Riley just got Chase down for a nap. Momma deserves a relaxing meal before he wakes up."

Grandma June is quickly becoming my favorite person in this room. Well, aside from Wes—but he falls into a different category altogether. I'd guess the woman to be about seventy-five, though she moves like she's sixty. It's clear she's the unspoken leader. The one commanding the room. The one no one dares cross. I never knew any of my grandparents, but when I dreamed about them, I imagined my grandma was just like Grandma June. I lean closer still to Wes and whisper, "I really like her."

"She's wonderful, right?" His thumb strokes my shoulder, making me momentarily forget we're at a table with five other people. Well, six when Katherine finally struts into the room. Her heels clack against the hard floors. Everything about her is expensive and refined. Her dress is better suited for a business dinner than a family meal. She's elegant, but she could be beautiful if only she smiled.

I look away before Kat catches me staring.

I shouldn't care so much about the family dynamics. Not when I really don't belong here. But I find myself filled with curiosity and absorbing every wonderful moment. Grandma June makes me feel like part of the family, making it harder by the minute to remember that this is all a farce.

"Grandma June," Ben says to get her attention, "Did Katherine tell you she put together a big merger this week? She's taking the business world by storm. Made the Forty Under Forty list."

"Impressive, dear." Grandma June's normally radiant smile doesn't reach her eyes as she passes around a bowl of mashed potatoes. Even I can see that from the opposite end of the table. Maybe it's because she catches me staring that she shifts her attention to me. "Avery, do tell us about your students. I'd love to hear about Caribou Creek's next generation."

I adjust in my chair, unaware that my hand has fallen to Wes' thigh until he lets out a quiet grunt. One that immediately takes me to a dangerous place. I slide my hand from his leg and put it back in my lap. "Well, I had a kid try to eat blue paint Friday. But it wouldn't be a normal day if there wasn't at least one disaster." Grandma June's laughter is music to my ears. "They're really wonderful kids. So bright. I feel lucky to be their teacher. Well, *most* days."

"When little Timmy Carlson isn't testing your every

last nerve?" Wes guesses, meeting my gaze. For a beat, my breath halts in my lungs. This close, I notice the gold flecks in his brown eyes, so dark they're nearly black.

"Right."

"There isn't a Carlson boy who won't test your patience in this town," Grandma June chuckles. "I taught second grade for a number of years before I left to start the brewery with Del." Grandma June glances at her husband, and it's as if the world melts away around them. The man isn't much for words, but he doesn't need them. How so much love can exist in one glance, I'll never know. But it makes me crave what they have. *Someday.* After my year of getting all my ducks in a row. Which will be quite the task since my ducks are all over the damn place doing their own thing.

"If you have any tips, I'd be happy to hear them," I say.

"We'll have to get a drink one of these nights."

"Oh boy," Zac says, hiding a smile behind his hand.

"What?" I ask Wes.

"I should warn you that Grandma June can drink anybody at this table *under* it."

"Really?" I ask, glancing at anyone who'll give me a straight answer.

"Don't go scaring her off," Grandma June teases. "I like this one."

"Me too," Wes agrees, caressing my shoulder again with his fingertips of fire. I know we're playing this up for the table, but it's so easy to pretend for a minute that this is real. That Wes and I are in love, too. That I've finally found someone I can trust not to hurt me. Not to turn on me.

"Katherine, you should join them," Ben suggests.

"What's that?" Katherine lifts her gaze from her lap, no doubt because she's been on the phone this whole time and hasn't even touched her plate. If I was lucky enough to be a part of this family dinner for real, I wouldn't mess up that opportunity by being so rude. Ben leans over and whispers to her, but the whole exchange is awkward and stiff. I make a mental note to ask Wes about it later.

"Oh yes, that would be nice," Katherine finally pipes up, a couple minutes after the conversation.

Grandma June seems to ignore her as she holds her glass up. "A toast everyone!" She taps her spoon against her glass until everyone—including Katherine—is paying attention. "I'm so happy my grandsons have such wonderful women in their lives. When Del and I left three years ago, I was worried the lot of them would end up alone." There's a light rumble of laughter across the table. "So thank you, ladies, for loving them."

Love.

The word should make me antsy. Activate my flight instincts. Have me plotting to escape out a bathroom window.

Instead, all it does is call to me. Tempt me.

Wes reaches for my hand in my lap and threads his fingers through mine, causing that feeling to intensify. My eyes widen in surprise, but I quickly recover my shock when I catch Ben staring—or more accurately scowling—at me. I may not be crazy about this fake relationship, but no way am I going to mess this up for Wes. Most importantly, I don't want to break Grandma June's heart.

"It makes my heart so full that each of us sits at this table today with someone by their side." She lifts her glass and seems to notice for the first time that it's empty. "Well, how about instead of a drink, we seal this with a kiss?"

I freeze.

My heart pounds against my rib cage.

A kiss?

I turn to meet Wes' gaze, surprised that he doesn't seem bothered at all by this request. He turns his head, resting his cheek against mine, and whispers in my ear, "Just a quick one, okay? For Grandma June."

He rests his forehead against mine, peering into my eyes. Seeking permission, just as he'd promised. I give me a subtle nod.

But I'm not prepared for what the simple brush of his lips against mine does. I don't expect my entire body to ignite from the inside out. Or jolts of electricity to travel the length of my entire nervous system. I certainly don't expect to cup his cheek and pull him back as he breaks away. Desperate for more than a mere brush.

The tender graze of lips becomes a deliberate joining. Our lips move sensually together as the world around us melts away.

He's the first to pull away, but we're both panting. Wes' eyes are the darkest shade I've seen them yet. *What* just happened?

"You two planning to skip dessert?" Zac teases, forcing us back to reality. Making me painfully aware that everyone at the table is staring. "Because I'm happy to eat your piece of blueberry cheesecake."

"Not a chance," Wes says to his brother, again taking my hand under the table. The rest of the family seem to return to normal, making it entirely possible that I'm the only one with the wildly racing heart rate. If I thought resisting Wes Ashburn was tough before, it's nothing compared to the fight ahead of me now that I know how enticing and all-consuming his kiss is.

CHAPTER 8

Wes

"Y ou can take me home," Avery says as nonchalantly as if she were suggesting something for lunch. We only made our escape from family dinner two minutes ago. I'm not even at the end of Zac's driveway. "I'll be okay there."

This is about that kiss.

A fucking dizzying kiss that'll haunt me for days.

I *know* she felt it too. She's the one who pulled me back in for more. But I suspect she's overwhelmed by my overbearing family and still skittish where relationships are concerned. She hasn't told me anything about this Lucas character, but I figured out all I needed to know in the two minutes I had to deal with him yesterday.

"It's not safe, Avery," I say gently.

"I'll keep my doors locked. And I have a baseball bat near my bed."

"Remind me not to piss you off." My attempt to tease falls flat, making me wonder if she's regretting that kiss. Perhaps regretting the whole fake relationship ploy because it's forcing her to do things she doesn't want to do. Which only makes me feel like an ass. I had no idea Grandma June would pull a stunt like that. She's a wild card, but even that toast seemed a bit excessive.

"I'm really tired, and I have school tomorrow."

I resist the urge to reach for her hand as we come back to city limits. "Garrett hasn't been able to get eyes on Lucas' car. I hope that means he left town, but until we know for sure, I'd really feel better if you stayed with me."

"And how will you know for sure?" Avery challenges, the playfulness from earlier gone. Hardly an hour ago she was all smiles and having fun through dessert and a game of Pictionary with my family. Now she's clammed up again. This is about more than a kiss that was supposed to be pretend.

"Garrett has contacts in Fairbanks keeping an eye out."

"Garrett's the police chief?"

"Right."

She plays with the silver bracelet on her wrist, as

she's been doing off and on during tense moments. I know she wants to fend for herself. I also know I can't keep her with me against her will. "Have you taken any self-defense classes?"

"No. I wanted to. Just...didn't get around to it."

I hesitate at a stop sign, and ultimately decide to make the right turn leading downtown. "Would you let me teach you?"

"I didn't realize kickboxing was used in self-defense situations." She flashes me a smirk, but I can't tell if she's actually teasing or injecting humor to hide her tension. I'd bet the latter.

"I have a military background." I pull into a spot right outside the vacant studio. There aren't any classes offered on Sundays, which guarantees we'll have the place to ourselves. "If you insist on sleeping at your place tonight—which for the record, I'm against—I want you to learn a couple moves."

Avery looks down at her skinny jeans, then back to me. "I'm not exactly dressed for this."

"What you're wearing is perfect." *Too* perfect in fact. I allowed myself to steal a few too many glances during family festivities, telling myself it was all to sell our fake relationship. But in reality, I just liked having the excuse to check out Avery's curvaceous figure which is all the more accentuated in those damn skinny jeans. "If you get attacked, it's not like you'll get a chance to change into gym clothes."

Avery lets out a soft sigh. "You're right."

"Hey," I say, daring to reach for her cheek with a single finger. Turning her face toward mine. "You're not in this alone, Avery. Whatever you have to prove to yourself, I get that. But if you need me, don't let your pride get in the way of your safety." My gaze flickers to her lips. I'm instantly taken back to the feel of her fingers combing through my beard as she dragged me back for more.

"Okay." A smile spreads on her lips, but it doesn't reach her eyes. "Teach me what I need to know."

Once inside the studio, we kick off our shoes. I lead Riley to a corner away from the punching bags already stationed for a morning class. "I'm going to walk you through some basic techniques. Then I'll have you practice them on me, okay?"

"On you?"

Though I suspect it's the close proximity she wants to avoid, I do my best to lighten the mood. "Don't worry, sweetheart. You can't hurt me."

"Is that a challenge?"

"Maybe it is."

She lifts her eyebrows, lips pinching into a tight and utterly kissable smile. But she doesn't say anything, and I slip into my instructor tone.

"The first thing is to memorize an attacker's weakest points. Eyes, nose, throat, chest, knees, and groin. It doesn't matter how big your attacker might be. If you remember these vulnerable places, you can use them to your advantage." I explain some basic moves she can use demonstrating on myself, but she doesn't seem to comprehend my explanation. I can see the frustration growing. It's in her expression, the way her fists clench at her sides, and in her cute groans.

"Maybe we should try this another way," I suggest.

"I think you're wasting your time. I have no idea how I'm supposed to remember all this. Maybe you should try teaching me how to swing a bat so I have a better chance of hitting an intruder instead of destroying your house."

"Let's try it another way," I repeat, keeping the words relaxed, void of the anxiety rolling off her. I'm used to kickboxing students getting frustrated when they can't seem to figure out a move, and I'm not about to give up on Avery. But it will also put me in her personal space, and I know I need to tread carefully. "Do you trust me?"

"Do I have a choice?" she teases.

"Of course you do. You always have a choice."

Her expression sobers as she stares at me. Those emerald eyes peer so deeply into mine I feel exposed. Naked. But I don't dare look away. Even if it makes the temptation to close the gap and taste those lips again almost painful. "I don't know why, but yes. I trust you."

"Hold out your hand."

She hesitates a moment before she complies.

"If someone grabs your wrist," I wrap my hand around hers, "Turn your arm up. Rotate in the direction of your thumb. Like this." I rotate her arm slowly, but it takes every ounce of focus to keep my thoughts on the demonstration. To ignore the electricity buzzing inside me at this simple touch. The pull I've felt to Avery all these weeks is only intensified by our close proximity. By our touch. "Now, yank your arm away."

She pulls too softly and isn't able to break the stronghold.

"I'm not going easy on you." I don't have to explain the unsettling truth.

Avery pulls again, this time much harder. "I did it!"

"Good job. Now, I'm going to come up behind you and put my hands on you. Like I'm the bad guy. Then I'll talk you through getting out of my grip. Okay?"

She nods.

If her safety weren't so damn important, I'd table this lesson for another day. For a day where the mere thought of being this close to her makes me want to do very naughty things to her. But I force all those urges down. I'll deal with them later, when she's learned how to escape an attack from behind.

I put my arms around her, pinning her own to her sides. "Attackers often come from behind because it's the easiest way to hold your arms so you can't move." I hold her tight, telling myself it's only to simulate reality. Not because the feel of her body molded against mine reminds me of the midnight banana pancake moment where I nearly kissed her.

"Now what?"

"The first thing you can try is to throw your head back and hit your attacker in the face."

She bends her head back and peers up at me. "Doesn't exactly work with you since you're nine feet tall. And I bet if I tried to backwards head butt your chest, *I'm* the one who'd end up with a concussion." The twinkle in her eyes is dangerous. It nearly makes me forget why we're here. "So, what's the second thing?"

"You're still going to give the first thing a shot. Because the whole point is to get your attacker to put his leg forward. Like this."

"And?"

"You're going to reach down and grab my leg with both hands."

She bends forward, and dammit if it doesn't make me near blind with desire. Her perfectly plump ass brushes against my cock. She seems completely unaware, but if I don't keep things moving along, she'll know exactly how I'm feeling in about three seconds.

"You're going to pull my leg forward as hard as you can and stand up at the same time."

"What?" she asks over her shoulder. Driving me wilder by the second.

"The point is to knock your attacker on his ass. Now pull my leg."

Avery shakes her head but does as I say. Only she forgets the part about her standing back up and sends up both tumbling to the ground. When I realize what's happening, I wrap my arms around her to soften her fall. We land in a pile on the mat, her back against my chest, both of us laughing. "I think I did it wrong."

"We can try again."

She looks up at me, those emerald eyes twinkling with mischief. And quite possibly a hint of desire. "You think that's wise? I might injure us both."

I can't stop staring at her lips. Remembering the way they felt against mine. Wondering what they might feel like circling my cock. I slide my hand up her arm to her shoulder and she starts to turn. Her tits press into my chest. I want to kiss her again more than I've ever wanted anything. I reach a hand to her cheek.

The front door rattles hard enough to startle us both.

Avery gasps and immediately climbs off me, the fear in her eyes impossible to miss.

I catch a glimpse of Ben peering in, looking irritated as ever. "Relax, sweetheart. It's just my pain-in-the-ass brother. Let me go see what he wants." I offer her a hand and help her to her feet. If it weren't for an obnoxious knock, I might've leaned in to capture those lips. "Fuck, he has no patience."

I march to the door and unlock it.

"You forgot your phone." Ben thrusts it at me, looking irritable as ever. It might be because Grandma June ignored Katherine most of the night while she doted on Riley and Avery as if they were her own granddaughters. Or because his relationship with Kat is a desperate attempt to deny his feelings for the woman who actually has his heart. But whatever the cause of his extra scowly scowl, I don't care tonight.

"Thanks."

"I think you're a fucking idiot," he mutters with a subtle nod at Avery.

"Back atcha."

Ben heads back to his truck, and I notice that Kat isn't inside.

"Everything okay?" Avery asks.

"Yeah. Just forgot my phone." I hold it up as evidence.

"You have a bunch of messages."

"That I do." I skim them, looking for the most important ones. But Garrett hasn't gotten back to me on Lucas. I slip the phone in my back pocket and look at Avery. "I'll take you home if that's what you want. But for the record, I think you should stay with me. At least one more night."

"You're worried Mr. Sprinkles will shit on your pillow, aren't you?"

"Yes." I don't mention that if she decides to sleep at her own place tonight that I'll be camped out in my truck down the block to keep an eye on things. I can survive on little to no sleep, but with the busy day ahead, I really hope I don't have to.

"Okay, one more night."

Avery

I give myself a once-over in the mirror the next morning, deciding I'm ready for combat. Or, in other words, another day with kindergarteners. But the truth is, I'm stalling. I'm getting too comfortable at Wes' place.

Last night I desperately wanted an excuse to kiss him again.

Hell, I wanted an excuse to crawl into bed with him.

I blame the family dinner and the self-defense lesson. In the blink of an eye, it feels as though I'm finally getting the life I've always wanted. The crazy but loving family. The perfect man. Except, it's fake.

Mr. Sprinkles weaves through my ankles and *meows* up at me. He cuddled with me most of the night and woke me up fifteen minutes before my alarm by sitting on my chest and staring down at me. I screamed, unintentionally summoning Wes to my door in a panic.

Thinking back on that moment, I should've told him to save me from the intruder. Would he have shoved open the door and crawled into bed with me? I groan, realizing I'm hornier than I want to be. After two miserable years with Lucas, I thought I'd never think about sex again. But the truth is, it's *all* I think about around Wes.

"Okay, let's go see what our breakfast prospects are." Mr. Sprinkles follows me down the hall to the kitchen, both of us sniffing the air trying to place that wonderful aroma. Is Grandma June here? No way Wes is cooking something that smells *that* good.

"Good morning," Wes says, handing me a plate. On it is some cheesy egg casserole that smells like heaven.

"What's going on?" I ask, setting my plate on the island and going for a cup of coffee. "Is Grandma June here?"

"What makes you think that?"

"Your complete inability to cook."

"Oh, that." His goofy grin is doing things to my insides that are entirely problematic. I find myself searching for any excuse to brush up against him. To touch him. When did this yearning grow so intense?

Oh right. That earth-shattering kiss. "Okay, full disclosure. Grandma June snuck me this casserole last night when we were leaving. All I had to do was preheat the oven."

"I knew it!" I playfully push his shoulder.

"I could've waited until you left to make it," Wes teases, taking a step closer to me. I think he means to pull me into his arms, except he reaches around me for a bottle of caramel creamer and offers it up. Damn this pent-up sexual frustration. "But it wouldn't be fair to deprive you of her cooking after what you put up with last night."

"Thank you," I say, meaning it. I'm touched by how effortless his thoughtfulness comes. It's genuine and without strings. I set my coffee mug on the counter and squirt a heavy amount of creamer into the cup.

"For what?"

"Thinking of me."

"Avery, it's hard *not* to think about you."

Setting the creamer on the counter, I dare to turn. Wes stands so close I can feel the heat radiating from him. Or is that coming from me? Probably both of us. Our mutual heat swirling a storm of desire between us. "You don't have to pretend," I tell him, fighting the urge to touch his chest. Though I seem to be losing that battle because I watch my hand make its way without my permission. "We're not in front of an audience right now."

Wes' deep chuckle causes a quiver low in my belly. "You think I'm pretending?" He brushes my hair back, combing it behind my ear. His fingertips brush my skin, making me shiver in the best possible way. He cups my cheek and tilts my face up to meet his gaze. Which is as dark as it was last night after our tumble onto the mats.

"That's what we agreed to, right?" But any resolve my whispered words might have lose their conviction as my hand fists his shirt. I don't realize I'm tugging his lips closer to mine until we kiss. Until our lips brush, then collide. I snake my hand around the back of his neck, sinking into the kiss I haven't been able to stop thinking about. Molding myself against his hard body as his arms wrap around me and hold me tight.

It's an explosive kiss. One that promises I'll never get enough of this, even if it were a hundred kisses. Our tongues tango as hands roam. I comb my fingers up the back of his neck, relishing in the feel of his soft hair against my skin.

"Avery," Wes pants, resting his head against my forehead. "If we don't stop now—"

"What?"

He starts to tug free, but I hold on. "Please.

Don't." I flicker my gaze up to his, revealing the slightest bit of vulnerability in doing so. "Don't stop."

He holds my gaze, his expression unreadable. I fear I've crossed a line, but it's too late to turn back now. Finally, Wes lifts one corner of his mouth, pulling me back against him. "You'll be late."

"Not if you're quick about it."

"Not as much fun as taking my time," he admits, already gathering one side of my long shirt in his hand. He tilts my head back and steals a kiss that leaves me both breathless and unable to stand. Wes scoops me up and sets me on the island, pushing my skirt the rest of the way up. "You're sure about this?"

"Yes."

"If you want me to stop at any—"

"I don't." I take his hand and firmly place it on my exposed upper thigh. "I want this, Wes."

Heat flashes in his eyes as he returns his lips to mine. I feel my panties being peeled away as his tongue swirls with mine. I moan as he drags a finger through my folds, teasing my clit. The simple touch is nearly enough to get me off. It's been so long since I've been intimate. So much longer since I've enjoyed it.

Wes pushes the plates and coffee out of the way. "Lie back." As I obey, he spreads my legs and lowers his mouth. His breath teases my pussy, warning me I'm not going to last long at all. I've been dreaming about this very moment for longer than I care to admit. Seeing Wes between my legs is so fucking hot I almost can't stand it.

He slowly runs his tongue up and down a few times, making me wish we had all day to enjoy this.

Though I love the show between my legs, I let my head rest against the counter and close my eyes. Surrendering to sensation as Wes fuses his mouth to my pussy. I feel his lips and tongue move in ways that seem to defy the law of physics. I moan his name as I gently rock my hips against his face.

When I feel his tongue plunge into my channel, I arch hard. It's all I can do to hold on to the island as Wes intensifies everything. Keeping his promise to make this quick. His tongue becomes a cyclone around my swollen button, taking me over the edge so hard and fast I nearly go blind from the pleasureful shock.

Still in the middle of recovering my breath, Wes looks up from between my legs. "Hope that starts your week off on a good note, Teach."

CHAPTER 10

Wes

After stopping by Avery's house to apply a proper, more permanent fix to the pipe beneath the kitchen sink, I head in to the brewery. I don't bother trying to hide the smile that stretches my cheeks. The taste of her pussy lingers on my lips. My brothers think I'm dating Avery, so why not lean into that? With any luck, Avery will decide we don't need to stage that breakup.

"All the empty fermentation tanks are cleaned," Tanner announces when I step into the brewhouse.

"Liam get his grain?"

"Yep. He picked it up the other night. That tank is cleaned too."

"I know."

"You do?"

"I stopped by to check things out over the weekend."

"Was that before or after you shacked up with Avery Nichols?" Ben's smug tone comes from behind. But even the grumpiest man in Caribou Creek can't wipe the smile from my face. Not today.

"Tanner, why don't you check on the wort?" I wait for the kid to walk across the brewhouse before I turn to face my brother. "Something I can help you with?"

"You're an hour late."

Ben is convinced everyone should be on a strict schedule, including the three of us owners. Never mind that he's been working from home more and more as of late to avoid being around Josie. I bet he's only here to harass me about dating a tenant. "I don't work on a schedule. I told you that the day we signed the papers."

"What kind of example does that set?"

Ben seems extra pissy today. I'm guessing Kat went back to Anchorage and he didn't get any. In fact, I don't think those two have that kind of relationship. That'd explain a lot about my brother's attitude as of late. Sexual frustration can make a man quite growly. Of course, in my case, it can also make a man giddy with anticipation.

I've avoided dating since I moved back to Caribou Creek. Sure, I've entertained an occasional out-of-town fling, but even that impulse has faded away. For the first time in years, I yearn to settle down.

With Avery.

A part of me has known since that first day she pulled into the driveway that she was mine. And now, with each day that passes, I'm only more certain of that. Eating her pussy this morning didn't hurt in reaffirming that conviction. Fuck, I could eat her out every day for the rest of our lives.

I *want* that. With her.

With any luck, Avery will hang around a couple more nights and give me the opportunity I need to make this fake relationship a real one.

Ben's hardened expression pulls me back to the brewery. Forcing me to table my dirty fantasies for later.

"Look, I'm here when I need to be. I check and maintain everything that's required of me and more. Just because that doesn't fit neatly into your rigid schedule doesn't mean I'm slacking. Zac isn't either." If Tanner weren't across the room, I'd really let Ben have it. But I'm not in the mood to start anything with him today. Which is why I switch tactics. "Look, I have an idea. Something I want to share with you and Zac. You going to be in the office for our next owner's meeting or you going to phone that one in?"

"I was in Anchorage last time." Ben folds his arms over his chest. "Networking."

"Just, make sure you're here this time." I don't wait for Ben to leave the brew house and walk out first. I head for the offices at the back of the taproom fully intending to give my *schedule* an overhaul.

But before I make it to the office that Ben, Zac, and I share, I notice Josie coming out of the janitor's closet. Her cheeks are puffy and I catch her wiping her eyes. I could kill Ben. I know this is his fault.

"Hey, everything okay?"

"Yep!" Her too-cheerful smile is instant and a complete front for what's really going on. "Everything's great!"

If I had to guess, Kat stopped by before heading off to Anchorage. Ben's way of reassuring Josie doesn't get any ideas. Some days I can't figure out how the hell we're related. The man's been in love with Josie since the day they met. She's been in love with him. But he won't allow himself to cross that line and makes her suffer instead.

"Josie, you don't have to lie to me." I follow her back to the main office and close the door. "Was the Wicked Witch of the West here?"

She cracks a smile. "It's not nice to call her that, Wes."

"I didn't mean it. Not really. Just wanted to make

you smile a real smile." I drop into Ben's chair and pull up his Outlook calendar. One look and I'm nearly blinded. The damn thing has more colors than a kaleidoscope. It takes me a beat to figure out I'm yellow. I go through and delete all the reoccurring yellow boxes.

I hear sniffles as Josie pretends to focus on whatever report Ben has her compiling. Frustration wells up inside me. I'd love to smack my brother for his ignorance. Josie's way too good for him. Much sweeter, kinder, and all around better than he deserves. But for some reason, she only has eyes for him.

"Hey, can you come to the brewery on—"

"What's going on in here?" Ben's baritone voice booms throughout the tiny space. His eyes are narrowed at me, sitting behind his desk.

"Making some schedule adjustments," I answer before Josie can. I pop out of his chair and meet him at the door.

To my surprise, Ben closes it behind us. Leaving Josie alone in the office and us in the hall. "What the *hell* are you doing? Isn't messing around with one woman enough for you? You know how I feel about fraternizing with—"

"Whoa, whoa." I hold up my hands. "I'm not going after Josie."

The rage in Ben's eyes dies down. I drag him down

the hall by the arm, away from the office door and eavesdropping ears.

"Why was the door closed?" Ben growls.

I just shake my head. "You're got it worse than I thought."

"What are you talking about?"

"You obviously want to be with her. But if you're going to parade Business CEO Barbie on your arm around Josie, you don't get to act like a fucking jealous boyfriend." It takes incredible restraint not to tell Ben that Josie came out of the janitor's closet crying. I won't humiliate her like that. But his silence reveals something interesting. "Why aren't you defending her?"

"Who?"

"Kat."

"Katherine."

"You're unbelievable. You know, I thought what the two of you had looked fake. But now I know I was right." I spin on my heel, headed back to the brew house.

"As fake as you and Avery?" he shoots back.

I stop and take a moment to collect myself. It's been years since I've been in a fist fight with one of my brothers, but the temptation to tackle Ben and knock some fucking sense into him is overwhelming today. I love him, but he frustrates the hell out of me. Finally, I turn. "You don't know what you're talking about."

"You think I don't know you're making this up? I *know* you, Wes. Even if we're not as close as we used to be. Avery Nichols goes out of her way to avoid you every time you two run into each other. And there's nothing cutesy about it. I don't know what you're playing at with her, but if it's to appease Grandma June—"

"Stop." My fists clench at my side. "This has nothing to do with Grandma June."

"Then what?" Ben challenges.

"I'm *protecting* her." Before Ben can ask from who, I storm down the hall and return to the brew house. I hate that what Avery and I have isn't real, but I'm working really damn hard to change that.

CHAPTER 11

Avery

S ilence falls over the classroom as the last of my kids hurry down the hall and out the door for the day. It was a challenging day to say the least. No blue paint, but there was a debate about where babies come from that got way out of control. I've never been so thankful in my life that six-year-olds are so easily distracted.

Yesterday, I was the one who was easily distracted. I could hardly focus in the classroom. Couldn't stop thinking about Wes eating me out on his kitchen island. I had no idea what to expect when I returned to his house after work. But it certainly wasn't a freshly run bubble bath with candles and a couple of Grandma June's famous red velvet cupcakes.

I had hoped he'd get in the tub with me, but after a

few sultry kisses and a neck rub that strayed a little south, Wes left me to enjoy my bath in peace.

It was surprisingly perfect. I'm craving one of those delightful bubble baths again. Maybe this time, Wes will get naked and join me.

"Avery, you're still here!" Grandma June's voice pulls me from my daze in front of the whiteboard I've only half-finished cleaning. "I was hoping to catch you. I wanted to see where my grandson would be going to school."

"He's got a few years yet," I tease.

"I do hope you'll still be teaching when he's old enough."

"I hope to be." For the first time, the words don't feel rehearsed. They don't feel like a lie. In the few months I've lived in Caribou Creek, I've fallen in love with it more each day. But I've always had one foot out the door ready to run should Lucas show up. But now that he has, I'm not so rattled. Not with Wes to help keep me safe from him.

"Good, good!" Grandma June wanders around the classroom, taking in the decorations and showering me with more compliments than I can count. She tells me some about her classroom and how we seem to think alike. The words warm me right to the core, making me wonder if what Wes and I have could become...real.

It would totally shoot my one year of being single to hell.

But I'm already starting to cave.

And it's not just his incredible mouth.

It's the whole package. His kindness, his thoughtfulness, and his family. I want to be a part of it so badly I could cry. Which is exactly why I have to keep my guard up. I can't let myself fall. Because if I do, it won't just be for Wes. Which is troubling enough. It'll be for the entire Ashburn clan. That's a heartbreak I don't know if I can survive.

"How long are you staying in town?" I hope my tone sounds nonchalant and not at all like I'm trying to do math in my head to see how long I'll have to keep pretending to be Wes' girlfriend.

"We're headed out on a red-eye Friday night. Which is why I'm hoping you and Wes will join us tonight."

"What's that?"

"Del and I would like to take you two out for a special dinner at MOUNTAIN PRIME. I hope tonight will work."

An intimate dinner with Wes and his grandparents. In the fanciest dining establishment for a hundred miles. My pulse races at unexpected speeds. This is a horrible idea. Yet, I can't tell her no. "Of course tonight will work."

"Oh good! I made reservations for seven. We'll meet you two there, okay?" Grandma June lunges at me, wrapping me in a hug like a python. For several beats I can't breathe, but I don't dare move. "I'm so happy Wes found you, dear. You're so good for him."

"How can you tell?"

"He lights up around you. He slows down."

I shouldn't pry, but I'm too curious not to. "What do you mean?"

"I shouldn't tell you any of this, but ever since Wes came back from Portland, he's not been the same. He does everything he can to stay busy. To keep his mind preoccupied. His ex did a number on him, you see. Did he tell you any about her? Camille?"

I shake my head, unable to cut her off. Because selfishly, I want to know all about it.

"It's been a number of years now. He was all set to propose to her. Right after he'd been offered a position at one of the prestigious breweries there, you see. But when he went to surprise her with the news of his promotion and pop the question, he caught her."

"Cheating?"

"Worse! She was dressed for a cocktail party when she was supposed to be home sick. She admitted to being a hired escort."

If the story wasn't coming from Grandma June, I'd have a hard time buying its validity. "An escort?"

"He was devastated by her deceit. She never let on. And the things she had to do for money." Grandma June shudders. "All those rich old men. So gross."

I make a mental note never to mention my one week as a stripper. Never mind that I needed the money for books during my first semester of college. Or that I hated every minute of it. I'm not proud, but I did what I had to in order to escape my toxic mother. Somehow, I don't think Wes—or the schoolboard for that matter—would see things the same way. Grandma June would be completely scandalized and probably retract her statement about me being good for Wes if she knew.

"Anyway," Grandma June says, waving her hand as if to wipe away that conversation. "They have the *best* prime rib at MOUNTAIN PRIME. You should wear a dress. You have the perfect figure for one." She squeezes me in one more hug, then hurries out the door.

CHAPTER 12

Wes

When I first see Avery in her black dress, I'm stunned. From day one, her beauty has been undeniable. She's gorgeous with or without makeup. With her hair in a messy bun or cascading down her shoulders. In a t-shirt or dressed up for school. But in this sleek dress, the sight of her is doing things to me. I *feel* things.

"Wes Ashburn, are you speechless?" she teases, strutting down the hall and purposely swinging those hips.

I've been eager to draw her into my arms all day, but when I arrived home to find out we have plans with my grandparents, there wasn't time. She's been locked in her room getting ready for over an hour. It was worth the wait. "You look gorgeous."

"Grandma June insisted I wear a fancy dress. I don't want to get on her bad side, you know."

I reach for her hand, threading my fingers through hers. "We could always skip dinner."

"You want to be the one to tell Grandma June?" The twinkle in Avery's eyes tempts me to do just that. What I wouldn't give to scoop her into my arms and carry her to my bedroom. To spend the evening pleasuring her. Memorizing her body with my lips. To taste every delicious inch of her. "Wes!"

"You're right. Even I'm not brave enough to go against Grandma June's wishes." I yearn to tell Avery I'm done pretending. That what is happening between us is more than pretend. More than some fun fling that'll end once she goes home. But until I feel that Avery's ready to hear what I have to say, I'll keep it close to the vest. "Suppose we better get going or we'll be late."

She drops her gaze to our interlaced fingers, no doubt because I refuse to let go just yet. I tug her closer and cup her cheek so quickly she gasps in surprise. I capture her lips in a soft, sensual kiss that tempts me to do very bad things to her in this dress.

It takes incredible restraint to break apart the kiss.

Avery's eyes are hooded. "What was that for?"

"Practice. For tonight."

"Practice." She repeats the word as if she's trying it

on for size. Before she can call me out on it, Mr. Sprinkles weaves his body around her ankles, meowing up at her. For once, the cat with attitude for days seems to be throwing me a bone. I knew there was a reason I was destined to adopt him.

Avery bends over to stroke his neck, giving me an unobstructed view down the top of her dress. I imagine running my dick through the valley of her tits, which makes me hard almost instantly. I adjust my pants. "We better go."

"Right."

The drive is quick, as there's a shortcut from my place to the restaurant on the edge of Caribou Creek. Avery spends most of the drive playing with her bracelet. One I notice she never takes off. "Did someone special give that to you?" I do my best to keep the jealousy from my tone. It's far more likely a relative gifted her that bracelet than an ex.

"I did."

"Oh?"

"It was my college graduation gift to myself." She looks out the passenger window, but I don't miss the faraway look in her eyes. "I figured if I didn't buy myself something to celebrate, no one else would."

"What about your parents?"

"Never knew my dad. And my mom...let's just say she's not much of a mom." Avery practically jumps out of the truck the second I put it in park. Either she's eager to see Grandma June again or she doesn't want to talk about her family. Her determination to take care of herself makes a little more sense.

"Wesley, you're five minutes late," Grandma June teases, tugging me into a hug. Against my ear, she whispers, "I forgive you. But only because I suspect Avery had something to do with that delay. I like her, Wesley. A lot."

My heart swells at Grandma June's approval.

I only hope that I can convince Avery to give this a real shot after my grandparents leave.

"I ordered a bottle of wine," Grandma June announces as we get situated at a window table. But I'm too captivated by Avery to notice the mountain view it no doubt offers. "Let me pour you both a glass. There's also some fresh bread on the way. Avery, this place is amazing. You can order whatever you want, of course, but I will tell you that people travel hundreds of miles to eat their prime rib and king crab. *Oh*! You two have to tell me how you met."

I nearly choke on an ice cube.

Avery busies herself sipping on her glass of wine.

Guess that leaves me.

Once I've stopped choking and can breathe normally again, I reach for Avery's hand and squeeze it. "I first met Avery when she pulled into the driveway of one of my rentals earlier this summer. She was driving this old clunker of a car that miraculously brought her safely to Caribou Creek." I turn my gaze to Avery's. "But more amazing than that car was the woman who stepped out of it. I couldn't speak. I couldn't breathe. Zac was there. He remembers how I looked like some love sick puppy."

"Really?" Avery asks in a whisper, as if she's working really hard to figure out if I'm playing this up or telling the truth.

"Really."

"Love at first sight!" Grandma June coos.

"Well, for me maybe. But it took Avery some time to warm up to me," I admit, stroking her hand with my thumb. "She's very independent and stubborn."

"I'm not stubborn," she says with a laugh. "Okay, maybe a little."

"Or a lot," I tell Grandma June. "But eventually, I wore her down with my endless charm and sheer determination."

"What about your first kiss?" Grandma June presses.

"June Bug, they don't—"

"Hush now, Del. A first kiss story is one you tell your grandkids someday. I bet Wesley can recite ours, can't you?"

I don't know how I'm going to get out of this one.

I don't know if Grandma June would find the humor in the truth. I do my best to stall, turning my attention back to Avery and answering the second question first. "Grandma June stole her first kiss from Grandpa Del when they were both covered in mud. They'd been riding on trails the day after a heavy downpour. She hit a bump and went flying into a mud puddle. Grandma Del rescued her and well, she thanked him."

"I did indeed." Grandma June's eyes sparkle. The love in both their eyes is very apparent. The kind of love I now believe is possible again. I never thought I'd recover from Camille's deceiving lie. The double life she felt no remorse for leading. I never thought I'd let anyone in again. But now that I've met Avery, I feel like everything is possible again. "So how did—"

"You never wore that slutty black dress for me." I recognize the voice before I turn my head over my shoulder. Lucas sways in place. His bloodshot eyes zero in on Avery. "Well, you wore some much sluttier things when you were a str—"

I'm out of my chair and in his face in half a second. The stench of whiskey is heavy on his breath. "You have two seconds to get the hell out of here," I say in a low growl, well aware the entire dining room is watching this. It's the only reason I haven't broken his nose. Yet.

"Or what?" Lucas spits his words at me, causing

him to nearly lose his balance. He tries to right himself by shoving me.

I grab him by the shirt collar, my fist raised in position to knock out a couple teeth.

"This the guy?" Garrett's voice is a welcome surprise. That he's in uniform is even better. I should've known he'd be here. The man can't get enough of their prime rib. I lower my fist right away but take my time releasing Lucas' shirt collar.

"Yeah."

"Want to press charges?" Garrett asks me. "I witnessed the assault. So did a dozen or more other people."

"I didn't assault him."

"I'll take it from here." Garrett grabs Lucas' shoulder and the back of his arm.

"Get your hands off me," Lucas spits at Garrett. "Avery, don't think I won't tell everyone. You're not good enough for him. You're just a little slut--"

Before I can take a swing, Garrett tugs Lucas a foot closer to the door. Though it would be very satisfying to break his nose, I appreciate my friend looking out for me. I can't convince Avery to give us a chance from a jail cell.

"You folks have a good night now." Garrett quickly nods at Grandma June and Grandpa Del. When his eyes land on Avery, I see the twinkle there that promises he'll have more to say about this later. Probably over a couple of beers. We had a bet going on who'd be single longer. We never made a clause for a fake relationship, but hopefully that won't matter. I'd love to lose that bet fair and square.

"Why do I have a feeling you have a warrant or two?" Garrett says to Lucas as he urges him forward out of the dining room. "You won't mind if I look that up before you go, right?"

I return to my seat, draping my arm around Avery. "You okay," I ask her in a low tone only she can hear.

"I will be." She reaches a hand onto my thigh. I think it's a caress of gratitude until her fingers slide dangerously high. I'm suddenly wishing we'd already eaten dinner, because there's only one thing I want for dessert. And I'd bet the brew house Avery wants the same. "Thanks to you."

"Well, that was certainly exciting," Grandma June declares, bringing our attention back to the table. "What do you say we order? I'm starving!"

CHAPTER 13

Avery

Throughout dinner, all I could think about was how instantly Wes stood up for me. He didn't hesitate to get in Lucas' face despite the audience that included not only his grandparents, but half the town. Never in my life has anyone come to my defense like that.

Never in my life, have I been so turned on.

The ride home is quiet, but the cab of the truck is filled with electricity. It practically crackles in the air around us.

Throughout dinner, Wes kept whispering things in my ear. Naughty things that made it very hard to pretend they weren't in front of his grandparents.

Naughty promises I'm hoping like hell he plans to fulfill.

Tonight.

I wait only until we're inside and the door's locked behind us before I pounce. I throw my arms around Wes' neck and fuse my lips to his. I expected to catch him by surprise, but the man doesn't miss a beat. His lips move against mine instantly. He runs those warm hands up and down my back. Over my ass. Up my sides.

"You've been killing me in this dress, sweetheart," he growls against my ear. He tugs on my earlobe. "I can't decide if I want to get you out of it or fuck you in it."

If I wasn't wet before, I certainly am now. "Why not both?"

Wes laughs low and deep as he nuzzles my neck, causing my nipples to pebble, straining against the silk. "I sure hope you mean that."

"I do."

In one quick motion, Wes scoops me into his arms as if I weigh nothing. His breath doesn't get heavy at all as he carries me down the hall and kicks open his bedroom door. Though I snuck a peek the other day, this is the first time I've been invited in. I've been dreaming about sharing his king-sized bed for days.

Wes drops me on the bed and sheds his shirt.

I shouldn't be surprised at his washboard abs. The man is a fitness instructor. But the sight is still shocking to behold. I yearn to run my tongue over those delicious abs. "Not even fair," I mumble, playfully shaking my head.

"What's not fair is how you've been teasing me in this little black dress all night long." He crawls onto the edge of the bed, slowly sliding the skirt of my dress up my thighs. "Oh the things I want to do to you." His eyes are darker than I've ever seen them. Drenched with more desire than I ever thought possible.

It's late.

I have to teach twenty-one kindergartens all about the letter F tomorrow. I need to be on my a-game for that endeavor. But right now, as Wes sheds his jeans and fixes his attention on my pussy, sleep doesn't seem so important. It's nothing a few cups of coffee can't fix.

"You've been wearing these sexy panties all night?" He strokes his fingers over the damp silk, groaning in that sexy way that only makes me wetter.

"You like them?"

"I do." He crawls up my body until our lips rejoin. As he kisses me into oblivion, his hand slips inside my panties and dives for my wet folds. His touch is gentle yet deliberate. Tender yet powerful. He strokes me in all the right ways that, along with his potent kisses, make me dizzy with pleasure.

It's almost too much.

I can't remember the last time I enjoyed something this intimate.

I can't remember the last time someone prioritized my pleasure.

I rock my hips against the methodical movements of his hand, moaning into his mouth as our tongues swirl together. He strokes me faster, flickering a finger against my swollen button. Applying pressure and speed with such perfection. I dig my fingers against the back of his neck as he moves his mouth to the v-cut of my dress. Though I picked out a dress that wouldn't scandalize Grandma June, Wes doesn't have any trouble licking what he wants.

The combination of pleasureful sensations is over-whelming in the best way. I can feel it all building low in my belly. "I'm going to—*come!*" The last word comes out in a dozen high-pitched syllables.

"I love this," Wes says, flashing me a wicked smile.

"What?" My question is more of a pant, but at least it's my normal octave.

"Everything about the way you come."

I should need a minute to be this turned on again, but Wes does something to me no one else ever has. I shove down the bubble of panic that does it's best to emerge. I'll deal with reality tomorrow. Tonight, I'm surrendering to passion.

"I think it's time to get you out of the dress, sweetheart."

CHAPTER 14

Wes

I pull Avery to her feet and take my time undressing her. When her black dress falls to the floor, I stand back and take in her curvaceous body. Admiring every inch. When she tries to hide herself, I take her arms and pull them above her head. "You're the most beautiful woman I've ever seen, Avery. Don't hide yourself."

"Say that to all the girls?" she asks with a playful eye roll that I suspect is a cover for her insecurity.

It makes me want to find Lucas and knock a couple teeth out after all. I'd bet anything he's responsible for how she sees herself. "No, I don't. I haven't been with anyone in a long time," I admit. After I found out the truth about the woman I almost asked to marry me, I grew bitter. I didn't date. What little I got out was in Anchorage and never anything serious. But I grew tired of that, too. It's been two years since I've been with a woman. Only now do I appreciate that I waited for the right one. For Avery.

"It's been a while for me, too. I know you've met Lucas, but it's not what you think. We haven't..." She shakes her head, clearly uncomfortable talking about this. Clearly ashamed. I cup her cheek and turn her head to face me.

"You don't have to keep anything from me, Avery. I won't judge you in any way."

"You sure about that?"

"Of course I am." I draw her in for a soft kiss that quickly becomes a hungry one. Our lips move with greed as arms tangle around one another. I shuffle us back to the bed and we fall onto it. My cock presses against her belly, begging to get out of my boxers. "Do you want me to use protection?"

"I'm on the pill," Avery says. "I'm clean."

"Me too."

"Good." She strokes my cheek, running her fingers through my beard. "Because I don't want anything between us tonight. I want to feel you. *All* of you." She reaches between us, wrapping her hand around my cock. "And from the looks of it, there's a lot of you to feel."

I groan at her touch, finding it hard to focus. It takes concentrated effort to strip away my boxers.

Avery spreads her legs, bending her knees wide in invitation.

"Fuck, that's a pretty pussy." I can't wait to plunge my cock into it. "I bet it's nice and wet, too."

"That's all your fault."

"Good." I steal another kiss as I lower my hips, lining my swollen head with her entrance. "You can blame me for that as much as you want." I push inside her channel slowly. Giving her tight pussy time to adjust to my size. I rock in an inch and pull out. Rock in another inch and pull out. I repeat the motion until I'm fully seated in her channel.

"Damn you feel good," she says, combing her fingers over the back of my head. "You're going to spoil me for all other men."

A pang of jealousy strikes me hard at her playful words. I start to move again, rocking slowly but thoroughly in and out of her cunt. "If I come in your pussy, sweetheart, there won't *be* any other men. You'll be mine. *Only* mine."

Though there's a flash of panic in her emerald eyes, it's quickly replaced by liquid heat. "I won't share you either, you know."

"There's no one else I want, Avery. Only you." I leave a trail of kisses from her nipple, to her collarbone, and up her neck. Against her ear, I say, "I don't want to pretend anymore. You're the one I want. The *only* one I think about."

When Avery doesn't immediately answer, I fear I've put too much pressure on her. I reach between us and stroke my finger against her clit.

"Can we—can we talk about—*oh!*—that later?"

"Only if you agree to have dinner with me when we do. Tonight."

"Are you cooking?"

"Not a chance."

Her carefree, sexy laughter does something to me. It makes me feel deeper than I ever thought I'd feel again. It's not just lust between us. It's a soul connection. A promise that forever would never be enough for us. I know in this intimate moment that I've fallen in love with Avery Nichols. Hell, maybe I did the first moment I laid eyes on her months ago.

She runs her hands up and down the back of my neck and shoulders, settling them on my cheeks. "Okay, I'll have dinner with you."

Our lips fuse together as our bodies find a perfect hungry rhythm. We're a tangle of arms, legs, and all the best parts. I could spend days worshiping her body. Bringing her to the brink of pleasure time and time again, never tiring of it.

I lean back on my legs and pull her hips up onto my thighs. One at a time, I stretch both of her legs straight up until her heels rest against my shoulders. I can tell by the look in her eyes that's she both intrigued and a little scared. "If it's too intense, you tell me, okay?"

"It's okay."

I lean forward the slightest, filling her pussy once again. I start slow, ensuring she's enjoying this as much as I am. "Fuck, Avery. You feel so good. My dick *loves* your pussy." I gradually pick up the pace, holding her legs against my chest with one arm. I'd be lying to myself if I said I didn't love the way her tits bounced with each thrust. Or the way she moans as I fill her again and again.

She reaches between her legs, playing with her button.

"Fuck that's hot."

The devious expression on her face promises she has something witty to say, but her words are swallowed by a series of moans as she unexpectedly reaches her climax. She cries out my name as her body rocks hard beneath me. Fuck, it's the hottest things I've ever seen.

I pump faster and harder, joining her in a release moments later. Filling her pussy with my seed.

Claiming Avery.

Claiming the woman I have fallen completely in love with as my own.

CHAPTER 15

Wes

I watch Avery sleep, not wanting to wake her. She looks so peaceful in my arms, her head against my chest. She still has an hour before she has to get up to get ready for another day in the classroom. Though all I want to do is nestle my cock her in tight pussy, I want her to feel rested for the day ahead.

Softly I stroke her hair, combing the stray locks from her face.

Sleep has been elusive for me.

Figuring out a way to keep Avery in my life, to be with her without pretending for the sake of anyone else, has kept my brain spinning. It's obvious she has a past that makes her afraid to believe in good things. To accept love. To trust it.

But I've made my decision.

Tonight, I'm planning a private dinner for two at

home. I already know if I ask Grandma June to whip up her shrimp scampi, she won't tell me no. Her invitation to dinner last night cements her approval of Avery. If she thinks her famous pasta dish will help me keep the woman I love in my life, I know she'll oblige.

"What time is it?" Avery mumbles, her eyes fluttering open.

"You still have some time to sleep."

She seems to drift off again.

Yeah, I could get used to this. For the rest of my life.

It's only the ping of my phone that shatters the peaceful moment. Avery stirs, groaning at the noise.

"Sorry." If it's Ben, I'm going to kill him. But the likelihood it's an emergency prompts me to reach for it. A text from Garrett lights up the screen.

Garrett: Ran Lucas Jenkins out of town last night.

Though I wish he arrested him, I know the law well enough to know you can't arrest someone for being an ass in a restaurant. All Garrett could do was escort him out and tell him to get the hell out of town. I'm relieved he's gone, but not convinced he won't come back.

My phone pings again.

Avery groans, again. This time she wriggles her

naked body against mine, as if trying to get comfortable. But her upper thigh rubs against my hard cock,
and her eyes open the rest of the way.

Garrett: State Patrol picked him up outside Aurora
Falls for drunk driving and an open warrant.

"What is it?" Avery asks as I shoot a *thanks* text
back.

"It's over."

"What is?" She rubs herself against my cock again,
as if ensuring I don't mean our under-the-covers
escapades.

"Oh, I'm not done with you, Avery." I set my
phone on the nightstand and grab her ass hard. "Not
by a long shot." I cup her cheek and drag her up for a
kiss that promises she's awake and ready for another
round.

"Don't try to distract me," she teases, shimmying
her body on top of mine. Her pussy lips smother my
dick. "What's over?"

"Lucas has been arrested. You can finally breathe."

"Really?" The relief in her eyes is impossible to
mistake.

"Really." A slight fear clutches my chest that Avery
might decide to go back to her place. That she might
use this an excuse to run away from what we're build-

ing. But when she climbs all the way on top and lines my cock with her slit, all worrisome thoughts flee. In fact, every thought that isn't relevant to her sinking down on me flees.

I lift my hips, pushing into her as she lowers.

Avery leans forward, dangling her tits in my face. I can't resist the urge to take one in mouth as she rides my dick. I give her tits equal attention with my mouth, tongue, and hands as she slams onto my cock over and over. Rubbing herself against me with each thrust. When she drops her lips to mine, it's game over for both of us.

She comes hard, moaning into my mouth as her pussy convulses. I follow right behind, shooting hot ropes of cum into her depths. Claiming her once again. Reaffirming my plan for tonight. I'm going to give Avery a key. Ask her to move in when she's ready. Tell her I can't imagine my life without her by my side.

I'm going to tell her I love her.

CHAPTER 16

Avery

I've always heard people talk about cloud nine, but until this morning, I had never experienced it for myself. I may be running on coffee and orgasm energy today since sleep was mostly elusive last night. But I have no regrets.

I'm falling for Wes.

Falling hard.

"You're all smiles today," Trinity says when she meets me in the parking lot. "Something you want to share?"

"Maybe later."

"Wow, I can tell you mean that, too."

Moving to Caribou Creek was the single best decision I ever made. It took me months to trust anything. To feel as if I could open up to people. To be vulnerable. Maybe one too many orgasms have gone to my head—who I am kidding? There's no such thing as *one too many* when it comes to orgasms given by Wes Ashburn. "I do."

"Any chance you'll come with me to kickboxing class tonight?"

I suspect Garrett is teaching this one because Wes will be all mine this evening. "I can't tonight. I've got... a date."

"Wes Ashburn?" she guesses.

"How did—"

"It's a small town, honey. Rumors spread faster than forest fires around here. The whole town knows you were out on a date with him last night. One with his grandparents. That's a pretty high compliment, by the way. June Ashburn doesn't give her approval so easily when it comes to her grandsons."

Any resistance I still had about falling the rest of the way for Wes fades away.

For the first time in my life, I feel safe.

I feel loved.

"Ms. Nichols," Ian Mathers, the superintendent, says when I reach the double doors of the school. His grim expression has instant knots forming in my stomach. Warning me that cloud nine might be too dangerous a place to linger for long. What the hell did I do? "I need you to come with me."

Trinity gives me a *good luck* look that makes my

stomach drop even more as I follow Mr. Mathers to the principal's office. He doesn't say another word until he closes the door. Principal Johnson sits behind her desk, her expression blank.

"Is everything okay?" I ask, knowing full well it's not.

"I'm afraid not. We heard a disturbing rumor and were forced to investigate," Mr. Mathers starts. But Principal Johnson takes over.

"You left something off your resume, Ms. Nichols." She slides a manilla folder across the desk. "Something you failed to disclose when we interviewed you."

With a shaky hand, I open the folder. Inside is a full-sized color photo of me hanging off a stripper pole with tassels hanging from my nipples. I slam it shut and shove it away, as if it's a contagious disease I want no part of. I'm sick to my stomach, thankful I didn't have time to eat breakfast this morning. It probably would've ended up on my shoes. "That was one week of my life, Principal Johnson. One week, a very long time ago."

"You don't deny that this is you?" Mr. Mathers asks, his expression filled with pity.

I pinch my lips together, forcing myself to choose my words carefully. Caribou Creek is everything I ever dreamed of in a home. I'm not about to let one fucking week of my life destroy that future. Not when I've worked this damn hard for what I have. "I needed money for books." Money my pathetic excuse for a mom promised me as a college gift. Only when it came time to buy those books, the money was gone. As was her latest boyfriend. Whether he stole the money or used it to buy them drugs before he jetted, I have no idea.

"We have to suspend you, Ms. Nichols," Principal Johnson says, her expression hinting at the slightest regret. I guess she's not completely heartless after all. "When the parents of your students catch wind of the rumor they can very easily verify with a quick internet search, they'll demand we get rid of you. There's a schoolboard meeting tomorrow night. If we don't suspend you now, we'll have to take action then anyway. We're trying to be proactive."

"What can I do?" I hate that my question is shaky. That I'm fighting tears just to speak it.

"I'm afraid there's nothing you *can* do. Your fate will be decided at that meeting. For now, please go home."

Home.

Fuck my life. I have to tell Wes. If he doesn't hear it from someone else first. Considering his history with his ex and the type of secret she kept from him, he might not be so understanding. All those sweet words and promises might not mean shit when he learns the truth.

CHAPTER 17

Wes

I've only pulled open my truck door when I hear the roar of an engine. Two seconds later, I see Ben's truck flying up my driveway like he's being chased. This better be a true fucking emergency and not some damn lecture about me erasing myself from his meticulously planned Outlook calendar.

"She here?" Ben demands before he's all the way out of his truck. "Your *fake* girlfriend. It Avery here?"

"Why would she be here?" I fire back, folding my arms over my chest. I don't have fucking time for this today. I'm teaching Tanner how to make wort today after I stop by my property on third street to check out the water heater. Not to mention I have to check on my secret brew and ensure it's ready for our owner's meeting tomorrow. I have a sinking suspicion I'll have to table that announcement for a while longer, though.

Considering the only way Ben might ever agree to add a seventh brew to our menu is if he tastes it for himself, I'm not breathing a word until I know it's ready.

"Where else would she go?"

"The school. Where she teaches."

"They canned her."

I scan my brother, searching for signs of a bump to the head or drunkenness. Unfortunately, the lug seems healthy and sober. I know I'm going to regret the question, but I ask anyway. "What are you talking about?"

"The schoolboard doesn't like to find out they've hired a stripper to teach a classroom full of six-year-olds. Is *that* what you were protecting her from? How the town would react if they found out the truth?"

Anger starts to boil in my blood. I've been itching for a fight with Ben for a while now, but until now, I've tamped down the urge to slug him. My fist balls at my side. "What the *fuck* did you say about Avery?"

"She used to be a stripper. You didn't know?"

I'm still trying to process the words he's speaking, certain he's got his wires crossed. Avery might be secretive about her past, but I doubt she'd hide something like that. Not from me. Not after telling her how my ex's double life derailed me.

"Man, you sure know how to pick 'em. First Camille the rich boy escort. Now Avery the pole

226

dancing sl—" He doesn't get a chance to finish his insult because I tackle him to the ground.

Fists fly as we roll in the dusty gravel. I land one square in his jaw. But Ben's not a meek fighter. He slugs me against the temple, temporarily making me see stars. He lands another one to my side before I can fully regather my wits. The jackass is using shit *I* taught him against me. I get back to my feet and put both hands up.

"Maybe what Avery and I had *was* fake. But it's not anymore. And you want to talk about *picking* them?" I yell at him. "At least I'm not the one picking woman for strategy. Do you even fuck Kat?"

Ben's growly expression softens for a single beat I nearly miss. But it's answer enough.

"You don't, do you? Because you're in love with Josie."

"This conversation is over." Ben wipes a trickle of blood from the corner of his mouth and marches back to his truck.

"You fucking started it!" I yell after him as he peels out of the driveway, kicking up a wall of dust.

The metallic taste in my mouth warns me I'm bleeding too. I turn to head inside to clean up, cursing my brother for fucking up my morning with his bull-shit, when I hear an engine again. My fists ball at my sides, ready to get back in the fight if Ben is stupid enough to come back for round two.

But it's not Ben.

It's Avery in my truck.

"Wes, what happened?" she asks, running to me. The sight of her instantly soothes me, until I remember she's supposed to be in a classroom.

"Why aren't you at school?"

She stops a foot from me, reaching for my hand. But I yank it away. There's only so much I can take this morning. Her showing up is confirmation that Ben isn't completely full of shit. "That's what I came here to talk to you about."

"So, it's true then?"

"Shouldn't surprise me you already know."

"Fuck, Avery. Were you ever going to tell me? Or just let me find out like everyone else?"

"I didn't think it mattered."

Her words are like a gut punch. "This isn't the kind of thing you keep to yourself. Not with me."

"I know that now. Grandma June told me about Camille—"

"Go home."

"What?"

"Get your shit, and go home. You're safe now. You have no reason to stay," I can't decide if I'm pissed at Grandma June for divulging the details of my past or even more at Avery for knowing about it and *still* keeping that secret from me. "We can tell everyone the breakup was mutual. Go."

"So much for never judging me," she mutters. "Fucking liar."

It takes all my restraint to stay mad when I see the hot tears run down her cheeks. I hate that I feel like I'm the asshole when she was the one keeping a doozy of a secret from me. As she disappears inside to get her things, I pick up a rock and chuck it as far as I can. But it does nothing to release the frustration that continues to build inside me.

As all the feelings from the past come rushing back, I remember the reason I put an iron clamp over my heart. I won't forget again.

"None of this is fair," Trinity says to me as we head down the sidewalk. After weeks of her insisting I needed to join her for kickboxing class, I finally took her up on it. It's only because Garrett's teaching tonight that I agreed. I'm hoping to work out some of my frustration. Even if I have terrible coordination, I know it'll feel good to punch and kick things.

"It was just one week," I tell her for the fourth or fifth time. Trinity called me on her lunch break to see if I was okay. Instead of lying like I usually do, I told her the truth. She was at my house the second the last kid got on the school bus.

I had hoped she'd bring wine, but I suppose a spare pair of kickboxing gloves was just as well.

I told her everything. I told her about my shitty

mom and how I would've had to drop out of school without books. I was lucky enough to get a scholarship for tuition, but I didn't bother with financial aid because my mom promised she'd buy my books. She made me believe that she actually wanted to do something nice for me.

I told her about Wes and our fake relationship that suddenly seemed not so fake at all. Until he found out about my scandalous week as a stripper. Something I have no doubt that Lucas managed to leak before he skipped town. "Stupid internet. If the owner found out someone was posting pictures online from his club, let's just say I wouldn't want to be the guy he caught."

"You should go to the schoolboard meeting."

"What?"

"Yeah. Plead your case."

"I can't show up there."

"They can't keep you from attending." Trinity helps me get set up in a spot right next to her as others fill up the studio. I can't help but scan the place for Wes, but he's not here. Only Garrett helping a boy at the end with his stance. "And if you want to speak, they have to let you. It's in the bylaws."

"Really?"

"Really."

"It's tomorrow night?"

"You're a fighter, Avery. You didn't make it this far without that being true. Don't give up now."

Her words stick with me throughout class. I'm surprised at how easily I'm able to catch on to the different techniques. It feels fucking amazing to punch and kick the foam-wrapped cylinder over and over. I would've thought with how poorly things went with Wes teaching me the other night that I'd be a lost cause. But now I realize I just couldn't focus with him so close.

"You're really getting the hang of this!" Trinity says during a quick break.

"I can't believe I avoided going for this long."

Another round starts. The music turns up. I get lost in myself. Faintly, I hear someone calling my name, but I'm in a zone. I don't stop. I punch and kick out all my frustrations. Not just the ones from this week, but from my entire life.

When two arms wrap around me, I don't think.

I act how I was taught.

I throw my head back until it hits something hard. I bend forward and drag the jean-clad leg forward as I stand. Effectively knocking my assailant on his ass. It takes about two seconds to realize where I'm at and that I might've just laid out the instructor. Except, Garrett wasn't wearing jeans.

"Wes?"

CHAPTER 19

Wes

I lie on the mat-covered floor, holding my nose. I should've known better than to put my arms around Avery. Or bend my head down. She was in a zone, and I only wanted to get her attention. I should've suspected the self-defense I taught her actually stuck.

"Did I break your nose?" Avery asks, her emerald eyes wide.

A huddle of people gather around me, including Garrett. He folds his arms over his chest and doesn't bother to hide his amusement.

"No, it's not broken. Just bleeding a little."

Avery kneels beside me, handing me her towel. "I'd say I'm sorry, but in retrospect, I'm not."

"I'm fine," I announce to the crowd of spectators.

"You heard the man," Garrett announces. "Back to your stations."

As the class resumes, I pull Avery to the side and sit down on a bench near the window. The music drowns our conversation so the whole damn class doesn't have to hear me grovel. But even if they did, I'd deserve it. It didn't take long after Avery left to realize I'd fucked up. Any challenges I had reaching that conclusion on my own were quickly overcome when I found a pile of cat shit on my pillow. Courtesy of Mr. Sprinkles.

That was moments before Grandma June showed up without any food and an expression scary enough to frighten an angry grizzly bear. She read me the riot act. I was so shocked at how wholeheartedly she sided with Avery that all I could do was sit there and take it. The wise woman made me see all the reason I couldn't see on my own.

"I'm sorry, Avery."

"For what exactly?"

Okay, she's not going to make this easy. That's fine. "I'm sorry I didn't wait to hear your side of the story. I'm sorry I jumped to conclusions. I'm sorry I compared you to my ex. That wasn't fair. You were never obligated to share any part of your past you didn't want to. I'm sorry I was a dick about it."

"They might fire me tomorrow night you know."

"I know."

"And if that happens? Then what?"

"Then you can work at the brewery. Or anywhere else you want to. I'll hire you to be Mr. Sprinkles' personal attendant. Whatever it takes to make sure you stay. Not just in Caribou Creek, but with me. I love you, Avery Nichols. I think I have since the moment you first pulled into that driveway in a car that defies the laws of physics."

I dare to reach for her hand, relieved as hell when she doesn't pull it away.

"Please give me another chance. Please give *us* a real chance."

"You're just scared of Grandma June, aren't you?" The twinkle in her eyes gives her away, and I finally let go of the tension that's been knotting in my stomach all day.

"*Everyone* is secretly scared of Grandma June."

"True enough."

"What do you say?" I ask her, cupping her cheek. Caressing her soft skin with my thumb. "Will you give us a chance? A real one?"

"On one condition."

"What's that?"

"Actually two."

"Name them."

"Number one, you don't judge me. Like you *promised*. I won't so easily accept your apology next time. I did what I had to do to get out of a bad situation. I'm not proud of everything I had to do, but I am proud of how far I've come."

"I promise."

"Good. Number two. You promise to *always* share Grandma June's goodies fifty-fifty. She's an amazing cook, and I don't need to be shortchanged of that amazing talent whenever she's in town."

"She came to visit you today, didn't she?"

"Maybe." Avery's smile grows wider. "I ate your half of the cinnamon rolls. But to be fair, our fake relationship was on the fritz, so..."

"I probably deserved that."

"You did."

"You didn't have to agree so quickly," I tease.

"Wes?"

"Yes, sweetheart?"

"I love you, too."

I draw her in for a kiss that quickly makes me forget we're in a public setting until the whistles and cheers start. When we pull back, we're both laughing and breathless. "What do you say we get out of here?" I pull the key I had made for her from my pocket and hold it out for her. "Start a *real* relationship."

"You want me to move in?"

"Only when you're ready." I place the key in her hand, covering it with mine. "But first, I want to get you home so I can make up for lost time. It's been a long time since I've been inside you."

"You were inside me this morning."

"I know. It's been *hours*. I can't wait any longer."

She chuckles, shaking her head. "Then take me home."

Epilogue

About nine months later...

As the last day of school lets out for the summer, I pull into the end of the pickup line to wait for my wife. Soon, we'll be headed for a long overdue honeymoon. Our bags are packed and in the back of my truck. The second the last kid leaves, we're heading to Anchorage to get on a plane.

Well, after we drop off Grandma June. She insisted she ride along to see us off before we left town.

Tyler Parsons throws his arms around Avery's legs as I've watched him do dozens of times this school year. This time, he holds on a little longer. Probably realizing this was the last day Avery will be his teacher.

"She's amazing, isn't she?" Grandma June asks from the back seat.

"She's the most amazing woman I know."

Avery has made such an impact on her students. An opportunity that was nearly stricken from her because her ex managed to run his mouth before he was run out of town. One stupid rumor blew up and put everything at risk. But Avery went to that school-board meeting and pled her case. It took courage to open up to an entire town about her past, but she did it without flinching.

It helped that Grandma June showed up in her defense.

"I hope I'll be coming back this time next year to meet another great-grandbaby," Grandma June says nonchalantly. As if she were discussing the weather and not suggesting we make a baby.

"We'll see."

"I don't know what you two are waiting for. You wasted enough time in the beginning pretending you didn't love each other."

I stare at my grandma as if she's a stranger. "You knew?"

"That Avery wasn't really your girlfriend when I first showed up at your house? Don't take me for a fool, Wesley. Of course I knew."

"Then why—"

239

"Because I knew you two were meant to be."

"How?"

Grandma June just sends me a devious smile, saved from answering because Avery opens the truck door. Her eyes lock on me, and it's as if the world fades away. Damn, I love this woman. "You ready for tropical paradise?" she asks.

"I'm ready to have you all to myself—"

Grandma June clears her throat.

"Oh hey, Grandma June!" Avery's voice is an octave higher. "Why are you sitting in the back? You should take the front seat."

"Nonsense. You two are dropping me off in a few minutes. I'm just here to wish you well." As Avery climbs into the truck and reaches for her seat belt, Grandma June sets a blanket on the center console. "I want you two to take this along to Maui. It's special."

"Is that...a baby making blanket?" Avery asks carefully.

"Of course not! It's a symbol of happiness. A reminder that you two should enjoy every minute together. Not just on your honeymoon, but for the rest of your lives." Grandma June leans forward as Avery studies the blanket. "If it helps get me another great grandchild—"

"Grandma June!" I playfully scold.

"Thank you," Avery says to her, her eyes shiny.

Family means everything to her. That mine has so effortlessly accepted her as one of our own warms my heart. "It's a beautiful blanket."

I reach for Avery's hand and thread my fingers through hers. In minutes, we'll be on the road to the airport. If that wasn't enough to make me smile, the fact that Ben has to go to North Haven for their local festival in my place is. It's been a long time since he's had to be the face of THE CARIBOU CREEK BREWERY much less man a tent to represent us. He hates the social events and does what he can to get out of them. But I've covered enough of them to last me a few years.

That Josie is going with him only pisses Benny Poo off more.

With any luck, he'll finally stop fighting the way he feels about her. Maybe then, when he's gotten laid, he won't be so pissed off all the time. Then, Zac, Ben, and I can act like brothers again.

"This is my stop," Grandma June announces as I pull into the driveway of Zac and Riley's place. Chase is playing in the yard. When he catches a glimpse of Grandma June, he pops to his feet, takes three steps, and falls. But he's too excited to see one of his favorite people to give up.

"Are you ready for all that?" I ask Avery. "For kids."

"Yeah. I am."

I turn to her, cupping her cheek to draw her in for a kiss. I let my lips linger. A promise of all that's to come on this honeymoon. "Then I guess we better get to Maui and make that baby."

THE END

Bonus Epilogue

AVERY

Bonus Epilogue: About four years later...

"This is perfect, Wes." I reach across the intimate table in one of Anchorage's finest dining establishments and clasp my husband's hands. Sometimes I'm still amazed that this is my life. That the man across the table looking sexy as hell with his beard and dangerous twinkle in his dark eyes is *mine*. My husband. The father of our two children. "Thank you for doing this for me."

"You deserve this and so much more, sweetheart." He strokes my hands with his thumbs. "Five years is a big deal."

This morning, I was hugging all my kindergarteners goodbye for summer break. The fifth round of them since I moved to Caribou Creek. Tonight, we're in Anchorage celebrating while Grandma June and Grandpa Del watch the kids for the weekend. Everything about our trip so far has been amazing, and it's hardly started.

"Are we ordering dessert—" I barely have a chance to finish my question before the server arrives with a beautifully plated slice of chocolate cake that makes my mouth water. Before I can sink my fork into it, the server places a stick in the center and holds a lighter to it. The sparkler flickers to life.

"Happy anniversary," the server says, departing with a nod.

"It's not our anniversary," I say to Wes, admiring the special dessert.

"It's your fifth teaching anniversary as Caribou Creek's kindergarten teacher," he clarifies as the sparkler dies down. "It's also the four-year anniversary of our honeymoon in Maui."

"That was a wonderful trip." I'm instantly taken back to dipping my toes in the beautiful sandy beaches and splashing through the ocean during the day and rolling around in the incredibly soft sheets at night. Wes and I spent so much time naked and tangled it's almost a wonder we got in any sightseeing. "I'd love to go back someday, but honestly, I love being in Alaska even more."

"Me too."

The chocolate cake is amazing but impossible to finish. It's not just its richness. It's my desire to check into the hotel. To enjoy this child-free weekend with Wes. To get naked as soon as possible. I miss my kiddos like crazy, but I know Nate and Natalie are in good hands. Grandma June is no doubt spoiling them rotten. Even Mr. Sprinkles is happy with the arrangement that guarantees him tasty bites of her cooking.

"Ready?" Wes asks when I set down my fork in defeat.

"More than ready."

Wes slips his hand in mine, lowering his mouth to my ear. "I'm going to spend the rest of the night exploring your body. With my tongue."

I shiver in anticipation.

Everything seems to take too long as we leave the restaurant, head to the hotel, and check in. It's a good thing Wes seems to have enough patience for both of us. I give up on the concept in the elevator. I pounce, wrapping my arms around his neck. Dragging him down for a kiss that is not appropriate for public.

Our lips move with fiery hunger.

Wes' hand slides to my ass and squeezes, pulling my hips against his. Revealing that the patience he's been displaying is merely an act. He's rock hard beneath those jeans. I cup his cock and give it a squeeze just as the elevator dings.

An elderly couple waits on the other side, appearing both a little scandalized and a bit jealous as we exit.

"We're on the top floor," I say to Wes as we roll our suitcases behind us. "I've always wanted to stay on the top floor!"

"I know." The look he flashes me is drenched with desire. It makes my nipples harden to peaks. I'm tempted to yank him to a stop and beg him to pin me up against a wall. The room is too damn far away. "I wanted only the best for you, sweetheart."

"Then why are we all the way at the end?"

He holds the key card up as we reach the door and looks at me. A devilish gleam in his eyes if ever I've seen one. "So we don't get as many noise complaints."

When the lock clicks open, I drag him into the room. Fusing my lips to his instantly. Thankfully Wes pulls our bags inside and locks the door behind us, because I couldn't care less about any of it in this heated moment. The one growing hotter by the second. My hands are in his hair. My body pressed against his, ready to climb him.

"I know you're excited," Wes says low against my

ear, his arms wrapped around my back. "But can you take a look first?"

"You don't want to fuck me against the door?"

"Oh, I do." He cups my ass, digging his fingers lower and giving my cheek a squeeze. "But this is for you." He nods behind me, and I follow his gaze.

I gasp.

The luxurious suite is dusted in red and pink rose petals. A bottle of wine sticks out of a metal bucket near a Jacuzzi that sits by a window with an ocean view. It's as if romance exploded in this room. Wes has always been thoughtful, but this is above and beyond anything he's done for me before. A small gift box with a red bow rests on the edge of the king-sized bed. "That's for me?"

"Of course it is."

I slip out of his arms, temporarily fixated on the long, narrow gift box tied up in ribbon. If I had to guess, there's jewelry inside. With shaky hands, I untie the ribbon and remove lid. Displayed inside is a beautiful white gold necklace with a small diamond pendant. "It's stunning." I remove it, letting it dangle in front of me. It's then I notice how closely it matches my bracelet.

Wes comes up from behind me, wrapping his arms around my waist. His beard tickles my neck. "You should be proud of everything you've accomplished since you moved to Caribou Creek. *I'm* proud of you."

I turn to look over my shoulder, accepting his kiss. Sinking into him. I snake my hand around his neck, pulling him closer. Our tongues slowly slide together as wetness pools between my legs, I moan.

Wes chuckles, possessing enough rational thought to take the necklace from my hand and set it on the desk along with the gift box before we start to undress one another. We take our time about it, peeling away a shirt or undoing a belt between steamy kisses. When my bra falls away, Wes grabs my breasts with both hands, lifting one up to his eager mouth.

We collapse onto the bed like this. Still half-dressed and Wes suckling my nipple. His jeans are unzipped and hanging low on his hips. Granting me the access I need to reach inside and wrap my hand around his cock. He groans against my tit as I stroke him.

"Fuck, I love your hands on my dick."

Wes peels away my leggings and panties, leaving me naked on the bed. From my back, I watch him shed the rest of his clothes. His hard cock stands at attention, causing my belly to quiver with want. Five years together and I *still* want him just as badly as I did that first night together. The night he stood up for me in front of half the town.

It was the night I realized I was in love with him.

Back then, I could only dream of the life we have now. The passion that still exists after two babies, birthday parties, brewery events, and the chaos of everyday life.

I snake my hands up his neck as he climbs up my body. "I love you, Wes."

"I love you more."

He kisses me before I can argue with him. His cock nudges my entrance, and I forget everything else. I spread my legs wider and lift to meet him. Inviting him in as I have so many times before. Only tonight, I can be as loud as I want. I don't have to swallow my moans and cry into a pillow when I come.

Tonight, waking babies isn't a concern we have to face.

Wes pushes into my channel until his balls brush against me. I moan at how fucking good he feels inside me. If I live a thousand lifetimes, I know I'll never experience anything as amazing as this right here.

He slides out, then slams back in. I cry out, arching my back.

"Fuck," he growls, fixing his attention on a nipple. "You're hot like this. All arched into me." He wraps an arm around my back, supporting me as he plunges quicker. I hold onto his neck and the headboard, surrendering to him completely. I'm at his mercy as he pummels my pussy over and over.

I don't hold back.

I cry out his name as each thrusts brings me closer to the brink.

"Sweetheart?"

"Huh?"

"You want to turn around so I can fuck you from behind."

I damn near come at the request alone. Because words are out of my grasp, I give him an eager nod. He helps me turn my body. As I bend forward, Wes runs his cock through my folds. Teasing my swollen button. It feels so fucking good that I reach between my legs and grab him. Pressing him harder against me.

"That's it, Avery. Use my cock to make you come. Then I'll fuck you nice and hard."

I grind against his shaft, using my hand to rub him against my clit. He rocks his hips from behind, intensifying the pleasure. It doesn't take me long to come apart. I feel the build of my orgasm seconds before it slams into me. My pussy shudders as I come on his cock.

Wes only gives me a few seconds to catch my breath before he takes control. Plunging his length into my pussy. Fucking me hard just like he promised. The bed rocks with us. Someone bangs on the wall. But none of that matters as he stills inside me, filling me with his seed. Claiming me as he has so many times before.

I love this man.

I'm thankful every day that the teaching position opened in Caribou Creek when it did. That the rental I found was his. That the leaking pipe under the kitchen sink forced me to call him. I'm grateful for it all, because even the shitty moments in my life led me here. To the best life I could have ever imagined.

A life where the most amazing man loves me more than I ever thought possible.

"You're *mine*, Avery."

"All yours."

"Good." He smacks my ass playfully as he pulls out. "Don't ever forget it."

"And if I do?" I tease.

"Then I'll fuck you again and again to remind you just who you belong to."

I bite down on my bottom lip, a mischievous twinkle in my eyes as I meet Wes' gaze. "I might get into that Jacuzzi and forget. Will you help remind me then?"

Wes captures my mouth, kissing me with his potent mixture of tenderness and passion. He scoops me into his arms and lifts me from the bed. "If you wanted me to fuck you in the Jacuzzi, all you had to do was say so."

"What about the water?" I ask as he carries me to it.

"We'll add that later."

"Wes!"

With me still cradled in his arms, he reaches down to turn the water on, allowing the tub to start filling. "I'm kidding. While we wait for the tub to fill, I have something I need to do."

"What's that?"

"Kiss every inch of your body."

THE END

Tipsy on Love

MOUNTAIN MEN OF CARIBOU CREEK
BOOK 3

CHAPTER 1

Josie

I reread the first paragraph of my resignation letter. One I've typed and retyped more times than I can count. The delete key and I have become well acquainted today as I've searched for the right words to tell the Ashburn brothers that I can no longer work for them. But every sentence I attempt feels too formal. Too emotionless.

Too much like Ben Ashburn.

A smile curls my lips for the briefest moment. Out of the three brothers, Ben is the grumpiest for certain. He keeps everything close to the vest. Doesn't let emotions factor in to a single decision. He's all business and no play.

Which is why I can't stay.

I've been in love with my boss for three years.

Three pitiful years.

I've worked my ass off trying to impress him. Hoping that one day he might see me as more than his personal assistant. But it's time to stop wishing for the impossible. I'm not Ben's type. That much was made obvious when he started dating the elegant and fierce Katherine Rollins last year. I foolishly hoped when they broke up—over a month ago—that Ben would finally see what's been in front of him all along.

But nothing has changed.

And the Cochran's have made me an offer I'd be an idiot to refuse. Head of marketing at their Anchorage brewery. I haven't *officially* accepted it, but I plan to as soon as I hand over my resignation letter. The same letter I'm having the hardest damn time writing without bursting into tears.

"It's time, Josie," I mumble to myself, refocusing on my computer screen. Forcing the unshed tears to stay off my cheeks. "Time to move on."

As I delete the opening line and prepare for attempt number fifty-two to get it right, the office door opens. I pretend not to recognize Ben's silhouette. I pretend my pulse doesn't go from zero to a hundred in half a second. He's been working from home a lot since the breakup, which is why I'm surprised to see him. I'd secretly hoped to avoid him my last two weeks here.

Quickly, I minimize my document. "Didn't expect

you in today, boss." I call him *boss*, wishing I could call him Ben. But the damn man's too formal for all that. If he had it his way, I'd call him Mr. Ashburn. I don't. I need *something* to rebel against. All his grumpy quirks drive me a little mad, but for some stupid reason I have yet to identify, it seems to make my attraction to him all that much stronger.

"There's been a change of plans." Leaving the door open, he folds his arms over his chest and looks at me. Except his gaze quickly drops to the floor, the way it has for three years. The man can hardly look me in the eye. His lips are hardened into their familiar straight line, but right now, they seem extra pinched.

"Something wrong?"

"Wes just took off for his honeymoon."

Wes, the brew master, was supposed to travel with me to North Haven this weekend for a local festival. THE CARIBOU CREEK BREWERY booked a vendor spot to hand out samples months ago. It's in a small town, but the festival promises to draw people from all over the state. Especially with the opening of their new hotel. I've been pulling data, running online polls, and making decisions about how much of each beer to bring. Including Wes' new secret brew. One he hasn't told his brothers about. Only his wife, Avery and me.

I'd planned to tell Wes that I was leaving first. I know he'll be kind about the news. Now I wonder if

I'll even get the opportunity to tell him in person. "I can make a call. Let them know we're not coming. But we won't get a refund for our booth this late—"

"We're going."

"We?"

"You and me."

I gulp a swallow, realizing I'm suddenly thirsty. *Very* thirsty. Ben never goes to these events. He can schmooze business professionals well enough. But I have a hard time picturing him smiling for eight straight hours. "Not Zac?"

"Not Zac." In typical Ben fashion, he doesn't elaborate. "Is this going to be a problem?"

"Nope." I don't notice that I'm fiddling with a pen until it goes flying out of my hand. Ben arches an eyebrow as it narrowly misses hitting him in the leg. He bends over to pick it up. I shouldn't steal a lingering glance. Not when I'm trying so hard to put him behind me. But I can't help it. Ben is all muscle beneath his suit pants and button-up shirt. He's so far out of my league it isn't even funny. But damn, is he nice to look at.

"We'll leave Thursday night." He starts to hand over my pen, but seems to think better of it, and sets it on the edge of my desk instead. "Be back on Sunday."

"Okay."

"Wes mentioned you had everything taken

care of."

"Yes. The kegs we need are headed on a delivery truck a day ahead of us. We have a contact in North Haven who's going to pick them up and store them for us until we get there. Do you want me to email you the checklist I've compiled?" Part of me hopes he says no, because Wes' special brew is on that bullet-pointed list. A beer that Ben doesn't even know exists. But then again, Wes disappeared without giving me a heads up. Whatever comes of that surprise isn't on me. I can't decide if I'm mad or excited to be stuck with Ben for a full weekend.

"No, that's okay. I trust you have a handle on things."

"Not my first rodeo."

Ben's gaze flickers up to mine, and I swear I see a hint of a smile form. Maybe that's why I'm so drawn to him. It's the challenge of making him smile that keeps me entertained. It's a nearly impossible task. For three years, I've hoped that if I could only make him smile, maybe *then* he'd realize what he means to me. What I *could* to mean to him.

"We'll go over the details tomorrow," Ben says, all traces of amusement fleeting. "I'll be working from home the rest of the day."

It's a challenge to keep the smile pasted on my face when all I really want to do is scream. "You have a call with Berkley Brewery at seven tomorrow morning about expanding distribution," I remind him. "They're on the east coast."

"Right."

"I added a calendar reminder."

Ben nods. His way of saying thank you. Then spins on his heel and leaves. Just like that. No *see you later*. No *goodbye*. No *thank you for being so accommodating*. If only I was a reasonable woman, I'd realize I was wasting my time when it came to Ben Ashburn. I'd realize he's never going to be the man I want him to be. He's never going to love me.

I pull my resignation letter back up, but the words all blur together.

A crazy idea strikes me.

One I know better than to entertain.

But it bounces around in my brain like a laser pointer and I'm the kitten unable to ignore it.

If I'm stuck with Ben this weekend, just the two of us, why not go for broke? Why not flirt my ass off and end the weekend with telling him how I feel? If he laughs in my face or, more likely, walks off without betraying a single emotion, I quit as planned. My heart might take a slightly more painful sting from the rejection than it's already feeling now. But at least I'd leave Caribou Creek never wondering what if.

I could move on without any regrets.

CHAPTER 2

Ben

"I'm going to kill him." I pace my kitchen, having a helluva time remembering what the fuck I even came in here for. My youngest brother, Zac, watches from a barstool, sipping on a beer and wearing an annoyingly amused smile. "I'm going to kill him and toss his body so far into the wilderness no one will ever find it."

"I don't see what the big deal is," Zac says. "You're the marketing director. This is your time to market the brewery. Get our name out there."

"You know this isn't my scene."

"You mean because the people you'll have to interact with aren't likely to be wearing business suits, or because you'll be alone with Josie for an entire weekend?" He lifts the bottle to his lips, but it doesn't hide the shit-eating grin I know he's wearing.

"This isn't funny."

Zac just answers with a wider grin.

For the past three years, I've been fighting my feelings for Josie Bennington. Hell, since the first day she came in for an interview. I've never met a more enticing woman in my life. She's intelligent and personable with a curvy figure that's plagued many of my nights. Robbed me of sleep.

But I have one very strict rule about our business. You don't date your employees. I've watched that scenario go south more than once for friends of mine. Josie is the glue that holds the brewery together. It's her acute attention to everything that keeps things running smoothly. Without her, we'd all be lost. *I'd* be lost.

If that weren't enough to keep me from making a move, I'm no good for her. She deserves someone without a dark cloud hanging over their past. But hell if I've met a man worthy of her. I'm irrationally consumed with jealousy anytime a man gives her too much attention. I know I have no fucking right to feel this way. No right to act as if she's mine to protect. To feel like she belongs to me when we can never be more than boss and employee.

"You still want to split all that wood or you want to go grab a bite instead? Rose served pot roast for lunch. I heard there's leftover, but you know it won't last long."

"You'd eat at the diner when Grandma June's in town?"

"She's at bridge night."

"You mean *poker* night."

Zac shrugs. "No one really knows what those little old ladies get up to. Plus, Riley and Penny are having a girls' night at the house. I need to eat."

Though it's tempting to skip out on cooking, I don't want to risk running into Josie. Caribou Creek is a small place. It's nearly impossible to avoid people. Which is why I've been working from home in my remote cabin. One halfway up the mountain with a stunning view of the range and a great deal of privacy. "Let's take care of this wood."

Zac empties his bottle, tosses it in the trash, and follows me out the back door. "Do you do anything *fun* anymore?"

"Who has time for fun?" I pick up one of two axes I set out early and hand one to my brother. Had I received the news that Wes was bailing on the North Haven weekend and forcing me to go in his place, I would've saved this task for myself. If only to work out the frustration welling up inside me.

An entire weekend with Josie.

It doesn't matter that we'll be in separate hotel rooms.

We'll be side by side for hours at a time, trapped together in a confined space. Likely brushing up against each other out of necessity. How the fuck will I resist her after that?

"You used to be fun," Zac points out, positioning a hunk of wood on a stump and swinging. Breaking it right down the middle. The wood splits perfectly. "We used to watch football together. Go salmon fishing. You remember that trip the three of us took to Homer?"

I check my phone, scanning a new email. But before I can think about responding, Josie has it covered. Never mind that she's off for the evening or that we don't pay her overtime. I make a mental note to bring that up at our next owner's meeting. "You mean the one where I caught the biggest halibut of the day?"

"Yeah. You wouldn't shut up about it." Zac swings his axe again. "I think it's the last time you smiled."

"Very funny." I leave my phone on the deck railing, pull off my shirt, and grab the other axe. I focus on the task at hand. Or try to. But when I swing and my axe misses the chunk of wood entirely, I know I'm in trouble.

"You're worried about this weekend, aren't you?"

"No." Another swing. I hit the wood this time, but it only splits halfway. Unlike Zac's that splits perfectly *again*. The competitive side of me is really fucking irritated at my inability to focus. I can split wood blindfolded. I shouldn't be having this much trouble.

"Why are you still fighting this?" Zac asks, his question casual enough to keep my temper at bay. At least if I have to be badgered about this today, it's by my youngest brother. The last time the topic of Josie came up with Wes, it ended in a fistfight and bloodshed. He hasn't bothered to say anything about her since.

"You know how I feel about it."

"I don't buy it."

My axe misses again, but this time, it's Zac's fault. "What?"

"I don't buy your bullshit excuse about Josie being your employee. She's worked with us for three years. She's practically family."

"Which is why I'd never jeopardize that." It's as much of an admission as I've ever given about the feelings I can't do anything about. Some days, I wish I'd never felt the stirring inside my frozen, dormant heart when Josie first walked through the brewery door. Some days I wish like hell that I didn't feel so drawn to her whenever I'm in her presence. Or that I didn't feel fucking antsy as hell when I'm away from her.

But most days, I gladly bear the burden. It's as close as I'll ever get to being with her.

"She loves you."

This isn't the first time one of my brothers has spoken those words. Not even the second or tenth. But I don't dare entertain it. Not as a possible truth or even their best of intentions. "She's infatuated. There's a difference."

"Maybe in the beginning. But not after three years. C'mon, Ben. You're not *that* stupid." Zac swings again, the sound of splitting wood silencing any retort I might throw back at him.

I return my focus to another block of wood.

And miss again.

"Fuck this," I mutter, tossing down my axe. "Guess I'm hungry after all."

Josie

Sitting in the driveway of Grandma Betty's house, I quickly type an email response to a customer who submitted their question about the different brews and purchasing options through the website. It's an old habit that'll be hard as hell to break once I leave. I love working for THE CARIBOU CREEK BREWERY. Feeling like I'm an integral part of their success.

The staff has become like a second family.

Outside of it, there's only me and Grandma Betty.

I let out a sigh as I grab my satchel, stuff my phone in it, and head inside.

Grandma Betty is the best woman I've ever known. When my parents were killed in a bush plane accident when I was only ten, she took me in. She never once made me feel as though I was a burden. She not only raised me, she was always there when I needed someone to talk to or a shoulder to cry on.

But I *still* live with her. At twenty-six.

The idea was to save up money after graduating college and moving back to Caribou Creek. But secretly, I'd hoped to be living with my future husband by now. When I first stepped foot into the brewery for my interview three years ago, I was struck by Ben Ashburn. I felt a connection stronger than anything I've ever encountered before.

I was certain it would lead to something.

I knew it in the depths of my soul.

And because Grandma Betty meant it when she told me I could live with her as long as I wanted, here I still am.

I bet Katherine doesn't live with her grandma. Probably never has.

"Did you do it?" Grandma Betty asks before I even get the door closed behind me.

"No." I stare at the floor so I don't see her disappointment. She coached me through turning in my notice during breakfast this morning. Though she's sad to see me leave town, she's incredibly supportive. "I chickened out. Again."

"Ben was there today, wasn't he?"

"If only that was the *only* problem," I mumble.

"What's that, dear?"

"Nothing." I'll tell her that I'm traveling with Ben to North Haven at some point before I leave tomorrow night. But right now, all I want to do is unplug. To try like hell to forget all about the alluring man who'll never see me as a woman. Only an employee. "Did you want me to make dinner?" I offer when I notice there's nothing in the oven.

"I thought we might head to the diner," she says. "Switch it up for a change."

"Rose made pot roast, didn't she?"

"I don't know how long the leftovers will last. She's at bridge tonight, or I'd have called ahead."

"Why aren't *you* at bridge?"

Grandma Betty looks away. "I don't want to talk about it."

I bite my bottom lip to hide my smile. I'd bet anything someone accused her of cheating last week and she's still sore about it. Though I've never been invited into their inner circle, I've put some pieces together from what little Grandma Betty has let slip over the years. It sounds like a fun, but cutthroat time. Whatever they're really up to, those little old ladies don't mess around. "Pot roast sounds wonderful."

We head across town to ROSE'S DINER, but it's not until we're out of my car and halfway to the door that I notice Ben's truck in the parking lot. My stomach ties in knots. If I had any sense, I'd fake a migraine. Insist we go home. But dammit, the urge to see him is stronger. Pathetic, but like trying to wrestle a lion.

I hold the door open for Grandma Betty and pretend I don't know my boss is already inside.

The place is packed.

Not a booth or barstool to be found.

"I guess we'll have to eat at home—"

"There's the Ashburn boys in the corner booth. I bet they can make some room for us." Grandma Betty's halfway to their table before I can fathom stopping her. Because Ben looks up from the menu and stares right at me, I have no choice but to follow. "You boys wouldn't mind making some room for us, would you?"

"Not at all," Zac says, sliding over for Grandma Betty.

Ben returns his gaze to his menu as he makes room for me, his lips pinched in an extra moody straight line. As if it pains him to be this close to me. Making me wish there was a cure for how I feel. If only I wasn't so hopelessly in love with him, I might be able to stay in Caribou Creek.

"Sorry if we stink," Zac says, freeing his straw from its wrapper and sticking it in a glass of ice water. "We've been splitting wood. Well, *one* of us was."

And now I notice how relaxed Ben looks in his t-shirt and worn jeans. He's always dressed up, like he's going to a board meeting or expecting billionaires to stop by the brewery for a chat. Dammit if my lady bits don't tingle.

"Did they run out of pot roast?" Grandma Betty asks, her question pointed at Ben.

"Not yet," Zac answers.

"Oh, I just thought with you looking at the menu..." She lets her words trail off, but they seem to do the trick. Ben tucks his menu behind the ketchup and mustard bottles, forced to join the conversation.

"Haven't been in for a while," Ben says, forcing a smile. One that seems to strain his expression. I've spent three years doing everything I can think of to make him smile a real smile. But it's a rare occasion at best. Like a comet that only makes an appearance once every fifty years. "Thought I'd see if Rose changed anything up."

"She knows better than to mess with a good thing," Grandma Betty says.

I feel the lightest brush of Ben's thigh against mine and hold my breath as my entire body responds. The heat swirling between us can't all be in my head. Though Ben is closed off and impossible to read most of the time, I swear I've caught a flicker of desire in his eyes. Part of me hopes that he's simply hiding his feelings for me.

Damn, I really *am* pathetic.

"Did Josie tell you she's stuck with Ben this weekend?" Zac asks Grandma Betty.

My head snaps up at those words. I'm sure I look panicked. But Grandma Betty doesn't miss a beat. "No, but we haven't had much time to catch up tonight. She was working late, you see." The twinkle in her eyes is somewhat intriguing, but mostly, it's frightening. She might come off a sweet old lady to someone who doesn't know her. But she's a force to be reckoned with when she sets her mind to something. That twinkle is a warning sign.

"Josie, you know we don't expect you to work late," Zac offers.

"I just had a few things to finish up since I'll be gone all weekend."

To my relief, Ethel comes to take our order. Giving me time to slow my rapidly beating heart. I don't know why it matters that Grandma Betty knows I'm going with Ben instead of Wes. Oh right. Because she knows about my embarrassing crush on my boss. A confession I gave up two years ago over midnight margaritas. *Not* my fault that Grandma Betty makes them with mostly tequila and little else.

"Josie, if you come back from North Haven and Ben's missing, we won't ask questions," Zac teases.

Ben clenches a fist beneath the table, releasing his

fingers after an extra-long beat. It's what he does when he wants to say something but knows better. His control is impressive, if not a bit scary at times. "Mrs. Bennington, have you been to North Haven recently?"

"Not in years. It's such a lovely place." Grandma Betty's eyes sparkle even more than before. *What* is she up to? "I'd love to see that new hotel!"

"Why don't you come with us?" Ben suggests.

I ignore Zac, but I feel his disapproval burning into me from across the table. No doubt he thought this weekend away with Josie would make me finally come to my senses or some bullshit like that. In fact, I wouldn't be entirely surprised if he and Wes planned this ambush together.

"You don't want an old lady cramping your style," Grandma Betty says.

"Nonsense," I continue, doing my damnedest not to look at Josie beside me. To pretend I don't feel the heat swirling between us or the insatiable pull that promises a thousand miles apart would never be enough to tame it. "We'd love to have you come."

"Josie?" Grandma Betty asks her granddaughter.

"You should come. You'd have fun," she says sweetly, encouraging my idea. Good. At least we're on the same page. If we have a chaperone, I won't so easily surrender to temptation. How badly I want Josie has made it fucking impossible to sleep as of late. Without a barrier between us, I know I can't be trusted not to act impulsively. "I heard the new hotel has spa treatments."

"Oh! I've always wanted to get a facial. And take one of those mud baths."

The server, Ethel Mayberry, delivers four pot roast meals, the aroma making my stomach growl. Though I'm still irked that the one time I decide to go into town for reasons other than work I run into Josie, I'm not sad about the hearty meal in front of me. Rose makes the best pot roast in the state.

"You save any for me?" Mason Reid sets his truck keys on the counter to claim the lone barstool that just opened up. He's a longtime friend and bush pilot. Because North Haven is more than a four-hour drive, I asked him to fly us down to the festival. The less time cooped up with Josie, the better. In someone else's plane, I can't succumb to the temptation of pulling over on the side of the road and dragging her into my lap.

"There's a few plates left," Ethel tells Mason, those stars in her eyes. Never mind that she's almost sixty to his thirty-five. She's just as dazzled by his good looks as the rest of them. "I'll grab you one."

"That's mighty sweet of you."

Ethel practically swoons when he flashes her that killer smile. One that's made him the target of every single woman's affection since he moved back to Caribou Creek. Better him than me.

"Go easy on her, will you?" Grandma Betty teases. "Ethel has a heart condition."

"Mrs. Bennington, a pleasure as always," Mason says with a nod.

"Betty, please. How many times do I have to tell you?"

Should I feel insulted that she didn't correct *me* earlier? I've made it a point not to care about things like that, but dammit, this one bugs me.

"Mrs. Bennington's coming with us tomorrow evening," I tell Mason.

"That's great. There's plenty of room for four."

"Room?" Josie's question is so soft I nearly miss it. My gaze flickers to her before I can think better of it. The usual calculation in her eyes is there, but there's something else too. Panic? Fear?

"Mason's offered to fly us to North Haven."

"Oh."

The urge to take her hand tugs at me harder than ever. Something's wrong. I can feel it in my bones. I hate that we're this connected when nothing can ever come of it. Or that I feel the need to fix it. I tamp it down, as I always do. Though this time, the feeling's not as easy to bury. "That a problem?" I ask her quietly.

"Nope." Her lips lift in a forced smile. "Not at all."

"If you made other arrangements—"

"Not a big deal." She stares at the mashed potatoes hovering on her fork. Her meal is mostly untouched. "Easy enough detail to change."

Ah, that's it. Josie is a meticulous planner. Her attention to detail is the most impressive I've ever encountered. It's the reason she's such a valuable part of the brewery. Nothing gets by her. "I didn't mean to disrupt your planning."

Zac's disapproving look is impossible to miss, even from my peripherals. Normally, I can ignore it easily enough. But this time it's nagging at me. Perhaps it's Grandma Betty's presence that pulls the rare apology from me.

"I'm sorry," I say to Josie. "I should've run it by you first."

"Write this one down in the books," Zac says with a laugh. "Ben Ashburn is apologizing."

I shoot him a glare that shuts him right up, then turn my attention to Mason. "We'll meet you at the flight line at seven." I look to Josie. "Will that work?"

"We're meeting Jasper Steele at seven-thirty. I'm

guessing we need to leave a little earlier. I'll let him know to come to the airport instead."

"Who's Jasper?" I shouldn't feel an instant bristling simply hearing Josie mention another man's name. A man she's obviously been in contact with since she started making these arrangements. But I do just the same. When Josie would leave for an event in the past, I never gave much thought to it. I never *let* myself. I was relieved to have some space. It never occurred to me that she was around other men. Men that might try to entice her. Make empty promises. Fool her into thinking their intentions were pure.

"Coast Guard pilot," Zac answers, giving me a funny look that suggests my irritation isn't as masked as I thought. "One of my contacts. He's doing us a favor, so be nice Benny Poo."

I narrow my eyes at him. It's usually Wes who calls me that, but I hate it just the same.

"Jasper's great," Josie says. "He's storing the kegs for us until we get there."

"You send some extra brew down to the J-Squad?" Zac asks Josie.

"Of course. I wouldn't leave them hanging."

I hate that I feel like the odd man out here. That I don't know who the J-Squad is or why it's important to keep them happy. Or that the very thought of Josie being around a bunch of coastguardsmen fills me with lime-green jealousy. I have no right to feel this way, much less act on it. But I feel protective of her just the same.

"You sure about going?" Mason asks me, pulling my attention from my thoughts.

"Why wouldn't I be?"

"Just worried you might scare all the customers away with your scowl." Mason's laughter turns the heads of every woman in the diner. Not because it's overly loud or obnoxious. But because it's like some fucking siren call to them. "You going to handle all that smiling without having a heart attack?"

"That's what Josie's for," Zac pipes in.

"She's a delight for sure," Grandma Betty says, patting the empty space on the table as if it was my hand and I was a child. "Certain to make up for Mr. Ashburn's broodiness."

"He'll do fine," Josie says, offering me a gentle smile I don't deserve. One that instantly thaws the ice in my veins. Never mind how cold I've been to her, even more so lately. Josie is the one who comes to my defense. Her kind heart is a reminder why I keep my distance. Though I wish like hell that I was the man worthy of her, she deserves someone better than me. Someone who compliments her bright spirit, not darkens it as I surely would.

"Breathe, Josie," Grandma Betty says, taking my hand and squeezing. She knows exactly how hard this is for me. I haven't gotten near a plane since my parents died. And bush planes? Forget it. Hell, I close my eyes when I see them flying overhead. To be standing twenty feet away from one now is enough to give me a heart attack. Which is why I keep my back to it. "We can drive down," she offers. "A road trip, just us girls."

I feel my pulse slow. Grandma Betty really is the best.

"I need to do this," I say to her. "I need to face my fear."

"If you change your mind, even half a second before takeoff—"

"Thank you."

When Ben announced we were flying last night, I froze. I thought I'd throw up my dinner right then and there if I tried to speak. He's never asked about my life. Not about my parents or what I like to do for fun. Nothing. He only asks about Grandma Betty from time to time because she stops by the brewery. He had no way of knowing about my fear of flying.

Because I'm still going full steam ahead on my plan to tempt Ben Ashburn this weekend, the last thing I needed to do is show him another sign of weakness.

"You ladies ready?" Mason asks as he and Ben approach us.

My pulse goes right back to over the speed limit, but I have no way of distinguishing how much of that is from my fear or from Ben's nearness.

Grandma Betty wraps her hands around Mason's arm and tugs him down to her so she can ask him a question. "You won't mind if I ride up front with you, will you? I've always wanted to be a pilot. Might be a little late for this old lady and her fuzzy eyesight." She adjusts her glasses. "But it'd be nice to pretend."

I feel the tension rippling from Ben beside me.

Great.

Just what I need.

Grandma Betty is abandoning me to flirt with a pilot young enough to be her grandson, and Ben is pissed off having to sit near me. I try to catch Grandma

Betty's eye, but Mason's already leading her to the plane.

"After you," Ben says to me.

I start to look over at him then think better at it. I don't need him to see the sheer panic in my eyes. When we get to North Haven, I'm going to have a word with Grandma Betty. Had I known she was coming along to play matchmaker, I might've tried to talk her out of the invite. She means well, but I don't think she realizes who she's up against. Ben Ashburn is not an easy nut to crack. I'll probably make a damn fool of myself trying to flirt and get his attention. I don't need to add insult to injury with her overzealousness mixed in.

Last night, I had a nightmare that I threw myself at Ben. Planted a wet one on his lips. But he didn't kiss me back. He peeled me off him like I was a piece of chewing gum he'd just stepped in. Needless to say, that dream didn't end well. As if I needed help increasing my anxiety level today.

"Josie?" Ben says, making me realize I haven't moved.

"Oh, right."

The back seat is cramped, to say the least. There's hardly enough room for Ben and I to sit without touching. His bicep brushes my shoulder, temporarily distracting me from my greatest fear. I turn my head, pretending to look out the window, and allow my eyes to fall shut. But the second the engine starts, they pop open. Fear clutches my chest. Never mind that it's been sixteen years since I lost my parents.

"You okay?" Ben asks, leaning closer to me, trying not to shout but still needing to be heard over the engine.

"Did you know that the rate of fatal plane crashes in Alaska is higher than the national average?" The statistic that makes me both look like a nerd and a scaredy cat spews from my mouth before I can stop it. It's something I do when I'm nervous. Spout random facts. Or sometimes not so random facts that might make the experience less exciting. Who wants to hear about plane crash statistics right before they leave the ground?

"Josie, are you afraid of flying?"

As the plane lifts from the runway, my stomach dropping into my shoes, I squeeze my eyes shut. "Nope. Not me. Not at all."

When I feel Ben's hand cover mine, I'm certain the plane has crashed and we've all died. Ben goes out of his way to avoid touching me. To avoid being any nearer to me than is absolutely necessary. It's why a single brush of his arm can damn near give me an orgasm. There's no way this is real. But I squeeze his hand anyway, pretending that it is.

"Why didn't you tell me?" he asks, his voice tickling my ear. His tone is surprisingly compassionate.

Yeah, I'm totally dead.

I force one eye open, spotting Grandma Betty in the cockpit clapping her hands excitedly. She's wearing a headset that allows her to talk to Mason. I open the other eye and find Ben leaning dangerously close to me. His cologne is nearly enough to make me forget the terrifying experience.

"Did you know almost forty percent of the general population has some degree of aviophobia? That's the fear of flying." *Shut up, Josie. You're embarrassing yourself.*

"I wish you'd told me," Ben says, sounding like me means it. His tender tone is tempting me to look into his eyes. But I know it'll only take half a second to get lost in them and embarrass myself even further. So, I keep my gaze pointed to our joined hands. "I didn't realize that's why you wanted to drive."

"This is faster."

"I'm sorry, Josie."

"Two in twenty-four hours. I must be dead," I mutter, referring to his sudden need to apologize, when he never has before.

"Dead?"

"Never mind."

Grandma Betty looks over her shoulder, sending us

a wave. I expect Ben to release my hand like we've been caught making out or something. But he doesn't flinch. Instead, he strokes his thumb along my skin. The motion is both soothing and seductive, whether he means it to be or not.

"I'm an ass," Ben murmurs.

"Are you expecting me to argue?" I dare to flicker my gaze to his in this playful moment. "Because I'm not going to."

"I deserve that."

My heart rate remains unsteadily high, but the longer Ben holds my hand, the less I can blame it on fear. It's almost comical that I'm *this* turned on by a single touch. Something that might only be scandalous in a Hallmark movie. It's about as PG as it gets. Ben has scooted closer, but there's still a gap between our legs.

It's better than nothing.

I accept that this might be the only affection Ben Ashburn ever extends to me and let my eyes fall shut again. Focusing on the warmth of his hand. The soft strokes of his thumb. This single memory might be all I have to comfort me after I move away from Caribou Creek.

The plane jerks, rocking hard enough to throw me against Ben. I shriek, instantly filled with fear all over again. Ben's arm goes around me and tugs me against him. Pressing my cheek to his chest. Calming the panic.

"It's okay, Josie. I've got you." He rests his chin against the top of my head. "I won't let anything bad happen to you."

When the plane touches down in North Haven, I'm almost disappointed. I don't want to let go of Josie. Not now. Not ever. Selfishly, I love how it felt having her cling to me like a lifeline. Having her nestled against my chest. My chin resting against the top of her head. I'll never be able to smell strawberries again without thinking of her shampoo.

But when the plane rolls to a stop, I know what I have to do.

I let go and move away, as if the entire flight was a blip of time in another reality. No way in hell was I going to let her suffer through her fear of flying alone. Especially since I'm the asshole who changed our travel arrangements without taking Josie into consideration.

It's my own damn fault I didn't know about her fear of flying. I've kept her at arm's length for three years.

But now that we've landed, it's back to business.

A black diesel truck rolls along the flight line, stopping short of Mason's plane.

"That must be Jasper," Josie says, her eyes glued to the window.

That irritating pang of jealousy hits me again. Harder this time. It's one thing to *think* about Josie with someone else. It's another to be confronted with the possibility in person. With any luck, Jasper will be in his sixties. A washed-up military pilot who doesn't fly anymore and has grandkids. "Better get our stuff. Can we set up tonight?"

"No," Josie answers. "They won't let us into the grounds until tomorrow morning."

"We could've flown down tomorrow morning?"

"We were supposed to drive," she reminds me, taking the hand Mason offers to help her out of the plan. If I'm not mistaken, there's a chill to her tone that's normally not there. Fuck, that's probably my fault.

I follow Josie out of the plane, meeting everyone on the flight line.

"Oh, this view!" Grandma Betty coos as she stares out toward the bay with its mountain backdrop. "I haven't seen the ocean in years. This old lady needs to get out more!" She reaches for my arm and squeezes it. "Thank you so much for inviting me along."

"Of course. Glad to have you."

She leans closer, tugging on my arm as if she wants me to meet her halfway. "Thank you for taking care of Josie. She hasn't gone near a plane since her parents... well, you know." Before I can tell her that I *don't* know, Grandma Betty skitters off toward Mason. For a woman of seventy-five, she sure has surprising energy and quick moving feet.

Josie waves me over and introduces me to Jasper, the coast guard pilot in full uniform. The one who is nearer my age than that of sixty. Definitely not a washed-up military member. Only a pilot with a sprained wrist from the looks of his brace.

Seeing the uniform takes me back for a beat, to the days when I wore a uniform myself. I was Army, not Coast Guard. But that doesn't make the memories any less prominent. Memories of a time when I did unspeakable things that shaped me into the hardened man I am today. A man who's not worthy of such a kind-hearted spirit like Josie Bennington.

But that doesn't mean I'm handing her over to Jasper. Not a fucking chance.

"Decker dropped off all the kegs earlier today," Jasper explains. "They're in my garage."

"Jasper, we hate to trouble you more. You've

already done so much to help us out. But we don't have a truck to take the kegs back and forth." The sweetheart that she is, Josie doesn't blame me for causing the kink in her plans. No doubt she had all the details ironed out before I fucked them up with my selfishness.

"I have one you can borrow."

"That's so kind of you," Josie practically coos at him. Or am I imaging it? That Josie has a crush on me is no secret. My brothers have noticed as much for years. But it doesn't stop the irrational jealousy I feel at the attention that she's giving this Jasper character. I sure as hell hope Zac is right about this guy.

"Why don't I take you folks to the hotel? I'm sure you're ready to get settled in."

"Is it really as fabulous as all the rumors?" Grandma Betty appears, holding on to Jasper's arm. "Is there a day spa?"

"It's quite the place," Jasper reassures. "My buddy's wife had a hand in the whole production. Serenity made sure it was top-notch and very accommodating to all its clients." Jasper pats Grandma Betty's arm, leaning down as if to conspiratorially share a secret with her. "Which means the day spa is out of this world. I'll make sure you get a discount on any service you want."

"I like you," Grandma Betty announces.

Mason helps me load our luggage into the back of Jasper's truck as the coastguardsman helps the ladies into his truck. Not surprising, Grandma Betty takes shotgun. I can't make out much through the tinted windows, but I see two heads in the backseat.

"I'll be back Sunday afternoon to pick you up," Mason says, holding out his hand to shake mine.

"Thanks for the ride."

"You owe me one." Knowing Mason, that probably means he'll drag me out fishing. At least then I can't be accused of not doing anything fun by either of my brothers.

I join Josie in the back seat, along with another woman I don't recognize.

"This is Vanessa. She's heading up this whole festival," Josie explains to me, likely unaware that she's leaning against my shoulder to share this bit of news. Or perhaps I'm not the only one in this truck feeling jealous. I have no interest in Vanessa or any other woman for that matter, which has proven very problematic for my dilemma with Josie.

For nearly a year I endured a relationship with a woman I knew didn't love me. Who knew I didn't love her. We dated for purely business reasons. Any attempts to make it romantic were laughable at best. It was clear early on we weren't attracted to each other. Not in the primal way I'm attracted to Josie. Apparently, that part of me can't stand the thought of being with another woman. So, I've stopped trying to force it.

"Wow, this looks so fancy!" Josie says leaning over my lap to look out the window at the hotel. I pretend that the intoxicating aroma of her strawberry shampoo doesn't make me fucking want her even more than I already do and check my phone instead.

"You *have* to get a massage while you're here," Vanessa insists to Josie.

I'm relieved as hell that the drive is short, because I'm in dangerous territory. My ability to act like Josie doesn't mean anything to me is wearing thin. Especially after that plane ride. My dick twitches against my zipper at the mere thought of her in my arms again.

"I'll get us checked in." I hop out of the truck, eager for distance. Desperate to make an adjustment below the waist so the whole fucking town doesn't catch wind of my true feelings for Josie.

At the front desk, I wait to be checked in. Unable to keep my gaze from the double sliding doors. Jasper helps Josie load our bags onto a luggage cart. I watch for any stray touch or smile that doesn't belong. Never mind that I'm certain he and Vanessa have something going on between them. I caught his look toward her in the rear view.

"Here you are. Room 305. The elevators are—"

"What about the other room?"

The woman behind the counter looks confused, though she manages to keep her smile. *Linda*, her name tag reveals. "There's only one room."

For the life of me, I can't make sense of this. No way would Wes and Josie have stayed in the same room. Even if Wes weren't happily married and on his fucking honeymoon right now, there has never been anything between those two. Their relationship is like brother and sister. "Can you check again? There should be two rooms."

Linda returns her attention to the computer, clicking and clicking. Her grimace telling me everything I need to know. "I'm afraid the second room was cancelled."

"Cancelled?"

She squints at the screen as Josie talks to Jasper. It doesn't help that Grandma Betty seems to melt all over him either. "There's a note here that Wes—"

"Son of a bitch."

"Excuse me?"

"Sorry. He wasn't supposed to do that. Can you please give me a second room?"

Linda looks at me almost as if she's afraid to tell me something. Damn, do I make everyone that uncomfortable? I do my best to soften my hardened expression. But a smile's too much when I'm distracted by

Josie, still loitering outside with the military guy. "I'm afraid there's no rooms available. We're fully booked because of the festival. The lodge is too."

The sliding glass doors part, the squeak of wheels echoing as Josie pushes the cart inside. She takes one look at me and her smile drops. "Is there a problem?"

I have no clue how to answer that question, so I don't try.

I stash the room keys in my wallet and take over steering the cart. I don't mind sleeping on the floor. I've slept on worse. That's not the real problem. "We're on the third floor." The *real* problem is being so close to Josie all of the time. Even with a chaperone I know it'll become harder and harder to keep my hands to myself.

"There's only one bed." I scan the single room we've been given, thanks to some glitch in the system. But no matter how many times I look, a second bed doesn't appear. There's no way the three of us are sleeping in the same bed. Even if it *is* king-sized. There's only so much weird I'm willing to entertain.

"The sofa has a pull-out bed," Grandma Betty points out, already inspecting it. "Ben, you can sleep here. I'll take the bed with Josie."

"I'm sorry about this, ladies," Ben says, wearing his familiar grimace. All traces of the compassionate man from the plane are gone. I shouldn't be surprised. In fact, I should be happy that I got a glimpse of that side of Ben Ashburn at all. "Hopefully it's only for tonight. I requested another room if it comes available."

"It's not likely," I say, focusing on my suitcase so I don't have to look him in the eyes. "I had to make reservations three months ago."

"You kids are going to be so busy you won't care about the room situation. You'll come back each night to simply collapse before you get up and do it all again." Grandma Betty unzips her suitcase and pulls out a nightgown. "If you'll excuse me, I'm going to get in my shower." If I didn't know she was seventy-five, I'd be surprised to learn it by how quickly her feet move.

Awkward silence falls over the room, filled only by the faint sound of running water.

I focus on unpacking my clothes. Hanging my carefully chosen outfits in the small closet space by the door. Pretending like the man I've craved for three long years isn't merely feet away.

"You okay now?"

I startle at Ben's words, spoken low and much closer than should be possible. He reaches out, touching my arm as if to steady me. Dammit if my nipples don't instantly pebble at the contact. "I'm fine."

"I still feel like an ass."

"Isn't that kind of your MO?" I tease.

"I mean it, Josie." His thumb moves up and down my arm, leaving a trail of fire in its wake. "I didn't know how you felt about flying."

"How could you?" I challenge, feeling surprisingly bold in this moment. Maybe it's because I no longer have anything to lose. Or because there's nowhere for Ben to run and hide if he doesn't like what I'm saying. "You don't know anything about me, *boss*."

He flinches, as if I'd slapped him. "For this weekend, you can call me Ben."

I wish it felt like something special. His permission to call him by his first name. But instead, it feels...disappointing. Though I may have every intention of seducing him—or I did until I realized the *three* of us would be sharing a room—I don't want to go back to Caribou Creek and pretend like nothing happened. It would break my heart beyond repair. It's better to keep my armor up. At least for now. "No thanks."

"Josie—"

"Tell me, *boss*. What *do* you know about me?"

"I know you're a master of spreadsheets."

I let out a disbelieving laugh. "You don't know anything about me outside of work, do you?" Before he can answer the question we both already know the answer to, I add, "Your brothers know a lot about me. They know a lot about all the people who work at the brewery because they take an interest."

"What do they know?" Ben asks, a mixture of

smug and curious. As if he expects to poke holes in my words.

"My birthday, for one." I stare at him, daring him to tell me the date. Hell, I bet he can't even guess the month. His silence is all the answer I need. "Zac knows my favorite band." He and his wife gifted me tickets to see Florida Georgia Line for my birthday when they came to Anchorage last year. "Wes knows how I like my coffee." I poke a finger into Ben's chest. "Hell, even Tanner knows I read romance novels by the truck-load." He's only been around for a year and everyone still calls him the *new kid*. But he already knows more about me than Ben likely ever will.

Ben's eyes widen a bit. "I've never heard you swear before."

"*That's* all you got out of this?" I shake my head, turning away to hide my embarrassment. A part of me hoped he'd secretly learned all those things about me. That he only pretended not to know them and would fess up when confronted. I adjust a blouse on a hanger, wondering if packing this risqué top was really worth the trouble. I could attend the festival naked and I doubt Ben would notice. "You don't know anything about me. Including *why* I have a fear of flying."

"Then tell me."

"No thank you." I go to move around him, but Ben has managed to corner me. My heart races, but not from fear. Oh no. It's out of control because it's rare to have Ben's delicious, muscular body this close to mine. The invisible pull I feel between us begs me to give in. To wrap my arms around his neck and suction my entire body to his. Never mind that right now I'm really fucking annoyed with him.

"Josie, please." His hand slides up my arm, settling on my shoulder. His warm fingers are inside my shirt sleeve, making it really fucking hard to concentrate right now.

"You don't care about me." I stare at his chest because those deep blue eyes of his are my kryptonite. "Not like that."

"Is that what you think?" His whispered words tickle my cheek, leaving me to wonder how we're so close when I don't remember moving an inch.

"It's what I know."

Ben's fingers tangle inside my sleeve as he grips it. "You're wrong."

I dare to glance up. To meet his gaze. It's filled with liquid heat. Something I've only ever caught glimpses of before outside my dirtiest dreams. I watch those baby blues drop to my lips. I've fantasized about this moment forever. I keep expecting to wake up from this lusty dream.

"Ben—"

The bathroom door flies open and we jump apart.

I bang the back of my head against the closet shelf and grumble. I probably deserve it for letting myself get so carried away. For allowing lust rather than common sense to take control.

"Now, don't make fun of my nightie," Grandma Betty says, seemingly oblivious to what nearly occurred between Ben and me. "I'm allergic to cats, but I love them so!" She holds out her arms and spins in a full circle, showing off her purple nightgown adorned in hundreds of cats.

I feel the swirling tension ease immediately. But more surprising than that is the sound of laughter. Coming from Ben.

"Am I dreaming?" I ask aloud.

"Hardly," Ben says, turning to me and proving that the laughter was his own. In fact, he's...smiling. I'm so stunned I don't have words. I've never seen him look so sexy before. That thing is positively dangerous. He takes a step closer to me, lowering his voice. "Your birthday's December tenth."

CHAPTER 8

Ben

There's not enough coffee in the world to save me from my night of restless sleep. Knowing Josie was sleeping only a few feet away kept me tossing and turning. I don't know if I'm still grateful I invited her grandma along or regretting it. Because if Grandma Betty hadn't been an obstacle, I would've crawled right in that bed last night and claimed what was mine. All my reasons to keep my distance be damned.

"You *are* a dear, aren't you!" Grandma Betty coos as I hand over her requested coffee. Slowly, I'm winning her over. Fetching her a coffee was a small price to pay to find out that Josie loves white chocolate mochas. She takes a sip and lets out a moan of satisfaction. "This hits the spot."

"Did Josie leave?" A quick scan of the hotel room

leaves little trace of her, aside from clothes hanging in the open closet and a curling iron plugged in on the sink counter. Did I miss her in the lobby when I returned with coffees? Did Jasper already pick her up—

"She's in the bathroom, Mr. Ashburn." Grandma Betty pats my arm. "No need to get those boxers in a twist just yet."

"I'm not—"

"I'm almost ready," Josie announces as the bathroom door opens the rest of the way and she steps out looking dazzling enough to stun me speechless. In those skinny jeans and red silk blouse unbuttoned low enough to make a blind man drool, she's never looked so sexy. How the fuck am I supposed to focus all day with the curvaceous beauty in tight quarters with me? With who the hell knows how many guys ogling her?

"You two'll be all right without me today, right?" Grandma Betty grabs her purse from the bed and loops the strap over her shoulder. "That handsome coastguardsman hooked me up with a mani and a pedi this morning!" She glances at her wrist, as if a watch resides there. It does not. "Already running late. I'll catch up with you two this afternoon."

Grandma Betty scurries out of the hotel room, leaving me alone with Josie.

My heart pounds against my rib cage at the very

sight of her. It takes every ounce of restraint to sit my ass on the couch and pretend to skim emails. I couldn't give a fuck about work emails right now, which warns me just how much trouble I might be in.

"You sure that's what you want to wear today?" I ask Josie without looking up.

"Are you kidding me?" she mutters.

I turn off my phone screen and casually glance her way, shocked to see the daggers shooting my way. "Josie?"

"Are you *fucking* kidding me?" Though her tone is quiet, it's bordering on scary. I've rarely seen Josie mad. Never have I seen her anger directed at me.

"What?"

"You don't want to *touch* me, but you have something to say about the way I dress? You're unbelievable." She spins around, facing the mirror, and starts to curl her hair. "For your information, I love the way I look today. So, *no*. I'm not going to change. And before you pull that boss card on me, remember I'm the one who knows how these events run. I'm dressed appropriately. It's *you* who looks like he's going to a stuffy board meeting."

I'm stunned once again, but this time by her bold words.

If I had any sense, I'd keep my ass in my seat and return to scrolling through my inbox. But apparently,

I'm a glutton for punishment, because I'm off the couch and halfway across the room before I even realize I'm moving.

I come up behind Josie, taking the curling iron from her hand and setting it on the counter. I stand so close a breeze could hardly wedge its way between our bodies. I comb back the wavy blonde locks from her neck allowing the softest graze of my fingertips to tease her sensitive skin as I lower my lips as close to her ear as I dare. "You think I don't *want* to touch you?"

In the mirror, I watch her eyes become hooded.

"That I don't ever think about kissing you?"

She whimpers, her eyes falling all the way shut.

"If you think I don't think about *fucking* you every minute of every day, you're wrong, Josie." I press my cheek against her head, inhaling that sexy strawberry scent before I force myself to step away. She lets out the softest moan that warns me to get the fuck out of the room before I do something neither of us can take back. I hurry to the door and call back to her, "I'll meet you down in the lobby."

Whatx. The. Actual. Fuck?

I pinch my arm for the third time, convinced I'm dreaming.

No way did Ben Ashburn just tell me he's *always* thinking about fucking me. *Me*. Josie Bennington. The spreadsheet nerd with a few too many curves. The one he's acted so damn cold toward since day one. The one who looks nothing like his ex, Business CEO Barbie.

I'm so turned on right now.

I nearly came just from those whispered words.

If I ever get the chance to sleep with Ben, it'd probably kill me. Death by pleasure overload. I shiver, remembering the way his breath felt against my ear. I need to finish getting ready. Our ride will be here any minute.

But dammit, I'm so turned on right now that I need a release.

Looking over my shoulder to ensure Ben did in fact leave, I dare to tug down the zipper of my jeans and reach my hand inside. I rest my other hand on the counter to balance myself. I only need to stroke my finger along the silk once to discover my panties are not just damp, they're soaked. I pull them to the side and rub my finger against my swollen bud.

I allow my eyes to fall closed and picture Ben standing behind me. I imagine his lips on my neck. His hands sliding from my waist, up my stomach, and onto my breasts. I rotate my finger faster, feeling my release building. His words echo in my mind. *If you think I don't think about fucking you every minute of every day, you're wrong, Josie.*

I cry out as I come, shocked at how quickly it happens.

I'm panting so heavily I might as well have run a mile. I lean against the counter with both hands and breathe deeply until my body settles. Though I feel some release, I know it's a far cry from what I really need.

A ping on my phone alerts me to Jasper's arrival. He's taking us to his place to pick up the kegs and loan us a truck.

"Shit." I zip up my jeans, grab my satchel, and

decide my hair is fine half-curled. After double-checking that I unplugged the curling iron, I run out the door.

By the time I make it down to the lobby, Ben and Jasper are already in deep discussion. Yesterday, I thought I was imagining Ben's jealousy toward our coast guard liaison. Especially since it's abundantly clear Jasper only has eyes for Vanessa. Now, I'm not so sure what to think. Not with Ben looking like he's giving that *don't piss on my tree* territorial look to Jasper.

Jasper looks my way first, but it's Ben's gaze that lingers the longest. As if he recognizes the flush on my cheeks and is giving himself credit for his words stirring me up. But I'm not about to admit to him what I did. Not about to give him the satisfaction of knowing he got to me like that. I may have waited three agonizingly long years for this type of attention from him, but that doesn't mean I'm simply going to swoon at his every touch or word. I've got more self-respect than that.

"I have a truck you two can borrow back at my house," Jasper explains, oblivious to the quiet tension between Ben and me as he rattles off the general details of the event. All things I thankfully have memorized from weeks of preparation. Because right now, my brain is fuzzy.

Today, Vanessa's in the front seat.

"He always look so pissed off?" she asks me, nodding at Ben.

I follow her gaze through the windshield, watching the men talk as if they're both getting along but also suspicious of one another. "Pretty much." Except when he's whispering dirty things in my ear. I'd describe that look entirely differently.

"You're a patient woman," she adds.

"Or a stupid one," I mumble.

"He loves you, you know."

If there's one thing I've learned in my twenty-six and a half years on this earth, it's that love and lust are two very different things. Ben wanting to fuck me definitely makes my lady bits tingle, but it doesn't promise my heart won't get broken at the end of this. In fact, I fear it's almost a guarantee.

Except, the man *did* know my birthday after all.

"What about you and Jasper?" I ask, eager to change the subject.

"We have a...complicated history. Not to mention I'm heading back to Houston once the festival is over."

"But you love him?"

"Somedays I really wish I didn't."

"Boy, do I know the feeling."

The opening of truck doors puts an end to our surprisingly intimate conversation. If Vanessa and I lived in the same place, I suspect we might end up being friends. I don't have many girlfriends. Though I can be social as a butterfly when the need calls for it, I prefer to keep to myself. If I'm not working, I'm reading or spending time with Grandma Betty. Not exactly the most attractive traits for friendship. Or a relationship for that matter.

Ben scoots close, but not close enough to touch me. The jerk.

"Sounds like they're expecting a large crowd," he says to me, sounding way too business again. It makes me want to scream, but I'm an adult. I can play this game, too.

"We can handle them."

"You said you have a checklist?" he asks, his voice low. Not that it matters. The two up front have tuned us out to have a conversation of their own. "Can I see it?"

I pretend I'm not completely aware of the way Ben watches me flip through the folders in my satchel. His attentive gaze is as good as a sensual caress. I'm *not* humoring what Vanessa said about him loving me. But it doesn't do much to keep my hand from trembling ever so slightly.

"Here." In my nervousness, I practically punch him in the chest handing over the paper. But before I can retract my hand and stare out the window to hide my embarrassment, I feel his fingers clamp around my wrist. His touch is like fire, but it's hardly a match for what's dancing in his eyes as he lifts my hand. His lips brush against my fingers as he ever so subtly inhales the scent that lingers.

His quiet groan is deep and sexy. "*That's* what took you so long," he growls, his words little more than a possessive breathy whisper. I squeeze my thighs together to ward off the tingling between them. But it's no use. I'm just as turned on as I was half an hour ago.

I yank my hand away, not wanting him to have this power over me. Never mind the audience in the front seat. "I don't know what you're talking about."

Ben leans over, his breath brushing my ear. "You naughty girl."

Shivers assault my body, making me wish we could head back to the hotel and settle this once and for all. Preferably, naked between the sheets. Maybe the two of us really just need some hot and heavy sex to get this out of our system. Why does love have to get involved? But my pride still has the better of me. I don't want Ben to think I'm so easily manipulated by him. "I'm mad at you," I mutter low as Jasper pulls into his driveway.

Maybe I'm imagining it, but the liquid heat in his eyes seems to darken at that. Is that the key? Playing hard to get? *Well Ben, game on.*

CHAPTER 10

Ben

"Why do we have a seventh keg?" I demand of Josie after recounting three times. Our brewery has always offered six brews, but there's seven kegs lined up. My head isn't exactly in the right place today. Not when I know Josie touched herself after I made my dirty confession. I know I crossed a line, but fuck it if I can help it right now. I can't stand her being mad at me. It...*does* things to me.

"It's an experiment," she says without looking at me. Without breaking her concentration on the tent setup. She's left no detail unattended in our booth. It's both eye-catching and intelligent marketing for the brewery.

"What *kind* of experiment?"

She holds up her hands as if to cement her innocence. "Look, I'm just carrying out instructions from Wes."

"Wes."

"Well, he was supposed to be here this weekend instead of you." She fixes the stacks of plastic sample cups for the third time. The booth is ready to go. In only a few minutes, the gates will open and a flood of people will move through the festival grounds. We'll be so busy pouring samples that we won't have time for anything else. Best to get this straightened out now.

"Just tell me what my idiot brother has been up to. Please."

Josie turns and stares at me, the usual gentleness in her eyes missing. I hate how unsettled that makes me feel. "He's not an idiot. He's actually a genius." She grabs a cup, fills it from the tap, and hands it to me. "If you don't believe me, try it for yourself."

"What's this?"

"Wes's new brew."

"His *what*?"

Josie lets out an exasperated sigh, warning me the patience she rarely loses is fraying. "Just drink it already. It's not poison."

"Are you sure?" The playful tone sounds foreign leaving my lips, as does the hint of a smile that forms. I know I'm not imagining it by the way Josie reacts. Her subtle intrigue masked by shock. She might be mad at me, but I've discovered her weakness.

"If it was, your brothers wouldn't blame me."

Cautiously, I sip the amber liquid. But not because I'm afraid of what's in it. If Wes has been secretly brewing a new type of beer behind my back, I want to make sure I find every criticism I can when I confront him. But to my utter surprise, the wheat concoction with a hint of pumpkin is...delicious.

"Good, right?" Josie asks as the gates open.

"Wes really made this?"

"Don't feel bad. Aside from Avery, no one else knew. Not even Zac."

"But you did."

"Only because he planned to bring it here to test on the crowd. He knew you'd want customer feedback and data to support adding another brew. Since I was making all the arrangements—"

"He had to let you in on the secret."

"No, he didn't." The first customers approach our booth. "But Wes knows I don't like to be blindsided."

Before I can say anything or even attempt to apologize again for the plane ride, Josie greets a young, happy couple. In two seconds flat, she goes from the shy, introverted, spreadsheet guru to an outgoing, bubbly woman who knows our beer inside and out. She could give Zac a run for his money in the taproom with the way she easily matches a person to the brew she thinks they're going to like best.

I'm fucking impressed.

And turned on.

The day is filled with an endless line of customers and not-so-accidental brushes as Josie and I shuffle back and forth between the different taps. I'm thankful as hell for the distraction that keeps me from pinning her up against the back of the tent wall and kissing her until we're both panting and desperate for more.

It's a big fucking problem.

"We brought more kegs!" Jasper announces, arriving with a few other guys. Each has a keg loaded on a dolly.

"You're the best," Josie gushes, making me jealous as ever. Never mind that it's crystal-clear Jasper only has eyes for Vanessa. Or that Josie is clearly attracted to me after she touched herself this morning. I feel territorial as ever, and I fucking hate that I'm powerless to do anything about it.

"Ben," Josie says to me, "meet the J-Squad. Jasper, Jaxson, Jordan, James, Jonas, and Joel." She flashes them a megawatt smile. "Did I get that right?"

"You got an a plus," Jasper says. My urge to punch him ratchets up several notches.

"They're all in the Coast Guard together. And, I

dare say, the brewery's biggest fans. Did you know they each have their own favorite brew?"

"Hmm."

"Where do you want these, boss?" Jasper asks Josie.

She directs traffic, effortlessly guiding keg switches for our empties without ignoring customers.

"She's really something, huh?" Grandma Betty's voice catches me off guard. She stands behind me in the tent, staying just out of the way. Where the woman snuck up from, I have no clue. Her ninja skills are terrifying. Something I'll definitely need to watch out for when it comes to Josie. The last thing I need is Grandma Betty catching me with my hand up Josie's shirt.

"Yes, she is, Mrs. Bennington." I wait, hoping this time she'll correct me. Tell me to call her Betty. But no such luck.

"I hope you're not taking her for granted." Though her smile is sweet enough, the penetrating look in her eyes warns me she's not as naïve as she might pretend to be. That if I hurt Josie, I'll be answering to her. Other than Grandma June, Betty Bennington is the only woman to make me quake in my shoes.

"I won't."

"Good." Grandma Betty pats my arm. "Now pour me a drink. I'm parched."

"Got a preference?"

"Give her the pumpkin brew," Josie suggests in between filling sample cups for the J-Squad, leaving me to wonder how much of this conversation she's overheard. She's a master at multitasking. Ninja must be somewhere in the family tree. "Trust me."

"I've always trusted you," I say without forethought, earning a stolen moment between us. The gleam in her chocolatey eyes warms me from the inside out. She might be annoyed as hell with me right now, but what matters most is still there. I'd never forgive myself if I was the reason that light in her eyes burned out.

"You two can flirt later," Grandma Betty says, reaching impatiently around me for the cup I've filled for her. "I'm thirsty." I step back to prevent the cup from bumping into me and inadvertently bump into Josie. She catches me with both hands braced on either side of my bicep. My heart stops. Hell, I think *time* stops.

"Ben."

"Yes, Josie?"

"Ben, the tap. You're going to spill!"

I catch the tap at the same moment beer spills over the rim of the cup, splashing onto my fingers.

"Here." Josie takes the cup to wipe it down, handing me a towel of my own. We're standing entirely too close. My heart won't stop its rapid pounding. "Here you go, Grandma Betty. This is Wes' new brew. Tell me what you think."

Grandma Betty coos approval after the first sip. It should annoy me that my brother's secretiveness is going over so well at this festival. That he knew *exactly* how to get around my objections to prove that his creation is a success. But we could add ten new brews for all I care right now. Because the only thoughts in my mind are of getting Josie alone the first chance I get.

CHAPTER 11

Josie

The first day of the festival is an incredible success. I'm relieved I arranged for extra kegs a couple days before we left for North Haven. It was a gut instinct, but one that proved to be right. Without them, we wouldn't have much left for the second day. I sit on the bed, browsing the website as Ben showers. I'm excited to share with him how many email signups we've collected for our monthly newsletter.

"Did I tell you my friend Carmelita is in town?" Grandma Betty asks from the sink counter. It's only now that I notice she's not dressing for bed, but fixing her hair. At ten-thirty. "I haven't seen her in almost a decade. We're going to grab a drink."

"Do I need to worry about you making it back?" I ask, half teasing, half serious. My grandma can drink me under the table any day, but there's at least one bridge night a month where I have to pick her up because she's too toasty to drive home. Going out this late seems a stretch, even for her.

"We'll just be down in the hotel bar," she says, slipping on a jacket. "Don't wait up."

Seconds after Grandma Betty slips out of the room, I hear the shower turn off. Making me suddenly *very* aware that Ben and I are all alone.

All day long, we shared flirty glances and touches. The man even *smiled*.

If it hadn't been for the endless line of festival-goers eager to sample the brew, I suspect something would've happened. Something more than a mere brush of our arms or graze of our fingers. Something *much* hotter.

Though I did my best to stay mad at Ben, I lost that battle quickly. I wasn't prepared for him to care that I was upset with him. I thought it might get his attention, but it was far more than I bargained for. Even now, the memory of those heated looks makes me wet with desire.

"Josie?" he calls from a small crack in the bathroom door.

"Yeah?"

"Can you grab my clothes? I left them on the couch."

It's impossible *not* to picture Ben naked as I retrieve his clothes. I can practically taste the water droplets my tongue yearns to lick from his skin. "Grandma Betty went out for a drink," I say, offering his clothes to the crack in the door and pretending not to look. "She said not to wait up."

"Did she now?" His tone is almost playful. It's enough to make me look back to the cracked door. Though I don't see Ben, I see his fuzzy reflection in the steamy mirror. I watch him wipe away a circle of it with a towel. Revealing the fact that he doesn't even have a towel wrapped around his waist.

"She ran into an old friend." The words come out half an octave higher, and I clear my throat. But damn if I can look away from the mirror as I greedily wait for the steam to fade further. To reveal the part of Ben I've always wondered about.

"Josie?"

"Mmm?"

"It's not polite to stare."

"Sorry." I rush from the door, embarrassed that I was caught. I crawl onto the bed and pull my laptop close. Pretending to skim statistics I couldn't make sense of if I tried. The data I usually find so fascinating is no match for my sexual frustration. I hate that I want Ben this badly. I hate even more that he seems to know it.

"You're not working, are you?" Ben asks, running a towel over his hair. He's missing a shirt and those shorts are hanging way too low on his hips. I don't need to stare to notice the V-shaped muscle that travels south beneath the waistband.

"I was just looking over some statistics. We got two hundred newsletter signups today. Isn't that great?"

Ben hangs the towel over the door and plops onto the bed beside me, lying on his side with his elbow bent and head propped in his hand. It's not his proximity that has my pulse tripling. It's his smile. Fuck, that smile is deadly. No wonder he only lets it come out and play on special occasions. Wait? Is *this* a special occasion?

"You were great today, Josie." He reaches for my computer, pulling it from my lap and setting it behind him. The heat between us is almost unbearable. The graze of his arm against my leg damn near making me whimper with want. I could give myself a hundred orgasms and still never find a release as satisfying as one with Ben.

I hate that I want this so badly. "Does that mean I get a raise, *boss*?"

"Would you settle for a bonus?" One corner of his mouth lifts in the most devilish grin I've ever seen him wear. It's not something appropriate for public. Hell, it's not exactly appropriate at all. But damn does it make my belly quiver.

"A bonus?"

Ben traces his fingertips from my ankle to my knee, slowing as he continues north. I have to be dreaming. There's no way this is happening. I mean Ben's *smiling* for crying out loud. That should be my first clue. But damn if I want to wake up. "Well, it might be a bonus for both of us."

His hand rests on my upper thigh, his fingertips teasing the edge of my shorts. "Grandma Betty might come back at any minute," I say in a raspy whisper.

"Then maybe we should hide under the covers." He runs a finger back and forth at the hem of my shorts, making me wish he'd just reach all the way inside and touch me already. "All you have to do Josie is sit back and enjoy." He locks his gaze with mine, those baby blues drenched with desire I never thought possible. "Unless you don't want me to touch you?"

"You know damn well I do," I grumble.

Ben has the audacity to laugh.

I want to play mad, but the smile that tugs at my lips is impossible to fight. "So that's what it takes to make you smile, huh?"

"That," Ben says, peeling back the covers and slipping beneath them. "And the thought of licking your pussy."

Oh, sweet Jesus I really *have* died and gone to heaven.

He tugs me under with him, pulling off my shorts and panties. Ben disappears entirely as I rest my head on a pillow and spread my legs for his eager mouth. There are a million reasons why this is a terrible idea, but for the life of me, I can't remember one of them right now. I surrender to Ben's magic tongue as it strokes my folds.

In the thousands of fantasies I've had about this man, never did anything feel so fucking good as it does right now. His mouth moves expertly, licking, suckling, and nibbling at my pussy in all the right ways. It's as if he's always known exactly how to pleasure me.

I rock my hips gently with his motion, moaning when one hand slides up my shirt and grabs a fistful of boob.

"Ben," I whimper. "Of fuck, Ben!"

He doesn't stop or even slow. Every stroke is faster than the one before it. More deliberate. Each flicker of his tongue against my clit is dizzying. He fuses his mouth to my core, feasting on my pussy like he's never wanted anything so badly.

I want this moment—this fucking incredible sensation—to last forever.

I want Ben forever.

My release hits me hard, like a tidal wave knocking

323

into my body from the inside out. I cry out as I come, rocking violently against Ben's face.

I hear the click of the lock and panic. Ben must hear it too, because after one last flick of his tongue, he rolls to the edge of the bed and drops onto the floor. Hiding in the spot between the bed and the window just in time for Grandma Betty to appear.

"Carmelita is *such* a lightweight!"

Where the fuck are my shorts? And my panties? "I'm sure it was nice to catch up though?" I force a smile as I search beneath the covers for my clothes. All the while Ben lies on the floor, both hands covering his face, a tent pitched very prominently in his shorts.

"I got a free margarita, so I can't complain." Grandma Betty drops her purse onto a chair. "Say, where is Ben?"

"He went to find a vending machine."

"Oh, well there's one right down the hall." She unzips her suitcase and pulls out her purple kitty pajamas. When she finally slips into the bathroom, I let out a deep breath. Ben pops up and runs to the pullout bed as I find my shorts and slip them back on.

Though Ben disappears beneath the back of the couch, out of sight from my spot on the bed, I hear my phone ping. I switch it to silent as I read the text.

Ben: That was close ;)

Josie: No kidding!

Ben: Now I know one more thing about you.

Ben: I know how to make you come.

Ben: Hard.

Josie: It might've been a fluke.

"I hope you kids won't mind that I'm spending the day with Carmelita tomorrow. She's getting a mud bath with me."

I don't dare ask Grandma Betty how she knows Ben is in the room. "Not at all. I'm glad you're having such a good time."

Grandma Betty looks at me, that mischievous twinkle in her eyes. One that says she's not the only one having a good time. "Goodnight, you kids."

Ben: It was no fluke, sweetheart. I'll prove it to you.

Holy orgasms, how am I supposed to sleep after *that* text?

CHAPTER 12
Ben

When it comes to Josie Bennington, I know I'm playing with fire. I've already crossed a line I can't uncross. I know it could fuck everything up. But that doesn't seem to stop me. Because the second Grandma Betty leaves the room the next morning for her spa day with her friend, I zero in on Josie.

She stands at the sink applying her makeup, looking sexy as hell in those skinny jeans that hug her ass in the best way.

"You sleep okay?" she asks, lining her lashes with mascara.

"Not really." I didn't sleep. Not with the blue balls I gave myself eating out Josie's pussy. My cock throbbed all night, tempting me to sneak Josie out of

326

the room so we could find somewhere to be alone. But it didn't feel right. It felt cheap.

Which is the fucking problem.

It's bad enough that I've given into my lustful temptations where Josie is concerned. But if I allow feelings to get involved, I'm totally fucked.

"I haven't applied my lipstick," she says over her shoulder. "Maybe I could...help." I meet her gaze in the mirror, the wicked twinkle in her eyes promising me she means what she says. "Unless you don't want me to suck your cock."

"Fuck," I groan, tugging her against me by the hips. My cock is half hard in an instant, not just at her suggestion, but at her dirty words. "I never knew you had such a mouth on you, Josie."

She snakes her hand around my neck, drawing my attention to her lips. I've thought about kissing her for so long. Tasting her lips. Devouring them. But one kiss and I'm certain I'll fall too far to ever turn back. If I fall, I'll never let her go. Even though I know I'm not the one who can give her everything she needs. Everything she deserves. The blackness on my soul is something that'll never go away. I may not have the nightmares like my brother had, but I'm still plagued by the horrific things I did in the name of duty.

"We don't have long," she points out, wriggling

her ass against my fully hard cock. "Maybe you could just *fuck* me instead."

"Josie," I growl in warning.

She reaches a hand behind her, cupping my length through my jeans. Jeans she promised me that'd be much more comfortable than my suit pants. I wore them to please her. Judging by the way she squeezes my dick through the denim, I've accomplished that.

I gently tug her hair, exposing her neck to me. Nibbling her sensitive skin. "You don't know what you're asking of me, Josie."

"I'm asking you to *fuck* me, Ben."

It has to be the way she practically moans my name that takes control of me. Forces me to surrender to her plea even though I fear I'll ruin her if I do. "I don't have a condom."

"I'm on the pill." She tugs the zipper down on my jeans. "I want you inside me."

Somewhere in the back of my mind, a warning whispers that this is a terrible fucking idea. It's one thing to fool around. Quite another to plunge into her sweet pussy. Knowing my dick won't know anything else but claiming a woman who deserves so much better than me. But when her fingers slip inside my boxers and wrap around my length, any rational thought that remained is gone.

"I'm not gentle, Josie."

"I'm not fragile."

I unzip her jeans and yank them down to her ankles. On the way up, I grab her inner thighs and spread them so I can drag my tongue through the back of her pussy. She tastes so damn good. I savor her flavor as she whimpers, leaning forward on the counter.

Standing again, I lock my gaze with hers in the mirror. I slide my hands up her stomach, pushing up her top with it. Exposing a sexy black lace bra that'll no doubt drive me wild the rest of the day simply knowing I'm the only one who knows it hides beneath her shirt. But right now, it's in the fucking way.

I unclasp it and push it up with her top.

"Fuck, Josie." I squeeze her enormous tits, damn near nutting from the feel of them in my hands. How many nights did I jerk off to this image? The one I'm watching in the mirror right now? "These are so fucking nice."

Later, I plan to give these tits all the attention they deserve. But my throbbing dick warns me time is against us. I have to fuck her hard and fast. I pull my length free and line it up beneath her plump ass cheeks.

Josie pants my name.

"Fuck, Josie. There isn't one single thing about you that isn't sexy as hell." I reach around her waist, spreading her pussy lips so I can run my dick through them. Priming myself for entry. I tease her clit with my swollen head until she's damn near writhing from it.

Then I plunge into her pussy.

Hard.

Fast.

All at once.

Filling her tight pussy.

She gasps, lifting up on tiptoes.

"You okay, Josie?"

"Omigod. I'm *more* than okay. Fuck you're so *big*."

"Hold on to the counter. It's about to get rough."

She leans forward, arching her lower back in the perfect angle for me to slide in deep. I slam into her pussy, over and over. My balls bounces off her as she pants my name. Fuck me, nothing has *ever* felt this good. Something warns me nothing ever will. Josie's pussy feels like home.

"Come for me, Josie," I order, rubbing a finger against her swollen button. "Come on my dick."

In seconds, her pussy convulses around my cock as she lets out a series of moans. I pump faster. Harder. I should pull out. Coming in her pussy will change everything. It'll make it impossible to deny my feelings. It'll make it impossible to ever give her up. But it doesn't stop the savage in me from claiming what I've wanted for three goddamn years.

I still inside her depths, releasing hot ropes of cum.

Claiming the one woman I'd hoped to never destroy.

I'm certain the regret will come later.

But right now, it's muted by the primal victory I feel. "You're *mine*, Josie. *Only* mine."

I t's a whole lot harder to concentrate on the crowd today because my dirty mind is back at the hotel room, remembering the way Ben's cock felt slamming into me. After three years, he's finally fucked me. And it was even better and hotter than any of my wildest fantasies. The only thing I wish is that he'd kissed me.

"The Amber's our most popular," I tell a couple of women. "But the pumpkin brew is pretty tasty, too."

I wait for them to decide, trying like hell not to sneak a side glance at Ben. But dammit, my gaze keeps landing on him every other minute. On his fine ass. On his thick biceps straining the brewery t-shirt I talked him into wearing. On the real smile I thought I'd never live long enough to see.

"You good?" he asks, dropping a hand to my hip.

"Better than good."

He squeezes me, his fingertips slipping beneath my shirt and teasing my lower back. "There's more where that came from."

"We'll try the pumpkin," one of the women finally says.

"Great choice."

The day is filled with extra flirty touches and looks. Promises of more to come. A promise that Ben meant what he said. I'm his. The way he possessively hovers around me when a guy is acting too friendly turns me on in ways I never thought possible. I've been on my own for so long that I never gave much thought to how good it would feel for someone to be so consumed by me.

I hope this is the start of something.

Something real.

We join the J-Squad for dinner at one of the local restaurants, THE ICEBERG, to celebrate a successful festival. It's great company. Though Ben keeps an arm around my chair throughout the meal, he finally relaxes when the wives join us, realizing most of the guys are spoken for. Even Jasper and Vanessa seemed to have worked through whatever was holding them back. Or at least their flirty touches and stolen kisses seem to imply as much. Ben and I are both inundated with invitations to visit anytime we want.

"What's Grandma Betty up to this evening?" Ben asks in a hot whisper against my ear.

"Apparently her spa day wore her out. She's hanging out in the room, watching HBO."

"Grandma Betty?"

"Don't ask," I tease, sliding a hand onto his thigh, digging my fingers in near his crotch. "We still have a truck for the evening. We could take a drive."

Ben's eyes darken, causing my nipples to pebble instantly. "Josie Bennington, you are full of surprises."

After we say our goodbyes and make arrangements for tomorrow with Jasper, Ben threads his hand through mine and tugs me out of the restaurant. We hardly make it to the truck before I'm pinned up against the side of it. He presses a thigh against my core. I grind against it, no longer caring if we might have an audience. Ben combs a hand through my hair, using his fingers as an anchor. He tugs my head to the side, blazing a trail along my neck with those magical lips of his.

But it's his kiss I crave.

"Ben?"

"We better go," he says against my ear. "I need to fuck you."

My breathing is heavy as Ben follows a narrow road out of town. One that hugs mountains and coast. He pushes the center console up and out of the way, and I scoot next to him. He drops his hand to my thigh, his thumb stroking me.

I search for the right words, but I don't find them.

There's a warning whispering in the back of my mine. One that worries I'm about to get my heart shattered into a million pieces. But I push it down until I can't hear it. Whatever happens, I don't have any regrets. I've wanted this for too long.

When Ben finds a deserted pull off a few miles from town, my pulse triples.

I've thought about him being inside me all day.

"Scoot over, Josie," he says nodding toward the passenger seat. He follows me there, lifting me onto his lap. I yearn to turn around. To face him so I can cup his cheeks and kiss him. But it's a tight fit. Not to mention the feel of his hard cock pressed against my ass is distracting the hell out of me. Making me wetter by the second.

"Get those jeans off," Ben orders as he unzips his own.

I lift from his lap, shimmying them down the best I can. He grabs my hips as I lower, guiding me onto his cock. As I sink down, my eyes fall closed. I surrender to sensation. To fantasy. To Ben.

He reaches up the front of my shirt, savagely pushing my bra out of the way without undoing the clasp. But I don't care because the way his rough hands feel kneading my boobs is so fucking good. He pinches my nipples as I slowly slide up and down his shaft.

"Fuck, Josie. Do you have any idea how much power you have over me?"

I let out a laugh at that. "Only took me three years."

"I've wanted you since the first day you came in for an interview."

"You're lying."

He lifts his hips, meeting me as I lower. A powerful thrust that seems to imply just what he thinks about that comment. "I've thought about this pussy for so long." He squeezes my breasts harder as he lifts his hips again. Slamming against me. He nuzzles my neck as we fuck hard. I cry out his name. I want to tell him I love him, but the words are lodged in my throat.

The weekend isn't over.

I promised myself I'd tell him how I feel before the end of it. I have until the plane touches down in Caribou Creek tomorrow morning.

Tonight, I just want to feel.

"Come on my dick, Josie. Come hard for me so I can come inside you."

His dirty words do something to me that I can't control. It's like a dial he knows how to crank inside me, turning up every sensation and amplifying it times ten. It takes me literal seconds to explode. My climax assaults me so hard I nearly crash into the dashboard.

Ben holds me tight, his hands still firmly clamped around my breasts. He thrusts hard once, twice, three times before he stills. I feel his dick pulse inside my channel as he releases his seed. Selfishly, I wish I wasn't on the pill. I wish he was putting a baby inside me right now. I've never wanted it more.

"You're mine, Josie. In case you forgot."

I lean my head back against his shoulder, wishing he'd drop his lips to mine. But we're both panting so heavily we can hardly breathe. I settle for nuzzling his neck instead. "I'll never forget."

CHAPTER 14

Ben

I'm not ready to leave North Haven. Not ready to face reality when we get home. Fucking Josie has changed everything.

It's awakened something inside me I thought long dead. Created a stirring in my soul. If soulmates existed, I'd dare to believe she was mine. I could live ten more lifetimes and never feel the same way about anyone as I do about Josie. Love like this isn't supposed to exist, but it does.

This weekend has changed everything.

Except what the future holds.

Fuck, I wish I was worthy of her. I wish I could give her everything she wants from me. But the darkness hanging over my soul will never go away. It'll always be there, crushing down on us both. I can't be the storm cloud in her life. We might be happy for a time, but my scars are permanent. The ugly things I did during war are unerasable. Horrible things I can never put to words. Things that have darkened me.

Josie deserves someone good. Someone worthy.

Even if it fucking kills me to admit it.

But until that plane touches down in Caribou Creek, I'm holding on to every last happy moment I can. It's selfish of me, I know. But it'll be the last selfish thing I ever do when it comes to the woman who will always have my heart.

"We don't have to do this," I say to Josie, nodding at Mason's plane. "We can borrow Jasper's truck and drive back."

"I need to do this." She folds her arms over her chest as she locks her gaze on the plane. As if settling something between them. I yearn to take her in my arms. To wrap her in the reassuring safety of my embrace. But I don't dare with Grandma Betty watching us like a hawk. The last thing I want to do is give her false hope that Josie and I will become something we never can.

"You never told me why you have a fear of flying," I say gently, hoping she feels comfortable sharing now. Hoping she realizes that I *do* care about her. That I always have.

"My parents died in one of those."

"Oh, Josie—"

"Load up, kids," Grandma Betty announces, waving us over. Robbing me of the last few seconds of bliss before everything changes. "There's a special bridge tournament tonight and I need time to make my famous carrot salad. I have some scores to settle."

"We better go," Josie says, brushing her shoulder against my arm.

The same jolt of electricity shoots through me every time. Warning me it won't be so easy to go back to how things were. To pretend that I don't want to spend every goddamn minute with Josie. I just hope I haven't fucked everything up by giving in to my greatest temptation. I suspect she might hate me for it all.

I sit closer to her than I should inside the plane. Taking her hand because I'm not a heartless asshole who's going to make her face her fear alone. To my amazement, she doesn't panic the same way she did on the way down. She squeezes my hand and leans against my shoulder. But she keeps her eyes open and focuses on her breathing.

We spend the flight admiring the Alaskan scenery.

I steal too many opportunities to press my cheek to her head, memorizing the sweet scent of her shampoo.

All too soon, we're back in Caribou Creek.

"Let me give you both a ride home," I insist when we step out of the plane. Pulling my hand free of

Josie's feels like a betrayal. It feels wrong. My heart squeezes as I catch a flare of rejection in her eyes. "My truck's still here."

Grandma Betty chatters at a hundred words a minute, saving Josie and me from having to speak. But the tension in the truck is heavy enough to slice with a knife. Yeah, she's going to fucking hate me all right.

Once all their bags are inside, I tug Josie outside and close the door behind me.

"Ben, I have to tell you something," she says, cutting me off before I can get out a single word. "Something I promised myself I would before the weekend was over. I already see the writing on the wall, but dammit, I'm not keeping this to myself anymore. I'm not living with regret."

"Josie—"

"I love you, Ben."

Her words are like a swift kick to the gut. Words that I've selfishly longed to hear for three years. But words I hoped she wouldn't ever speak. It would be so much better for both of us if she didn't feel this way. If I didn't know for sure. If I didn't love her too.

"Nothing?" She folds her arms over her chest, shaking her head. That angry fire returns to her eyes, extinguishing all the gentleness I've come to know so well. "After *all* that, you have nothing to say?"

Fuck, I feel like an ass. But since that's kind of my

forte, I lean into the part. I need her to believe I don't feel anything. This will be so much easier if she hates me. At least for now. "It was a fun weekend, Josie. Nothing more." I shrug, hoping that seals the deal. "I thought you knew that."

Shininess glosses in her eyes as they narrow at me. "Just a good time, then?"

"Yes."

"You are unbelievable. You spend three years sticking to this bullshit story about how you don't sleep with your employees, and *now* you act like it's not a big deal? God, I'm so stupid. You *used* me."

Her words clamp my heart in a vise-grip. It takes everything in me not to tell her I'm full of shit. That every word I've just uttered is a lie. But she's better off finding someone else. She deserves true happiness. "I'll be working from home next week, Ms. Bennington. Forward my calls to my cell."

With those coldhearted words, I do the hardest thing I've ever done in my life.

I walk away without looking back.

CHAPTER 15

Josie

"Here, drink this," Grandma Betty says, sliding a giant strawberry margarita in front of me.

"It's ten a.m."

"It's five o'clock somewhere."

The stench of tequila is strong, promising one helluva a headache later if I finish this. But before I feel like there's a midget inside my head beating on my skull with a hammer, I'll feel nothing. I'll be numb to the pain. I won't feel like I'm dying inside. Like my heart has been ripped from chest, thrown to the ground, and stomped on.

I tug the glass to my lips and gulp.

"There's more where that came from," Grandma Betty promises, taking a seat at the kitchen table to join me.

"God, I love you, Grandma Betty."

"You must be a lightweight if you're already professing your love for everyone in your sightline after a single sip."

"I mean it." I reach for her hand across the table and squeeze. "And let's be honest. There's enough tequila in this cup to knock out a linebacker."

"I don't know what's wrong with that boy," Grandma Betty says with a headshake. "I think he's in his own way. Might always be, I'm afraid."

I know what happened between Ben and me this weekend was more than lust. I know there was a reason he wouldn't kiss me. That he kept things from becoming too intimate. He was holding back. I only wish I knew why. At least having that closure would help me put this all behind me when I move on.

"I'm going to take the job," I say to Grandma Betty. "The one in Anchorage. You should come with me."

"I'll support you whatever you decide, dear. But my home is here." She stands up and returns to the blender.

"I'm not done with this one yet."

"I feel left out."

My laughter feels both soothing and hollow as it's drowned out by the blender. My heart aches in ways I never thought it could. Never mind that Ben left me on the doorstep with tears streaming down my cheeks only an hour ago. It feels as though a lifetime has passed since that dagger pierced my heart.

Together, we drink our margaritas. And then we drink a couple more.

I'll deal with reality tomorrow.

CHAPTER 16

Ben

"Your brother's right. You can't swing an axe to save your fucking life." Mason appears around the side of the house, a six-pack dangling from his hand. Had I known he'd still be in town today and not out on a route, I'd have told him to leave me the hell alone too. "Put that shit down and get your fishing gear."

"I'm fine." But another swing and a miss makes me eat my words. I toss the axe aside, muttering under my breath.

"I bet your poles are collecting dust in your garage somewhere," Mason says.

"I'm not fishing."

"Then you can come watch me fish and drink your beer."

"*My* beer?"

"I stole it from your fridge. I won the bet, so you owe me."

I use my tossed aside t-shirt to wipe the sweat from my brow. I've been out here all day fighting with the wood. Successfully splitting about ten percent of everything I touch and fucking up the rest. I've never called in sick before, but lately I've been doing a lot of things I said I never would. "What bet?"

"The bet on who'd cave to a woman first."

"Fuck," I mutter, more annoyed at his unsolicited visit than ever. The last thing I want to discuss is Josie. She already plagues my every waking thought and any attempt to sleep. I emptied a bottle of whiskey last night, but it wasn't enough to numb the pain. "The bet was who'd be single last. So far, we're both still standing. And considering Willow doesn't live here anymore, the odds have been stacked against me this whole time."

"Leave her out of this."

"Hit a sore spot, did I?"

"You're just be an extra big asshole because you're fucking lying to yourself." Mason invites himself into my garage and starts gathering poles and tackle. Looks like this pain in my ass isn't going anywhere until I humor him. At least out on the river we won't have to deal with anyone else but the salmon. To be entirely truthful, I don't care if they bite or not.

"I'm not with her."

"But you want to be."

"That doesn't matter."

"Why?" Mason challenges, setting my six pack on the hood of my truck and helping himself to one now that I've started collecting my fishing gear. "You love her, right? She loves you. Don't tell me you're still hiding behind that boss-employee bullshit excuse. No one buys that anymore."

"I'm no good for her. I've done things that have made me this dark person inside. She deserves better."

Mason stares at me in disbelief, beer hovering halfway to his lips. "You and I were in the same war, Ben. You're just afraid."

I don't entertain that bullshit theory with a response. "You want to go fishing or not?"

"When are you going to stop running from the truth?"

"When *you* do."

Mason's up in my face in half a second, ready to relocate my jaw. I'm rarely so bold—or stupid—to bring up his past. The way he still reacts four years later confirms what I feared most. I'll never recover from losing Josie. I'll never move on.

"I didn't run from Willow. She ran from me. You were the best man, after all. You had a front row seat."

"Everything good here?" I can't decide if I'm relieved or irritated to hear Zac's voice. What the fuck does everyone *not* get about leaving me alone for one goddamn day?

"We're going fishing," I say to my brother.

"Not today."

"You were the one telling me I needed to have more fun," I growl back at him.

Zac slaps a piece of paper to my chest hard enough to force me back a step. "You can go fishing *after* you fix this."

I grab the document and storm off to the opposite side of the garage where the light's better. I expect an angry customer email or some unpaid invoice. I'm pissed off at the disturbance, which is why I'm knocked off my feet when I see what's on the paper. With legs refusing to hold me upright, I drop to a dusty chair.

"It's effective immediately, in case you missed that part."

Josie's resignation letter.

Signed and dated today.

Effective immediately.

I crush the paper into a ball and toss it across the garage. Later, I'm setting the damn thing on fire. "This is all your fault," I bark at Zac. "You and Wes. You two fuckers set me up for failure. You *knew* what would happen if I went to North Haven with Josie. You fucking knew it and you staged the whole thing anyway. What the hell are we going to do without her?"

What am *I* going to do without her?

The thought of never seeing her smile again when I make the rare appearance in the office wrings my heart. I don't give a fuck about all the work that'll go undone. The reports that won't generate themselves. I only care that I won't get to see that smile.

It's...everything.

"She's leaving town *today*, Ben." No surprise, Zac is back in my face. "Are you going to stop her?"

"And say what?"

"I thought that was pretty fucking obvious," Mason mutters. "You're afraid, Ben. Hell, we all are. Love is scarier than war. More painful too. But this bullshit about you not being good enough for Josie is a copout. There's only darkness hanging over your soul because you refuse to let it go to make room for something better."

Something clicks.

Like a key I've been blindly searching for but unable to find.

Until now.

"What if she won't forgive me?"

"Then you get down on your knees and beg," Zac chimes in. "You put aside your fucking pride and grovel as if your life depends on it. Because Ben? It *does*."

CHAPTER 17

Josie

Ît takes every ounce of strength I have to back out of Grandma Betty's driveway and head down the road. It feels as if a piece of me has been ripped away. Which is why it's the *worst* time for my gas light to come on.

Because there isn't another gas station for a hundred miles, I have no choice but to stop and fill up.

If I believed in things like signs, I'd think fate was trying to tell me something. This isn't the first dilemma I've encountered today. First it was the busted zipper on my suitcase that unceremoniously caused all my clothes to dump out on the front lawn. Then it was my elusive phone charger disappearing. I found it sandwiched between my mattress and box spring—that one was probably Grandma Betty.

I pull alongside a pump, praying today is not the day someone wants to be chatty.

I need a few days alone to reset.

To accept that the biggest dream of my life has been shattered.

To come to terms with the harsh truth: Ben will never admit to loving me. Because the big, dumb idiot *does* love me. But for whatever reason, he can't accept his feelings. I've waited three years. It's time to move on.

"Josie? You headed on a road trip?" Hattie Kohl calls to me as she exits the convenience store.

Inwardly, I cringe at yet another obstacle. Considering Zac married her granddaughter, Riley, I have no doubt she's already heard the news. She's simply saving face by allowing me to put it in my own words. "Hi, Mrs. Kohl."

"Your backseat is mighty full. Will you be able to see out your rearview mirror?"

My attempt to answer results in me bursting into tears.

Hattie hurries to me, gathering me in her arms. Hugging me as tightly as Grandma Betty did half a dozen times before I made it out the door. I wish I could stand staying in Caribou Creek. I wish I could pretend like nothing ever happened with Ben. That I don't feel anything for the jerk. But the only way I stand a chance of getting over him is to leave. To start over fresh.

"I'm so sorry," I say to Hattie when I finally pull back.

"You sure this is what you want?"

"I don't think—"

"You can't leave." Ben's voice freezes me in place. He must've pulled in when I was sobbing on Hattie's shoulder. Dammit, fate. I'm trying to make a clean getaway here. "Josie, please. Don't go."

Hattie squeezes my hand before she abandons me. Leaving me to face Ben Ashburn on my own.

"Josie, I love you."

I fold my arms and slowly turn around, pinning him in place with my laser-beam glare. The words I've waited three years to hear do their best to make me feel all gooey on the inside, but I've got a bone to pick with him before I surrender to that warm and fuzzy feeling. "Took you long enough to figure that out. Seems like everyone else has known for months."

When he steps closer, my pulse doubles. My resolve to stay upset is weakening. Damn the heat between us that makes it impossible to think straight. One thing we've never lacked is sizzling chemistry. It's more potent than ever before now that love is on the table.

"I didn't think I was good enough for you, Josie."

My reflex to fire a retort at him fizzles out when I see the pain in those baby blues. He's being genuine and vulnerable. Something that's never come easily for him. There's more under the surface of this statement. I'm sure of it. "What are you talking about?"

"I've loved you from the first moment I saw you. From the moment you walked into the brewery. You were wearing that blue dress that twirled each time you turned, even when you didn't mean for it to." When he reaches for my cheek, I don't fight it. Damn I've missed his tender touch. "You're the most beautiful woman I've ever laid eyes on. I thought about you every moment of every day since."

"You get this line out of a movie or something?" My words are barely more than a whisper, my attempt to tease him tugging the gentlest smile across his lips. And dammit if that doesn't do me in.

"I tried to convince myself of all the reasons I couldn't be with you."

"You thought because you'd been to war—"

"It was an excuse I was hiding behind. Because I was afraid to let myself fall so completely for you. I've never felt anything this strong before. The thought of losing control—of being destroyed by it—kept me in denial for so long." He strokes his thumb across my cheek, tilting my face closer to his. "I was afraid to kiss you because I knew if I did, I'd have to surrender to these feelings whether I wanted to or not. I knew I'd be more helpless than I'd ever been in my life. But you know what?"

"What?"

"I realized something important."

"Oh yeah?" My gaze keeps dropping to his lips, desperate to feel them against my own.

"I realized that if my heart's in your hands, I have nothing to be afraid of." He leans the rest of the way, capturing my lips at long last. The kiss is everything I dreamed it would be and so much more. Every nerve ending tingles. My toes curl. My soul sings. It's not a secret that the sex is off the charts, but this kiss cements what matters most—we are meant to be.

"Wow."

Ben rests his forehead against mine. "Wow is right."

"Ben?"

"Yes, my love?"

If I wasn't swooning before, I am now. "Is it too late to take back my resignation letter?"

"Considering I set it on fire, I think we can pretend it never existed." He kisses me again, causing a quiver low in my belly. One that wants to revisit all the naughtiness of this past weekend. And not just tonight, but all the nights to come.

Epilogue

BEN

About a year later...

"You all packed?" I ask Josie as I enter the brewery office with her favorite white chocolate mocha and hand it over. I come around behind her chair and drop my hands to her shoulders. She moans softly as I start kneading the knots from them.

"My suitcase is by the front door," she says, melting into my touch. "And everything's in order for our festival booth, too."

Working with my wife *can* be distracting, but we're both so work-driven that we've found a balance that gets boxes checked and itches scratched. Earlier this morning, before anyone else arrived at the brewery, I fucked Josie in this spot. With her bent over the desk and me pummeling her from behind. But that didn't prevent a single email response from being sent out in a timely manner.

"You sure you're up for flying?" I ask her.

"Of course. Grandma Betty likes pretending she's a pilot. Aka flirting with Mason. He's headed in that direction anyway, right?"

"Yeah." On occasion, Mason picks up small passenger groups from Anchorage and flies them into smaller communities. Which is why he offered to drop Josie and me off in North Haven a couple days ahead of the festival. "You confirmed Grandma Betty has her own room this time, right?"

"If you mean did Wes monkey with the reservation, no he didn't. I called an hour ago to make sure."

"Good."

The relationship I have with my brothers is night and day from what it was a year ago. Turns out I was only a giant pain the ass when I was denying my feelings for Josie. Now that I've embraced her love, I feel like a new man. Gone is the dark cloud that hung over me for so long. I can't change my past, but I've learned to not let it dampen my future.

I'm present for family events again instead of simply tolerating them. I'm an uncle to two amazing little boys. My brothers and I go fishing and watch football together. I don't even get bent out of shape when Wes calls me Benny Poo anymore. Our wives get along and often come up with reasons for our families to gather.

Life has never been better.

Next week, Grandma June and Grandpa Del are heading up north for a visit. I can't wait to have them try Wes' newest brew. We've added two more to the menu since his pumpkin beer was such a hit last year.

But until then, my only focus is taking care of my wife. In every possible, pleasure-filled way I can imagine.

"Josie?"

"Hmm?"

"We still have an hour before Mason plans to take off. You think it's enough time to head back to the house and make sure you packed everything?"

"I did—" She playfully rolls her eyes at me. "You want a nooner."

"And you don't?"

I bend down, pressing my lips to hers in answer. That my hand slips down the v-cut of her shirt isn't my fault. My hands are drawn to her tits like magnets. I slide my fingers inside her bra and pinch her nipple. "If we go now, I can lick your pussy before I bend you over the counter."

Josie's logged out of her computer in three seconds.

"You two in a hurry?" Zac asks as we rush out of the office. His smirk says it all. He knows exactly how we feel. Hell, I'd bet twenty bucks he's already been by the clinic to see Riley for a lunch visit of his own today.

"If you need us," Josie calls back to him.

"*Don't* call us," I add.

THE END

Bonus Epilogue

JOSIE

About three years later...

"This is heaven," I say in a near-moan, letting my body sink into the naturally hot water. I've heard about Aurora Springs and their natural hot springs, but this is the first time experiencing them for myself. Loose tendrils of my hair frost instantly against my cheeks at the negative twenty-degree temperature, but I'm not cold.

"I know this place isn't exactly North Haven with its fancy hotel and spa—" Ben says, joining me.

"It's perfect." This is the first time my husband and I have gotten away from Caribou Creek since our little Livy was born. She's the youngest of the Ashburn cousins, but that might change in the near future. I swear my sister-in-law, Riley, looked as though she had a secret when we dropped Livy off.

"That brilliant brain of yours is still turning, isn't it?" Ben asks, kicking off at the steps and gliding over to me. His arm is around my lower back a moment later, his breath tickling my ear, as he settles a hand on my hip. And I know, right then, best weekend *ever*.

"It never stops. You know that."

"Oh, it does," Ben says, sounding more devilish than ever. "You just need the right distraction."

My body shivers, but not from the cold.

Ben kisses my jaw, his beard scraping against my neck. The frosty strands tickle my sensitive skin, making me giggle. I comb my fingers through his beard, brushing away the white layer that has formed. My fingers feel the chill until I sink them back into the water.

He moves his mouth to my shoulder, oblivious that half a dozen others wander the hot spring pool. The steam rising from the water gives us a curtain of privacy as long as we keep our distance from the others. Which is why I dare to grip Ben's hip and slide my hand inside his shorts. Squeezing his muscular thigh.

"Josie, you're going to make it hard for me to get out of the water," he growls against my collarbone. He backs me against a boulder as his hand slides down my body and grips my ass. Those deliberate fingers dig into a place that makes me dizzy with want. "Of course, I could make you come first. Finger fuck you against this boulder. But you'd have to be quiet. We don't want to get kicked out on our first night."

I tease him further, moving my hand inward beneath his swim trunks until my fingers graze his half-hard cock. "I can be quiet."

The hand on my ass moves to my hip. "If you make a single sound, I'll have to stop." He runs a finger back and forth along the waistband of my bikini. Something I never would've dared to wear a few years ago. But Ben makes me feel so fucking desirable in anything and everything. The way he looks at me says it all. He *loves* my curves.

How did I get so damn lucky?

Ben looks over his shoulder, ensuring the steam is giving us the privacy we need. But it wouldn't matter with the darkness overhead and the way his brick-house of a body blocks me from sight.

Leaning back against the boulder, I lift a leg up and wrap it around his lower back, offering him easier access to what he wants most. His hand slips inside my bikini bottom, his fingers on a mission for my pussy. His strokes are rough and hard, making me damn near go blind with how hard it is to keep quiet.

When we get back to our room, I know we'll slow

things down. Enjoy the quiet evening that promises no interruptions. But right now, the urgency that's been building since we set out on the road this morning has hit its limit. We spent the day visiting local shops to expand distribution for the brewery. It was all business.

But now...*fuck!* I dig my fingers hard into his shoulders, swallowing my moans so we won't draw any attention.

I buck my hips when he slips a finger inside.

"I'm going to make you come quickly, Josie," he says in that low, deep tone that makes my entire body ache with need. As if it wasn't already. "Then I'm going to take you to our room and fuck you all night long." He slips in a second finger and pumps faster. "Slowly and thoroughly." He curls his fingers, hitting that spot that makes me see stars behind my eyelids. "Again and again."

I explode.

I bite down on my lip so hard I'm sure there's blood.

But it's taking every ounce of restraint not to cry out. To ride this tidal wave of pleasure without drawing attention. Ben fuses his lips to mine, helping me swallow the pleasureful cries that yearn to escape.

When I finally start to come down from my high, I dare to open my eyes.

Ben's baby blues are drenched with desire. "You're so fucking hot when you come."

If there wasn't a cloud of steam around us from the water, my heavy breathing would no doubt produce one of its own. It takes a few minutes for my breathing to steady. When I lean my head back against a chilled boulder, I notice the northern lights dancing overhead.

"Look," I say to Ben, nodding toward the sky.

He looks up and together we watch the greens and purples dance above us. As if an invisible, giant hand is using a paintbrush in real time to entertain us.

"I know I've lived in Alaska all my life, but I'll never get tired of seeing those," I admit. "They're so beautiful."

"They are," Ben agrees. "But not nearly as beautiful as my wife."

I return my attention to my husband, still surprised sometimes by his words. It's been years since he's been the coldhearted grump. A time I hardly remember anymore, aside from the insatiable pining I felt for him. But when he says such kind things with sincerity, it makes my heart sing. It makes my soul radiate happiness I never thought could exist.

I drape my arms around his shoulders and anchor my hands at the back of his head, pushing his lips toward mine. The kiss quickly turns heated and slightly inappropriate for public consumption.

"I better get you back to the room before I fuck you in the hot spring."

"We'll be banned for life if you do that," I tease.

My body is shaky with nerves and anticipation as I dry off and change in the locker room. Even after nearly four years together, the idea of being intimate with Ben makes me giddy and overwhelmed in the best way possible. Since Livy was born, we haven't had as much time to ourselves. But I wouldn't change a thing. Our daughter is the most beautiful, precious soul on this earth. Of course, I'm also really glad to have this weekend away.

Back in the room, Ben flips the deadbolt behind us. The metallic click of the lock echoes in the suite, a signal that things are about to get heated.

I feel my husband come up behind me, his chest pressing into my back. He's fucking hard, that delicious cock teasing my lower back. Wetness pools between my legs as his beard tickles my neck. A beard his brothers convinced him to grow now that they all get along. The three have some ridiculous contest about who can grow the longest. But none of us wives are complaining.

The thought of Ben between my legs, his beard tickling my pussy as he devours it, makes me whimper.

"First," Ben says, dragging his tongue down my neck, "we're going to shower. Then, I'm going to spend the rest of the night worshipping every inch of your body." He strips me out of my clothes, getting quite handsy about it. Making me hornier by the second. We barely fucking make it to the shower.

Ben turns on the water and lathers us with my favorite body wash. Over the years, the man has proven he can be incredibly thoughtful. All those years, when I thought he wasn't paying attention, I was either wrong or he's making up for it now.

I surrender to his touch as he slowly and thoroughly lathers my body in floral body wash. The urgency from earlier builds again with each caress of his hand. I reach behind me and grab his cock. Squeezing it to tug him forward.

Ben groans. "Josie," he says in warning.

"I want you to fuck me, Ben."

"Oh, I will. All night long."

I give his shaft a couple slow, twisting strokes. "Don't pretend like you don't need a release first. That you don't want to push me up against the tile and fuck me hard." I squeeze him again. "Do it, Ben. Fuck me. Empty your cock into my pussy. We both know it's what you want."

He growls against my ear as he traps me against the tile wall. I arch my back, popping my ass in invitation.

"You're fucking dirty talk gets me every time." He saws his cock through my pussy lips, his swollen head teasing my clit. I could so easily come with a few more strokes. But my husband has been driven impatient by my bluntness and plunges into my channel all at once.

The powerful thrust lifts me up on tiptoes. If it weren't for his hand on my hip, I might've toppled over.

Ben fucks me hard and purposefully, moving his hands to my tits once he's set the pace. My shaky hands are braced against the tile, but I move one between my legs. Intensifying all the sensation.

"Fuck, Josie," he groans.

A wicked smile spreads across my lips. I know how much he loves watching me touch myself. "Harder, Ben. Make me come. Then come in my pussy. I know you want to."

He slams into me, his thrusts almost savage.

I come apart suddenly. Without much warning. Crying out his name and hearing it echo off the shower walls.

Ben pumps harder as my pussy convulses around his dick. He plunges faster and faster until finally, he stills inside me. Emptying his cock inside me. He collapses against me, his chest pressing into my back as his cock pulses inside me. "Fuck, Josie. You're trying to kill me."

"Hardly," I tease, my word escaping as more of a pant. "I need you to make good on that promise to fuck me all night long." I turn my head, glancing back over my shoulder so I can kiss his bicep. "This was just the warm-up."

His hands slide possessively down my sides, then back up again. Wrapping me tightly in his arms. "You're right about that," he says in that deep, sexy voice that gives me shivers. "I'm going to spend hours make you come over and over again."

"God, I love you."

Ben kisses my neck, teasing me with that delightful tongue along my collarbone. "Not as much as I love you, Josie."

THE END

About the Author

Kali Hart writes short & sweet with plenty of heat. Instalove is the name of her game. She loves penning protective heroes with hearts of gold who'll do anything for the women they love. As a military veteran herself who served in the Army and completed a tour overseas in Iraq, Kali often writes characters with military experience and backgrounds. Because who doesn't love a good man—and sometimes woman —in uniform?

Visit her website: https://kalihartauthor.com/